BEWITCHING FIRE

BEWITCHING BREWS
BOOK 1

SHERITTA BITIKOFER

Contents

Dedicated to all those who believe in magic, miracles, and the mystical power of a good cup of coffee.

Chapter 1

"I already fed you, Artemis," Krystal whispered to the long-haired – and slightly pudgy – Siamese cat that brushed in and out between her legs. The cat meowed loudly and looked up to his owner with crystalline blue eyes as she inspected her hair in the hall mirror.

Krystal plucked at her black bangs to even out the strands, even though she knew the autumn winds outside would toss them about. She shushed the greedy cat again and stepped over him once she was somewhat satisfied. Her sister, Sierra, was still asleep in one of the upstairs bedrooms, and the walls in this old house weren't soundproof. Krystal knew how grumpy her sister became when she was woken up too early.

It was a good thing that Krystal was a morning person; otherwise, waking up at five o'clock every day might have been unpleasant. Apart from the fact that she had to practically tiptoe across the hardwood floors, she enjoyed taking her time to fix her breakfast, have her first cup of coffee, and read a little before stepping out onto their front porch.

Artemis couldn't care less about silence or food rations, and Krystal was sure that Sierra was sneaking the fat cat treats and extra helpings after she left for the coffee shop each morning.

Krystal checked the time on her phone. Right on schedule, as always. She fled from the begging cat to sit on the antique mahogany hall butler bench and slipped on her knee-high black boots that accented her creamy, heavy, woven skirt. Artemis thought he was awfully clever when he hopped onto the other side of the bench and pranced down to rub against her elbow.

"I told you no," she hissed as she snatched up her canvas coat from the hook above her head.

Artemis gave her a displeased look and watched Krystal grab her purse as she hurried toward the door. Krystal knew something would get peed on during the course of the day; that is, if Sierra didn't dish out the cat's second breakfast before he grew too impatient.

Krystal locked the intricately carved set of doors behind her. The house, almost a century and a half old, was the jewel of the Goldcrest Cove Historical Society. It had been passed down through her family for generations, and it was her and her sister's turn to be its caretakers.

Sometimes that meant calling a specialist carpenter all the way from Boston, nearly an hour's drive away, to fix some of the resin details on the staircase balusters. It also meant paying an arm and a leg for careful repair work on the electric wiring that had been installed throughout the house long after it was first built.

Krystal made her way to the sidewalk and looked up at her beloved home. No matter the cost of the maintenance, it was worth it to keep this precious piece of her heritage alive. If only her older sister felt the same.

The sun hadn't risen just yet, but the night was slowly chased away by the coming dawn. Krystal loved this time of the morning when the sky was a light, smoky blue. Birds that hadn't flown south for the winter already could be heard chirping and twittering in the nearby trees that lined the road leading into town. Otherwise, Pinkerton Street was peaceful and quiet.

The Perfect Books and Brews Coffee Shop wasn't far from her home, just five blocks, and nestled on one of the main thoroughfares that snaked around the center of town. Johnson Avenue and the south side of Goldcrest Cove were the picture of small-town America. The gardens lined the front walkways that led up to Victorian homes, and the independently owned shops and restaurants that had kept tourists flocking here for decades.

Nestled on the north Massachusetts shore, Goldcrest Cove attracted people from all over the northeast – and some from the south – with its seaside harbor and marina. It was a quaint retreat from the bigger cities. That meant Goldcrest Cove was considered a haven for the weary and exhausted businessmen from Boston and New York. It also meant her coffee shop would never go out of business. Someone had to serve tourists their caffeine.

Krystal stepped up to her glass-paned shop door, and already there were some motorists making their way up the avenue. She looked down the sidewalk and saw the lights in McRae's Morsels flicker to life. She and the old woman who ran the shop made an agreement long ago that as long as Krystal didn't sell pastries, Mrs. McRae wouldn't serve coffee. That was the kind of "help-thy-neighbor" attitude that she loved about this town. With luck, it would never change.

The tinkling of the little brass bell chimed above her head as she stepped inside. The overhead lights behind the counter were still on from the night before and helped her maneuver her way through the darkened maze of café tables that were spread out across the floor.

Krystal stopped when she bumped her hip into one of the sharp table corners, and silently berated herself. "Lights on," she sighed with a flick of her hand toward the backroom where the main switch was located. Instantly, the inset can lights popped on, and she could see her way around even better. A lot of good her magical powers did if she didn't use them every once in a while.

Krystal first got the idea to open a bookstore-slash-coffeeshop when she was a senior in high school. She and her two best friends, Alex Boyer and Valerie Lloyd, decided that as soon as they were able, they would open the shop together. The community needed a casual meetup place besides restaurants and gas stations.

Five years ago, they did it, and life had never been better. Sure, it was a little rocky at first, but Alexa's knack for numbers came in handy. She had even earned her degree in accounting at the community college once the three of them found out that running a business wasn't going to be all sunshine and roses.

While Alexa served as the bookkeeper, Valerie set out to design the interior. It was her idea to lay real bricks against the sheet rock walls to give it that vintage, cozy feel. She even picked out the distressed oak flooring that matched the countertops and tables. Floor-to-ceiling bookcases consumed the far wall of the coffee shop, every shelf filled with novels and reference books that were available to her patrons to browse through or buy. She didn't go to school for design, but they all agreed that she had an eye for matching colors and finding out what looked warm and inviting.

That was what they wanted this coffee shop to be. Warm and inviting. Krystal wanted it to be a home away from home for loyal customers. It became that and so much more. Like the historical landmarks and statues on Main Street just a couple of blocks to the north, Perfect Books and Brews had become part of the community. A live and breathing piece of their local culture.

She wouldn't have had it any other way.

Krystal was the one who came up with the personal touches that made Perfect Books and Brews so appealing. She hung her coat on the driftwood plank coatrack just beside the sales counter. Every guest was offered a hook if one was available. Behind the counter were several shelves where personalized coffee mugs sat, waiting for their owner to come in and use them. They had a mug for the police chief and his officers, the mayor, some of the other shop owners on Johnson Avenue, and many other citizens like teachers, lawyers, single moms, doctors, construction workers, and anyone else who came here to take a break from their everyday lives.

Krystal picked up her mug, a beautifully crafted piece she bought at a fair years ago with a shiny, green, and blue glaze. The images of leaves and vines encircled the body of the mug and wound around the handle.

After starting up the coffee grinder on the far back counter of their brewing station, Krystal set to making her own drink for the morning. The coffee she kept at home was fine, but she couldn't really start her workday without her chai tea latte.

Just as she was sprinkling the bits of cinnamon on top of the white foam, the shop door opened, and the bell heralded the arrival of Valerie.

She glanced up as her friend shuffled across the floor and her hip bumped into a corner of one of the tables, the same one Krystal had bumped into just a couple of minutes ago.

Valerie let out a whimper and continued on her zombie-like walk toward the sales counter.

"Want me to make your café mocha?" Krystal asked as she pulled back her long, straight black hair into a high ponytail, leaving her bangs to tickle the tops of her brows.

Valerie let out a groan and blindly grabbed for her simple black mug from the shelf behind the counter. She dropped her messenger bag on the floor and deftly set to work on her own morning wakeup juice, as if her friend hadn't said a word to her.

"At least you're on time," Krystal remarked as she turned and sipped on her latte. Perfection.

Valerie ran her fingers through her short brown hair, and in this light, Krystal could see the streaks of dark red stand out. Sierra, another entrepreneur of Johnson Avenue, had dyed Valerie's hair dozens of times, trying out new and exciting colors that her friend would have never been able to get away with at other jobs.

"Shane was playing video games all night," she grumbled.

Shane Stokes was a history teacher and a roommate of Valerie's since she moved out of her aunt's house just a year or two after high school. He was at least five years older than the girls, but you would never guess it, judging by the way he behaved like one of his own students.

"And the noise kept you up all night?"

Valerie turned around and leaned against the counter. Dark circles hung under her heavily lined green eyes. "No, I was playing co-op with him," she replied. "I didn't even realize what time it was until I checked the clock and saw it was two in the morning."

Krystal winced. "You'd better put some more espresso in that mocha then."

"Blessed be!" a cry came from the door, preceding the brass bell. Krystal didn't need to turn to know that it was Alexa who came skipping between the tables, her loose blonde curls bouncing against her shoulders.

Valerie rolled her eyes and slumped against the counter. Krystal couldn't help but smile. Alexa had enough energy for all of them, and probably enough to power the whole city. If only they could find a way to bottle it and sell it with their house blend coffee grounds.

Alexa hung up her white cashmere coat and stowed away her designer purse under the counter with Krystal's. "And how are you two lovely witches this morning?"

If they weren't alone, Krystal would have shushed her friend. The shop didn't open for another few minutes, and they were free to talk all they wanted about witches, magic, and their charm goals for the day.

"Val's sleepy," Krystal said with a sympathetic flavoring to her words.

Alexa snatched up her bright purple fairy mug to make her usual caramel macchiato.

Like she needed any caffeine.

"Sleepy is an understatement," Valerie corrected as she pumped chocolate into her coffee. Krystal wondered if she had realized she just put in twice the usual amount, but she wasn't going to question it.

"Okay, Val's running on fumes," Krystal corrected with a shrug.

Alexa set down her mug and skittered over to her tired friend. "Here, let me help."

Valerie quickly edged away and lifted her coffee out of reach from the petite blonde. "No way," she barked. "The last time you charmed my coffee too early in the morning, I was shitting glitter for a week."

Krystal laughed, remembering that time when Alexa snuck a quick joy charm into Valerie's drink.

Granted, she was being a grouch that day, and Alexa was just trying to help.

She crossed her arms over her chest and pouted. "How am I supposed to get better at charms if you guys won't let me practice?"

"You can't practice on the customers," Krystal countered. "And we do let you try sometimes."

Alexa rolled her pretty blue eyes. "Yeah, only the really basic ones. I'm ready to move on from charisma charms."

They had been working with Alexa for almost all her life, and she still struggled with the simplest of spells and charms. Being only a half-blooded witch, many of her charms didn't go exactly according to plan. Some could have nasty side effects, which was why Krystal and Valerie were in charge of charming the coffee while Alexa served the customers. With her peppy attitude, it was a good fit, and their patrons appreciated her smiling face first thing in the morning.

Krystal, Valerie, and Alexa were witches and had been since birth. Krystal was older just by a few months, but they had been the best of friends since they could walk. Krystal's parents encouraged the playdates, especially when Valerie's parents died and Alexa's single mom became busy working long nightshifts.

Out of them all, Krystal was the most fortunate. She had come from a long line of witches and warlocks, and her family had always been supportive in her training. Her two friends were not so lucky, and they clung together, somewhat out of necessity. There were other witches in town, but these three were so close in age that they became instant friends.

When Krystal confessed her motives for opening the coffeeshop, she wasn't too shy to tell them the truth. The cardinal rule of their witchcraft order was that they could never use their powers on non-magic folk. Krystal never agreed with that.

What good was having these miraculous powers if they couldn't heal and help people?

The coffee shop would change all of that. If a customer came in with a problem, anything from their hair falling out to a disagreeable pending divorce, the girls helped in what way their magic would let them. They charmed the drinks with exactly what the customer needed, whether it was a little confidence to finally ask their secret crush out on a date or a financial blessing that would help them get through a rough patch in the month. It was their way to give back to the community, to pay it forward, and use their powers for unselfish reasons. Valerie and Alexa were totally on board as soon as Krystal was done explaining her plan. They, too, wanted to take their magical creed of "Do No Harm" a step further.

At first, they were a little reckless with their charms and helped everyone who came in with the tiniest of problems. It might have become too obvious. So Krystal had to set a quota limit for them each day. They would only pick the most desperate customers, the ones who were diagnosed with cancer or at risk of losing a job that helped to feed their family. They had to carefully choose who would benefit from their powers. Five became a fairly comfortable number.

Krystal had set up a little chalkboard by the counter, and they would keep a daily tally.

"We can work on different charms on your day off," Krystal told Alexa as she hung the small chalkboard back on the hook after wiping it clean.

"You mean half-day off," Alexa quipped as she turned back to her half-brewed macchiato.

To Krystal's chagrin, she was right. There were plenty of perks to being a witch running a coffee shop, but one major downside was that they could only hire magic folk. There was no shortage of them in Goldcrest Cove, but they all had stable jobs of their own.

Sierra owned a salon down the avenue, Amber McCain ran her own bed and breakfast on the outskirts of town, and Taylor Morrow had her plant nursery just a little farther south of Krystal's home. Unless another witch came to town looking for work, the three girls were slap out of luck. And with the holidays just around the corner, Krystal may have had to beg and plead her friends to take extra shifts to handle the hours.

However, Thanksgiving was still a month away and the annual Fall Harvest Festival was in the forefront of Krystal's mind. They had a lot todo to prepare for Samhain and Halloween this year, including making sure that they were well stocked on everything they would need for their hot chocolate booth on Main Street.

It was hard work running this shop. But with her friends, all the long nights, the headaches, and the careful planning were worth it to see the happiness in their customers' eyes when they took the first sip of their morning coffee.

"Walking two blocks to this coffee place is worth it?" Devin complained after his new partner, Aaron, tried to convince him that braving the task of finding a parking spot along Johnson Avenue was well worth the effort.

"Totally," the cop replied as they passed by an older couple on the street, both holding to-go coffee cups with the Perfect Books and Brews logo printed on the sides. "It's the only coffee shop in town and I want you to get a taste of what real, small-town coffee tastes like."

Devin's mouth quirked in a disbelieving grin. "Seriously? Coffee in Boston is nothing special, and the coffee at this place won't be either."

Aaron held up a cautionary finger. "You haven't had an espresso brewed by these girls. I don't know what they put in it, but it's nothing like any I've had before."

Devin shrugged and hooked his thumbs into his uniform pockets. "Again, an espresso is an espresso. Just don't be disappointed when I'm not impressed."

They passed by a donut shop that boasted a long line inside. Devin peered through the bay window and saw some of the customers eating their breakfast pastries and treats at the little café tables.

"Why not get coffee there?" he asked. "They've got bagels."

Aaron hurried a little farther ahead and didn't even seem to notice the scent of deep-fried dough and powdered sugar. "Mrs. McRae's doesn't sell coffee."

Devin's brows shot up as he hustled to catch up. "A donut place doesn't sell coffee?"

A chilling breeze blew down the street, another sign that autumn was in full swing for Massachusetts. Devin was glad for the warm uniform shirt and jacket that the department issued for the coming winter season. The light windbreaker with the police department logo on the chest and upper arm was warm enough to fight off the cold, but when winter fully set in, he knew he would need something heavier.

Aaron ran his fingers through his blonde hair to push aside a strand that had fallen in his face. "That's right," he replied. "McRae's doesn't sell coffee, and Perfect Books and Brews doesn't sell pastries."

"That seems a little counterintuitive for business, don't you think?"

Aaron chuckled just as the bright gold and purple sign of the coffee shop came into view. "Not at all. It's actually a pretty good setup. No competition."

Devin looked ahead, and somehow, he had hoped that the line of customers that had been standing outside on the walkway didn't belong to the shop. Upon Aaron's insistence, he hadn't had any of his usual coffee that morning, and though he'd already been awake for a few hours, he was ready to crawl back into his wrought iron bed and call it a day. It wasn't even nine o'clock yet.

"Did they just open?" he asked as they stepped up to the end of the line that was straddling the curb. Devin cast a glance down either end of the street and saw how the line of parallel-parked cars seemed to stretch on indefinitely. The same went for the other side of the narrow, two-way street lined with thick, manicured bushes and towering trees that were beginning to lose their leaves. He imagined spring in Goldcrest Cove would be absolutely beautiful, especially on Johnson Avenue.

"They've been open for probably five years," Aaron answered.

Though he was impressed that such a business was doing so well, even after five years, Devin shook his head. "No, I mean, did they just open a little while ago? The line seems pretty long."

Aaron checked his watch. "They open at seven in the morning."

"And they're still this crowded?"

Aaron slapped a hand on Devin's shoulder. "Come on, man. Just be patient. It'll all be worth it."

That's what he kept saying, but Devin still had his doubts. The line moved surprisingly fast, and once they were inside the warm lobby, Devin stole a glance toward the front counter. His brows furrowed in confusion.

There were only three women working the morning shift.

That didn't seem right for the kind of traffic they had to handle. These kinds of lines warranted at least five, maybe six baristas running around filling coffee cups and taking orders. There was only one cash register open. For being in business for five years, he imagined they should have been more efficient than that.

That didn't improve his first impression of the place, but the interior certainly did. He could see why people loved to come here. Sunlight streamed through the expansive windows at the front of the shop, giving the place an informal and sheltered feel. The air was warm and saturated with the strong, savory smells of coffee and herbs. Neither was it too loud, despite the fact that he couldn't see an open table anywhere.

It was hard to miss the bookcases that lined one of the long walls of the shop. That's when he noticed that several customers were reading while they sipped on their drinks. A couple of college kids were huddled around a bigger table, tapping away on their laptops. A few were reading the morning newspaper, and couples were enjoying each other's company while their hands wrapped around their steaming mugs.

"They've got real mugs," Devin commented quietly to his partner.

He nodded. "Yeah, that's another cool thing about the place. The customers who come in almost every day bring their own mugs or have the girls keep their mugs here so they can just fill them up whenever they come in. Less waste that way."

Devin also nodded in approval. "I assume you've got a mug?"

"Yep," he announced proudly as they neared the front counter. "I snitched a mug from the station and told them to keep it here for me. It's bigger than the other mugs I have at home."

"Remind me to tell Chief Nickels that you stole department property."

Aaron shot him a devious look. "Chief Nickels has his own mug here, too. It's the one with the basset hound on it."

He heard the bubbly laugh of the barista manning the counter and leaned around the portly businessman in front of him to take a peek. The blouse the woman wore sported billowy, long sleeves that were pulled up around her elbows by pull cords that scrunched up the grey-blue fabric. Her long ponytail of shiny black hair draped over her shoulder, and her brown eyes danced with genuine delight that made Devin stare a little longer than he normally would have.

She certainly was beautiful with her slender nose and high cheekbones. His heart thrummed hard in his chest as the line moved forward. Soon, he'd be the focus of those brilliant eyes that were offset by her dark bangs that curtained over her forehead. The shop lights caught the tiny fragments of gold in her irises, and one corner of his mouth twitched into a smile.

"Do you know what you want?" Aaron asked, snapping Devin out of his daze for a moment. Yeah, he knew exactly what he wanted, but it wasn't anything that could be poured into a mug.

He finally looked up to the huge menu board above the barista station and blinked at the wide variety of choices. Their selection was just as varied as any big-name coffee shop like Starbucks or Dunkin Donuts. There were coffees, teas, and other drinks like hot chocolate and smoothies.

"Don't they just have regular black coffee?" he mumbled as his eyes poured over the options.

"Sure, but you'll probably get a weird look from Krystal."

"Is that the girl at the front counter?" Devin hastily asked, hoping his partner wouldn't pick up on his obvious interest. The last thing he wanted was an earful of ribbing in the squad car while they patrolled the town.

Aaron slid him a knowing glance. "Yeah. The blonde is Alexa, and Valerie's the one with the red streaks in her hair. Don't cross her on a bad day, or she might put something in your coffee."

"You speak from experience?" Devin chuckled, watching the way the taller girl with short brown hair fixed the mixed hot drinks with such speed that he couldn't begin to figure out what she was doing.

Aaron laughed. "Oh, yeah. One time, I made some crack about a piece of studded jewelry she was wearing. After I left with my coffee, I had gas all day. And not the good kind."

Devin held his lips tight so he wouldn't laugh out loud, because they were next in line.

When the businessman paid for his highly modified and customized espresso, the two cops stepped up to the counter. Krystal didn't look at him right away, but turned to Aaron first.

"Good morning, Aaron!" she said with just about the prettiest smile he'd ever seen, then turned to fetch his Goldcrest Cove Police Department mug off the shelf.

"Good morning, Krystal," he returned. "You girls are a little busy this morning."

"Tell me about it," said the little blonde barista, Alexa, as she came forward with two cardboard drink holders loaded down with to-go coffee cups. She delivered the order to another lady waiting near the counter, wearing a black polo and pair of faded jeans. The logo on her left lapel told that she worked for a furniture store just down the road. She must have been sent to get the company their coffee.

When Krystal came back to the register after handing off Aaron's mug to Valerie, she finally looked up to Devin. He gave her his best, friendly smile, and he could see the faint pink color rising to her cheeks. At least he knew he was making a good impression already.

"You must be that new cop from Boston," she said.

"How did you guess?" he asked, his smile faltering a bit. Did news of what had happened on his previous job reach all the way to this little coastal town?

Krystal leaned against the counter, and he saw the way she popped her hip out just a little. Her navy blue apron covered much of her front, but he could tell she had a nice set of curves underneath.

"You're a new face," she replied. "The entire department has come in here at least once or twice, but I've never seen you before. I hope you'll come around more often."

Devin wanted to think that something in the way her gaze roamed over his torso made her say that, but it was far more likely she just wanted his business.

"If Aaron has his way, I'll be here every morning," he half-way promised.

"I guess we'll get to see a lot of each other, then." There was a little glimmer in her eyes that he couldn't ignore. A hungry, flirty look that made his pants feel a little tighter. What the hell?

"You having the usual, Aaron?" she asked his partner.

Aaron shot her that corny finger-gun gesture and winked. "You got it."

Krystal glanced over her shoulder at Valerie, but before she could call out the order, her coworker waved her off.

"Yeah, yeah, I know. Double espresso with coconut."

Devin looked to Aaron in utter disgust. "Coconut?"

"And what can I get you, mister..."

He immediately snapped back to Krystal. "Devin. Devin Daniels."

Almost out of reflex, he offered his hand to her over the countertop. He had gotten so used to shaking everyone's hand nowadays that it had grown into a weird sort of habit.

Krystal didn't seem bothered and shook it in return. He loved the way her hand felt so warm in his. More than that, he admired her strong grip. It wasn't every day a lady could return his handshake with just as much force. "Krystal Hayden. Owner."

"Yeah, Aaron was telling me how you and your friends run this place. Impressive."

She shrugged one slender shoulder, making the fabric of her blouse slide in ways that made his heart thump a little harder. "We try."

It was then he realized they were still shaking hands, and he finally let go, though he would have loved to keep touching her skin all day long. "And I'll just have coffee. Black."

Krystal seemed surprised. "We can make anything your Boston coffee shops can make," she said. "No need to go plain on us."

Devin slid his hand into his back pocket to fish out his wallet. "I got black coffee in Boston, too. I've just never been one for all these fancy drinks."

Krystal nodded and passed the order on to Alexa as she came back around the counter. "Well, I think you'll like our house blend. It's a dark roast, and I've been told it has a hint of nutmeg. Totally unintentional, but it's pretty popular."

She took their money, but Devin kept his eye on Krystal, studying the way she typed in the orders on her register screen. Everything about her was absolutely entrancing, from the way her lips moved when she formed her words to the slight scent of flowery perfume that seemed to fight its way past the overwhelming aroma of coffee grounds.

There was something about her that beckoned to him to fling himself headlong into getting to know her. It made him forget just about everything. His new job, this new town, what happened in Boston, it all faded when this girl looked at him. Had he lost his mind?

She handed Devin his credit card, and their fingertips brushed. His lungs nearly seized at the slight twinge of shock that passed along his skin when they touched by accident. He looked up and saw that there had to be something just on the tip of her tongue. She had that look that some people did when they were ready to confess, but didn't know quite how to say it.

Aaron moved to the side to wait for his order, but Devin didn't budge.

"You were going to say something?" he questioned as he returned his wallet to his pocket. He was well aware that there were customers waiting in line behind him, but he didn't care. Probably the only reason they weren't throwing a fit about tying up the barista's time was because he was a cop. He normally wasn't the kind to misuse his authority, but he'd take full advantage of it if it meant he could talk with Krystal a little longer.

She seemed flabbergasted, but spoke anyway. "I'm usually pretty good at judging someone based on their choice of coffee."

"Oh?" he asked and leaned his elbows against the high counter, so they could talk more intimately. "And what does my coffee say about me?"

Krystal mimicked his pose and grinned, forgetting herself just as he did. "That you're a realist," she said softly, just loud enough for him to hear. "You don't like your reality watered down or sugar-coated. You want to experience every bitter and bold moment that comes your way. So naturally, you appreciate honesty and justice, which is probably why you're a cop, right?"

Devin prided himself on his poker face. He'd had to use it a lot in the last few months while he gathered up the sharp, broken pieces of his life, so he could move on from Boston. He didn't want to use it on Krystal, but for the sake of his image, he had to. If he let his face do what it wanted, she would have seen the look of utter shock that mirrored what slithered down his spine when she pegged him so unerringly.

"Well, I'd say you do have a knack for judging people," he replied, and then reverted the conversation right back to her. "And what does your coffee say about you?"

The tip of her hair grazed the polished wooden countertop. "I like chai tea latte with a little cinnamon on top. Have you tried that before?"

Devin shook his head, staring into her dazzling, almost hypnotic eyes.

"You should try it sometime. I like to say it's like a holiday craft store exploding in your mouth. It reminds me of when my mom would take me shopping with her when she needed to get more yarn or beads for her little projects. I add the cinnamon on top because I love the flavor."

If he wasn't completely enraptured by her before, he was now. "I'll certainly have to try one of those sometime," he said through a grin. "Sounds like I could get to know you pretty well just by sipping on a drink like that."

That coquettish glint in her eye reemerged. "There are plenty of other ways you can get to know me, but I will definitely make you a chai tea latte whenever you're ready. On the house."

Oh, yeah. His pants were definitely getting a little tighter around his crotch. He nodded. "I'd like that."

Valerie broke into their discussion when she came up with a to-go cup in one hand and Aaron's mug in the other. "You mind wrapping that up?" she quipped as she blew a strand of her hair out of her face. "We do have other customers."

Devin laughed, took the drinks, and thanked her. "I guess I'll see you around," he said to Krystal as he began to move out of the way, so the lady behind him could step up.

"You know where to find me."

Chapter 2

From the moment Aaron and his new partner stepped into the coffee shop, Krystal could feel a disturbance in the air, as if it had been electrified. That same energy pulsed through her skin, seeping into her blood. When she looked to the front door and realized the strange force was wafting off the unfamiliar, hot cop standing next to Aaron, Krystal was ready to vault over the counter to tackle him.

Damn, he was fine. The police department jacket he wore did little to hide his strong, built frame beneath. His arms alone bulged against his sleeves and she nearly salivated at the way his button-down black uniform shirt hugged his trim waist. His square jaw was covered in a layer of dark scruff that must have broken some kind of police department dress code. All of their other cops were clean shaven, including Aaron. His short black hair looked soft and Krystal wished she could run her fingers through it.

She wasn't so sure she could keep her composure when he stepped up to the counter. Those blue eyes were so easy to get lost in that she completely forgot her hands had been shaking up until that moment. Talking to him came easier than she anticipated, and a warmth spread across her body whenever he gave her that smoldering look. All anxiety melted into a kind of comfortableness that she hadn't expected. As if beneath this man's stare was where she belonged for the rest of eternity.

He looked every inch a cop, but talked just like any other regular guy. She loved that. With Aaron being an exception, some cops came into the shop with poles up their asses when they were on duty, like they weren't allowed to socialize like a normal human just because they were wearing a badge. She hated when people took themselves too seriously.

She couldn't deny that something happened while they exchanged banter about coffee. Something deep within her seemed to awaken, and a whole new woman came out. She was on the clock with a long line of waiting customers, but it might as well have been like the whole world didn't exist as long as Devin was gazing at her like that, so intense and fixated.

Long after the two cops left, Krystal could still feel that fire burn in her chest, threatening to consume every bit of logical reasoning she possessed. She had never been so drawn to a man before, never craved his company like she did with Devin. If they still weren't in the middle of the morning rush, she would have thrown her apron at her two friends and run out the door to chase after him. What she would do when she caught him inspired a whole new level of excitement.

The moment Krystal could take a break from taking orders, she took a long, cold drink of water to douse the blaze Devin had ignited. She coached herself into keeping a level head, not to think about Devin or how he was seemingly perfect and totally fascinating. If she let her mind wander, she might as well have gone home. She'd be useless on the job.

Things finally began to slow down around eleven that morning and Krystal turned to see her two friends fixing themselves another cup of coffee.

"How many did you do today?" she asked with a drop in her tone as she folded her arms. She knew that both Valerie and Alexa could hear the customers as Krystal greeted them. She knew some had expressed their personal issues, but she had never given them the cue to whip up a special cup.

Alexa slipped a furtive glance to Valerie. "Nothing for me."

Valerie didn't look sheepish at all about it. "I did three," she proclaimed as she took the honors of picking up the chalk board and scoring the first tick marks of the day. "Mrs. Gregory said her carpal tunnel was acting up again and Doctor Jones was panicking over a new surgery technique he had to learn for a patient next Friday. The last one was Maggie and you heard her talking about how freaked out she was over her dog going missing. I slipped her a tiny charm just to calm her nerves."

Krystal crooked an eyebrow. "Your memory is impeccable, but you do realize we still have half a day left."

Valerie lifted her chin defiantly. "That means we have two charms for the rest of the day. I say that's good enough."

It was only a couple of days ago that she had told them she would rather keep the morning charms down to one or two, knowing that customers usually brought their problems into the shop toward the end of the day after everything went all to hell during their work hours. Alexa probably sensed the storm coming and stepped in, gripping her mug between her dainty hands. The painted image of the glittering fairy was obscured by her fingers.

"The new cop's a hotty," she nearly squealed. The coffee shop was about half empty, so she wasn't all that concerned about her friend causing a disturbance.

"I wouldn't mind being arrested by that tight ass," Valerie quipped from the corner of her mouth as she turned to add the finishing touches on her second café mocha of the day.

Krystal bit her lips together, refusing to openly agree with either of them. Though, they were completely right. She checked out Devin's behind when he left, and it was definitely a delicious sight.

"Think he always carries a pair of handcuffs?" Alexa offered with a sly grin.

Valerie brought her coffee over and the three of them congregated behind the register. "I love a man who comes prepared."

Alexa's gaze went a little distant. No doubt she was thinking of some erotic fantasy involving Devin and those handcuffs. "I wonder how comfortable the back of a squad car would be?"

"I wonder if his favorite form of foreplay is reading me my rights." Now it was Valerie's turn to smile and nibble on her bottom lip.

"Ma'am," Alexa began in a deep voice, "you have the right to remain sexy and naked."

Krystal held up her hands. "I'm cutting you two off. No more caffeine today." If they kept going, she knew for a fact she'd have to go get a change of underwear. Imagining Devin in that way was only going to make things worse. How could she possibly take his coffee order again, knowing that such images had been conjured in her mind? Though, she was achingly curious to see what was under that uniform.

Alexa reached out and flipped Krystal's black ponytail playfully. "We're just having a bit of fun. You were making goo-goo eyes at him too."

She looked heavenward. "I was not making goo-goo eyes. I was just being friendly."

Valerie nearly snorted coffee out of her nose. "Excuse me? You were totally flirting with him."

"And it looked like he was flirting back," Alexa nearly sang and wiggled her hips eagerly.

Krystal couldn't deny that. "So what if I was flirting? Doesn't mean anything. He'll come in here for his coffee with Aaron every morning and that's it. Ten second interaction and we're done for the day. I don't plan on getting arrested anytime soon."

Alexa gasped and grabbed Valerie's arm, nearly making her spill her mocha. "Oh! What about sex on a jail bed?"

Valerie made a face. "I still think the squad car would be more comfortable."

"You two are impossible," Krystal laughed. "Why come up with these things when you know they're never going to happen?"

Alexa shot her an impatient look. "It's just a little fun. You know, that thing that people like to have when they're not working. Oh, wait, you always work!"

Krystal sighed and cast her gaze to the ceiling. "I don't always work."

"I drove by the other night around eleven o'clock and you were still here," Valerie stated.

"We close at eight," Alexa added.

She shrugged. "I had some extra paperwork to do, that's all."

Krystal wasn't about to say it out loud, but they were right. Again. She worked all the time, making sure this place ran as smoothly as possible. If that meant spending a few extra hours sorting through receipts and researching new marketing strategies, she was all for it.

Alexa held up a hand in surrender. "All I'm saying is that you need to take some time for yourself every once and a while. Go home, pet your cat, cook something, I don't know."

The recipe board on Krystal's Pinterest account was getting pretty full. Each night before going to bed, she would browse the app and pick out new dishes she wanted to try whenever she had the free time – which was proving so elusive nowadays. Cooking was one of the few joys she had apart from work and her life as a witch.

Then again, there wasn't much she could do while cooking that didn't remind her of her witchy roots. Herbs all had their separate meaning and uses, and she could never take hold of a sprig of rosemary or pinch a basil leaf without thinking on those principles. The lessons her mother taught her as a child in the kitchen wouldn't be willed away in one lifetime. Within the same thought, however, she could thank her upbringing for showing her how to garden with purpose.

"If I go home, I'm just going to see all the things I need to repair and clean, and I won't get to relax at all. And Artemis doesn't like too much attention, you know that."

"Maybe you need someone with you when you go home to distract you from all the stuff you feel you have to do," Valerie proposed, giving her a furtive glance from behind the rim of her mug.

Krystal shook her head. "I'm not going to invite a guy over to my house just because you two think I need a diversion from life."

Valerie looked away. "Who said anything about inviting a guy over? I only said you needed someone with you when you go home. He could invite himself."

Alexa giggled. "Could Devin get a search warrant or something? Then he could come in without having to be invited."

Krystal took a deep breath and untied her apron. "That's it," she said. "I'm going to Taylor's early to get that cocoa mix. You two are driving me nuts."

Valerie and Alexa laughed together, something that rarely ever happened.

"You go get that cocoa mix, then," Alexa said once she could take a breath. "We'll hold down the fort."

When she was just on the other side of the counter, she remembered the long walk she would have to take to get to Taylor's nursery. It was nearly double the distance she had to walk this morning to get to work and she didn't want to be gone for that long. That, and the box Taylor would have for her might very well be more than she could comfortably carry.

She turned to Alexa. "Can I borrow your car?"

"Sure!" Alexa reached down to grab her keys from her purse and tossed the tiny bundle to Krystal. Alexa's keychain probably only had a couple of real keys on its rings. The rest were a confusing myriad of trinkets and charms she had collected over the years, some dating back to high school.

Krystal hurried out and found the Volkswagen bug parked across the street. It was hard to miss that bright yellow car, even in a snow storm. Since she lived so close to work, Krystal never bothered to drive. She enjoyed getting the fresh air anyway.

As soon as she revved up the engine, peppy pop music blared through the speakers. Without thinking, Krystal cringed and flicked her fingers to mute the audio without ever touching the radio on the dash. Ever since she learned the simple rules of magic, Krystal had a bad habit of using it reflexively. Whenever she needed something quick, she just did it with her magic. At least she was getting better at controlling those impulses.

She let out a breath and pulled away from the curb.

It was probably only a five-minute drive, if that at all, but Krystal found herself zoning out as she traveled down the long residential streets. Mostly, she thought of Devin.

Rumors had been floating around town ever since Aaron's first partner, Mr. Kenny, retired after serving on Goldcrest Cove's police force for nearly forty years. The old man wasn't as spry as he used to be, and now that his wife – who had been the elementary school principal for just about as long – was retired too, he was eager to stay home during the day.

Goldcrest Cove wasn't a dangerous place by any means. They could have transferred Aaron to a desk job if they wanted and the place wouldn't have been any less safe for one less patrol car out on the town. Yet, Chief Nickels thought Aaron needed another partner.

When she'd heard customers talking about the new cop from Boston, she had been mildly intrigued, but wasn't about to go poking around for details. Whoever the new cop was, she just wished that he would be a good fit for the town and for Aaron.

Seeing Devin interact with his partner that morning, Krystal was sure that they would get along just fine. They were about the same age, which was in his favor. That had been a bit of a barrier between Aaron and Mr. Kenny over the last six months since they were paired together.

As for whether Devin would be a good fit for the town, she wasn't sure. The few minutes they spent talking across the counter at the coffee shop wasn't enough for her to gauge whether he would be one of those stuck-up city folk who needed their organic produce and exciting clubs. He already admitted that he didn't like fancy coffee, which might have been a good sign.

Right on the corner of Lavender Lane and Kellie Drive, Krystal finally looked in her rearview mirror and saw a cop car coming up behind her. Its lights weren't on, and she couldn't help but strain her eyes to see through the tinted window. Maybe it was Devin and Aaron's car. She couldn't quite tell.

She stopped at the stop sign and waited an extra second longer than she normally would before proceeding through the intersection and taking a right turn.

Then, the red and blue lights started flashing.

She groaned and pleaded with the Fates that it would be someone she knew and they would let her slide without a ticket. Honestly, she didn't even know what she had done wrong.

Either way, she pulled along the curve in front of the two-story blue house that used to belong to one of the lawyers in town, and shut off her engine. It was only then that she realized she had completely forgotten her purse in the mad dash to escape her two dirty-minded friends at the shop. She didn't have her driver's license at all.

She groaned again. All she could do was wait, receive her ticket, and she'd have to go down to the court house on her half-day off to pay the fee. Her hands gripped the fuzzy steering wheel cover and she waited for the cop.

She glanced in her side mirror and swallowed back the lump in her throat when she saw Devin angle out of the driver's seat. Without realizing, she squeezed her legs together a little tighter as she watched him swagger up to her side of the car. Once more, her core came alive with desires and feelings that she couldn't even begin to process.

When they locked eyes, a slow smile spread across his face. "Fancy seeing you here," he said as he leaned down and crossed his arms over the car door so his face was level with hers.

Krystal stammered for a moment, her heart hammering against her ribcage. Up close like this, he smelled good enough to eat. "I was just going to pick up something from my friend's house. This isn't even my car."

Why she admitted that, Krystal would never know. Maybe it was the way those blue eyes danced at the sight of her, or the way his pearly white teeth seemed to gleam in the morning sun.

Devin looked around the interior of the car. "I should have guessed this wasn't yours," he said. "Seems a little too... extra for someone like you."

She wasn't sure exactly what that was supposed to mean, but "extra" definitely described Alexa.

"I can't imagine why you'd pull me over, though."

Devin jerked his thumb toward the tailgate. "The driver's side break light is out," he informed her. "I'm actually kind of glad, because we've been bored stiff all morning."

Krystal could have extrapolated out exactly why he was glad for a break from the monotony of patrol duty. Some of the cops had come into the coffee shop complaining that they hadn't made their quota for tickets written that month. If Devin was looking for an easy traffic stop, he certainly found it.

There was no way she was coming out of this without the little pink slip of paper.

Then again, maybe he was just happy to see her. Everything in the way he looked at her and how he was standing now, so engaged and totally against regulation, told her that he was glad to have pulled her over. In all honesty, she was thrilled that he was the one to be giving her the ticket. It meant she could see him one more time before the following morning.

"Since this isn't your car, can I at least see your driver's license?"

Krystal wasn't sure why she would even get the idea that she could flirt her way out of this ticket, but she tried it anyway. "Why? Wanna find out where I live?"

Devin smirked. "I'm sure I could find that out without your driver's license. I know your name and I'm sure there isn't another Krystal Hayden in a town this small. I can just look you up in our system."

"Something tells me you're not the stalker type, though," she said, easing back against her seat and letting her hands drop to her lap.

"You're right," he replied with a nod. "I'm not, but you might just convince me to do something like that."

Krystal bowed her head and felt heat plume through her body again like it had at the coffee shop. Hopefully, he didn't see her blush. "Well, you just might have to, because unfortunately, I don't have my driver's license either."

Devin made a displeased, clicking sound with his tongue and she couldn't help but think of all the nasty little ideas Alexa and Valerie had planted in her head when he said, "That's a shame. I may have to take you into the station now."

Krystal's eyes went wide and Devin let out a hearty laugh when he saw her shock. His hands lifted in capitulation. "No, no. Don't worry. I won't take you in."

She let out the breath she had been holding, though she was tempted to be furious with him for joking that way.

"I will, however, have to give you a ticket for not having your license. And you'll need to tell the owner of the car that they have a break light out, so I don't have to pull them over too."

Krystal peered at him. "I've never heard of anyone getting a ticket just for not having their license."

"You have twenty-four hours to bring it to the station and the fee is waived." He held up a finger. "However, I think I can work my way around the system."

Krystal felt the corners of her lips spread into a new smile, despite her circumstances. "Oh?"

"Yep. See, if you go out to dinner with me tonight and show up with your driver's license, I don't think a ticket would be necessary. Since you came and showed it to me, I think that's good enough."

She wanted to burst out into a fit of giggles. It wasn't exactly the direct way to ask her out on a date, but it was definitely unique. Who could resist an offer like that? No ticket and she would get to go on a date with quite possibly the hottest guy in town.

Krystal's face wrinkled when she remembered it was Thursday. "I have to work this evening."

"How late?"

"The shop closes at eight," she replied, wishing he had pulled her over the next day instead when she could get off at four in the afternoon."

"That should work fine. Most places don't close until midnight, right?"

Oh, the ignorance of city folk. "I'll let you know now that a lot of places close at nine or sooner. I think the only place that's open later is the grocery store on the north side of town. You can't eat dinner there."

Devin turned pensive for a minute.

"We can go to dinner tomorrow night?" she offered with a shrug.

"Nah, that won't work. You wouldn't have shown your license to me soon enough."

Krystal wasn't sure how serious he was about the license thing. She thought that was just an excuse, but now he's making it sound like it's a damn near requirement. "Well, then I guess you better write me the ticket."

"Do you think Alexa and Valerie can close up shop for you?" he asked. She could hear a little feathering of desperation in his voice. "It doesn't take three girls, does it? I mean, who's going to be getting coffee at eight o'clock at night?"

"Cops who are working the night shift."

Devin nodded in agreement. "Okay, you got me there. But, seriously, you're one of the owners. Can't you make an exception for a new guy in town? I don't know a good place to eat anyway. You should show me around."

Krystal smiled. "I'm sure Aaron can show you around. Besides, I may be one of the owners, but that means more than just my signature on a lease. I have a responsibility to my business."

All of the sudden, the words of her friends came back to her. Maybe she *was* taking everything too seriously. Here she was, with a handsome cop who was obviously interested in her, and she was turning him down just because she had to work hours that were fairly flexible, especially in the evening. There was no way she was going to make Valerie cover her shift, not after the way she had dragged her tired ass in that morning. She needed her rest, and though Krystal totally trusted Alexa to do a good job of cleaning up the store, the little nagging voice in the back

of her mind told her that she needed to do it herself rather than leave all the work
to her friend.

Yet, her heart and that tender spot between her legs were screaming different
orders at her. Devin was handsome, and absolutely interesting. She wanted to
know all about his life in Boston, and especially what would bring him nearly fifty
miles north to Goldcrest Cove – of all places. There was something more behind
those pretty blue eyes and she needed to know what it was.

Just when Devin looked to be losing hope, Krystal shifted a bit in her seat. "But,
what the hell. I'll have dinner with you."

Devin flashed her another smile. "Excellent. How does six sound?"

Krystal nodded. "Sounds just fine."

"Where should I meet you?"

It didn't take her long to figure out where she wanted to have her first date with
Devin. "There's a little Italian place down the street from the coffee shop called,
Mama Pazzini's. I know the couple who owns it. Have Aaron show you where it
is and I'll meet you there."

Devin straightened. "I love Italian food, so that works perfect. Don't forget to
bring your license."

With that, he tapped his hand on the hood of the car to dismiss her, and turned
to walk back to his squad car. Krystal watched him in the side mirror and licked
her lips. Damn, he was fine.

She let Aaron and Devin drive away first, and then Krystal pulled out onto
the street again to drive slowly – and carefully – toward Taylor's nursery. All the
way, she asked herself why she was so willing to throw away her unspoken code of
business ethics just for a guy. Devin might have been worth it, but how could she
tell until she got to know him better? For the past five years, she had practically
slaved to make sure Perfect Books and Brews was the go-to place for coffee.

So far, she had done all of that. One night on the town wasn't going to undo
years of planning and hard work. Right?

First thing's first. She needed to take care of that brake light. At the next stop
sign, Krystal stuck her head out the open window and flicked her finger toward

the tailgate. "Work," she commanded, and she faintly saw the driver's side brake light blink to life, and then beam a strong red.

Chapter 3

On principle, Krystal generally refused to wear dark clothes. There was too much hype around witches, but when Sierra walked into her bedroom with that stunning, midnight black dress from her own closet, Krystal could hardly turn her down. She had been going out of her mind trying to find the perfect outfit ever since she came home early from work.

Her own closet was filled with long skirts, loose blouses, and warm sweaters of earth tone shades. Far too casual for a date like this. It was just Mama Pazzini's, a place she had been going to with her family since she was little, but she wasn't looking to impress Mr. and Mrs. Pazzini. It was Devin she needed to amaze. Though, she had probably done that already.

She stood in front of the full-length mirror and twirled a bit before fingering the lacey, scalloped neckline that came off the shoulders. The long silky sleeves would ensure she wouldn't get too cold, but she worried about her legs that were exposed from the knees down. She never wore anything with a hem that high.

"Don't even worry about your knobby knees," Sierra slated from her open doorway. "It looks great on you."

After a few magical alterations to the bust and waistline, yes, it did look great. Krystal would have to let it out again when she took it off at the end of the evening. There would be no other way to get off the form-fitted gown.

"It's not too suggestive, is it?" Krystal winced, pinching at the hemline.

"Honey, even if it is, would that be such a bad thing?"

Krystal let out a nervous laugh. "I don't even know."

Sierra flipped her wavy, chestnut brown hair over her shoulder and leaned against the doorframe. "You said this guy was hot, so what's the problem?"

"Sierra," Krystal said, walking barefoot across the hardwood floor. "I know plenty about magic and making coffee, but I don't know the first thing about guys. I haven't gone on a date in like, four years and mom set me up for that one."

Her older sister grimaced. "Yeah, but that warlock wasn't exactly your Twin Flame. It sounds like you and Devin have some real chemistry."

Twin Flames. Krystal had considered that, but didn't want to admit it to anyone. It was a one in a six billion chance that Devin would be the missing part of her soul. Their connection gave the illusion that he could very well be her Twin Flame, but she wouldn't give it any credibility. This was just a date, and he was just a hot guy, the only one who had shown any real romantic interest in her for years. It wouldn't go further than that. She couldn't think of it. Couldn't believe in a fairy tale idea that magic folk put on too high of a pedestal. It just wasn't rational.

Krystal retreated to her closet to find a suitable pair of shoes. There was no way she was going to walk all the way to Mama Pazzini's in high heels like Sierra had suggested. "Well, maybe," she said as she knelt down to pull out several shoeboxes. "But, I don't know a whole lot about him. What if he got fired from his job in Boston, because he did something really bad, like killed a guy that didn't need to be killed or something?"

Sierra entered the bedroom and sat down heavily on the four-poster bed, making the old plush mattress bob under her weight. "If he did something like that, Chief Nickels would have never hired him."

She cracked open the lid of a big shoebox to check the contents, then shoved it aside. "What if he's got some weird fetishes or dark secret that's a total turnoff?"

"Like being magic folk?"

Krystal shot her sister an annoyed look and continued searching. "Well, I know he's not a warlock, that's for sure."

"Werewolf?"

She snorted. "No."

"What about a golem?" Sierra questioned.

"Nope." Krystal peeked into the last box and found the black felt boots she had been looking for.

"Then, seriously, what kind of dark secret could he possibly have? We've ruled out the worst scenarios."

Krystal shrugged, and she could feel the lacey fabric scratch her skin. "I don't know. Maybe he's just got hobbies or interests that just don't appeal to me? What if we have nothing in common?"

Sierra let out a dramatic sigh and rolled her dark eyes. "You're doing it again."

"Doing what?" she asked as she rolled up her socks and slipped on the boots.

"You're looking for an excuse to get out of this date, so you can stay miserable and alone."

"But, I'm not miserable and alone," Krystal argued as she stood and checked out the combination in the mirror. "Do you think these fabrics clash?"

Sierra didn't even bother looking. "Yes, they do. And you *are* miserable and alone. All you ever do is work and get up at an ungodly hour in the morning, so you can work even more."

Krystal frowned at the shoes she had on, then to the other shoes that didn't fit for the occasion. "Owning your own business takes work, you know that."

Sierra wrapped her hand around one of the tall posts on the footboard. "I'm not doing a whole lot of work and I'm still making a profit."

"That's because you have other stylists renting out space in your salon. If I can't find any shoes, I'm not going."

Sierra pointed accusingly at her. "See! You're doing it again. Here." She redirected her finger down to Krystal's boots and muttered a few words in the ancient Celtic tongue. Slowly, the felt material turned hard, rigid, and shiny. "Leather goes with everything."

She took another look in the mirror and nodded. "Much better. What time is it?"

Sierra fished out her phone from her back pocket. "A quarter until six."

"Shit!" Krystal exclaimed before darting out of the bedroom. "I'm already late. It's going to take me at least twenty minutes to get there."

The flat soles of her boots made her slide across the upstairs hall as she scampered to the steps.

"So what if you're five minutes late!" Sierra called out as she hurried to catch up. She had already dressed down into her pajamas for the evening and wore a pair of wool socks that were equally slippery across the floor. "Live recklessly!"

"I don't want to make him think I'm careless!" Krystal complained as she bounded down the steps, nearly tripping over Artemis who looked utterly confused by the ruckus.

Sierra laughed. "No one could ever mistake you as careless."

Krystal snorted as she grabbed her purse, which completely clashed with her outfit. Made out of patches of dark, patterned fabric scraps, it fit well with her earthy sense of style. With this dress, it stuck out like a sore thumb, but there was no time to switch contents from this purse to another.

"If you saw me today, you would second guess that."

Her sister caught up with her in the foyer and held her hand to her chest, feigning shock. "You? Careless? I don't believe it."

Krystal nodded and told her about how Devin pulled her over and she didn't even have her driver's license. She was never so forgetful. On that note, she made triple sure that her wallet and license were tucked away in her purse, just in case he actually asked for it.

"Not only that, but I kept messing up today when I was giving people their change. I even got an order wrong."

"Gaia forbid!" Sierra exclaimed, her eyes wide.

She had been living with her sister long enough that she knew Sierra was just making a show. "I swear, Devin is messing me up. Badly."

Sierra opened one of the front doors for her. "Well, maybe this is your chance to demystify him. Maybe he'll turn out exactly as you predict, and he's got some skeletons in his closet."

Deep down, Krystal hoped that he didn't. She desperately wanted him to be the real deal, someone she could really like and maybe this date would just be the first of many. Devin had been so amazing and sexy up until now and she didn't want anything to taint that perfect image.

But, she had to know if he was too good to be true. Maybe that was why she agreed to the date in the first place. She had to know about those skeletons in his closet and if they were worth overlooking for the sake of having her first real boyfriend since high school.

"Whatever you do," Sierra continued, "don't tell him you're a witch."

Krystal gave her a look. "You seriously think you have to tell me that?"

She shrugged, the collar of her oversized shirt sliding off her shoulder. "Hey, if you say this guy is messing you up that bad, maybe you'd talk a little more than you should."

At this point, that sounded like a complete possibility. "Do you think we need to do a secrecy charm?"

Sierra thought about it for a moment. "Do you?"

The two sisters stared at one another for a long moment. Secrecy charms weren't hard, but it also meant that it would limit Krystal's openness during dinner. It wouldn't just block her from talking about witches, but everything else about her that Devin didn't already know, which was practically everything. She wouldn't be able to talk about her family, her interests, not even Artemis.

"No," Krystal answered with a confirming nod as she took down her long coat from the hall butler hook. "Everything will be fine... Right?"

Sierra returned the nod. "Right... One more thing." Her sister reached behind Krystal's head and slowly pulled out the hair tie. Her black hair tumbled down around her bare shoulders, the tips nearly disappearing against the black lace and fabric. "There. Much better."

Though she didn't have time, Krystal hurried toward the hall mirror and primped her hair a little before rushing out the door. "Don't wait up for me."

Devin checked his phone one more time. He shouldn't have been so jumpy. It was only a couple of minutes past six. The moment he and Aaron drove away from Krystal's car, he knew he had made a grave mistake. Not in asking her out on a date, but in the way he did it. Going over the conversation in his head later, it nearly sounded like blackmail or bribery.

He didn't tell Aaron about that part, though. He only said he made the date and let her go with a warning. Devin had taken a stab at power flirting a little too eagerly and with Krystal being late, he wondered if he might have scared her off.

Heaven knows he deserved it.

He wondered how many people inside the tiny restaurant could see him standing on the sidewalk, a single rose in his hand, watching the darkened streets for any sign of his date. He didn't know if she drove a car, or if she'd come walking in from one of the residential streets that came to Johnson Avenue. The thought occurred to him that he should have offered to pick her up.

Why was he so damn nervous? This wasn't his first date. Krystal wasn't the first girl he had ever asked out. He'd had plenty of dates before, and a girlfriend here and there when he lived in Boston.

None of them were serious relationships, though. And none of them were like Krystal.

He didn't even know that much about her, but she had already made such an impression on him that it was borderline enchantment. Krystal was insightful, real, beautiful, and any woman who had the guts to start a business and keep it so successful had to be determined and strong-minded. She was nothing like the flitty airheads in Boston that just wanted to date a cop. Most couldn't handle being tethered to his kind of work anyway, but maybe Krystal could.

He spotted her coming from Kellie Drive, her long coat wrapped around her thin frame and purse slapping against her hip as she hustled down the sidewalk. Devin caught himself smiling at the way she looked both ways down the practically lifeless avenue and then hurried toward him. Her long black hair bounced and swayed around her shoulders, the light of the streetlamps gleamed against it to reflect that healthy shine.

"I'm so sorry I'm late," she said breathlessly as she came bounding down the sidewalk. "I was having the hardest time finding shoes that would match and – "

Her gaze trailed down to the rose in his hand and he realized he had been staring. Again. Devin offered it to her.

"This is for you," he said, feeling slightly awkward about it all of the sudden. Not even on the second date did he give a girl flowers. He usually reserved those for gift giving holidays like birthdays or Valentine's Day. It was an easy go-to gift, but Devin knew he couldn't be basic with Krystal. Nothing about her was generic. Even a bouquet of roses might have been more appropriate, but she seemed like a minimalist, so he decided to get one rose instead.

Why the hell would he try to be so thoughtful? Why was he trying so damn hard?

Krystal didn't smile, nor did she accept it right away. Her hand reached out and pinched the stem. "Can I be completely honest with you?"

Devin's heart sank into his shoes. What did he do wrong? "Please," he replied with a ghost of a laugh.

"I'm not really one for flowers," she said. "I mean, I like them and all, but I hate cutting them. I'd much prefer them to stay alive and cutting them just expedites death, you know?" Regardless, she took the rose and smelled the petals. "It is lovely, though. Thank you."

Devin let out a slow breath. "If we can both be candid, what should I get you next time?"

A soft smile graced her lips. "If there is a next time, you can just get me chocolates, or maybe seeds."

"Like sunflower seeds?"

She shook her head. "No, sunflowers are so hard to grow."

It then occurred to him that she meant seeds that she could plant, not eat. "So, you like to garden?"

A tiny sparkle of enthusiasm came to her warm brown eyes and Devin's heart might have skipped a beat. "Absolutely. My sister and I have a big garden in our backyard. We grow all sorts of vegetables and flowers."

"But, you never cut them. The flowers, I mean."

Krystal glanced down to the rose in her hand. "Right. We eat the vegetables, obviously, but we prefer to just admire the flowers."

They weren't even seated at the dinner table yet and he was learning so much about her already. Yeah, he had screwed up and thought she would be like any conventional woman. She didn't appreciate the flower as he had hoped, but at least she was honest and chose not to resent him for it.

What girl would have such patience?

"Oh, before I forget," Krystal said as she opened up her rather large and eclectic looking purse. She retrieved her wallet and Devin immediately waved her off.

"No, no. I was just giving you a hard time about the license. It's all right."

Krystal shot him a fiendish look and stuffed it back into the open compartment of her purse. "You really freaked me out about that," she scolded playfully. "I've never gotten a ticket in my life."

"Well, I'm sorry I freaked you out. I was just messing around. At least I can make up for it with dinner, right?"

Krystal looked to Mama Pazzini's and blinked as if she had completely forgotten that they did have a dinner engagement. "Right, yeah. You ready to go in?"

In all truth, Devin was content to stand with her in the cold all night, talking about gardening and whatever other secret, eccentric hobbies she might have. But, he was hungry, and the garlic bread smelled way too good to ignore.

He led her to the front door and opened it, letting the warm, herb-infused air out to greet them. Soft violin music played over the hidden speakers, nearly drowned out by the low roar of conversation coming from the couples and families already seated.

A young lady, probably fresh out of high school with big blue eyes and pinned up blonde hair, came to them and picked up the menus and silverware packets from the hostess desk.

"Hey, Krystal!" she greeted with a grin. "How are you?"

The hostess came forward and gave his date a quick, but sincere hug.

"I'm great, Tammi. How's that thesis paper coming?"

The girl, Tammi, pulled a face. "Well, it's coming. Just working on getting my sources right. If only the professor would allow Wikipedia as a valid reference."

Krystal laughed. "I know, I hated that too. I'm sure you'll get it figured out."

"Thanks." It was then Tammi finally acknowledged Devin. "Table for two, then?"

"Yes, please," he replied with a nod. He already spotted a booth near the corner and hoped they would be seated there.

No such luck. Tammi led them to a little table near the middle of the dining hall. He hadn't been in the restaurant for more than two minutes and he had already picked out the nearest exits, the hall that led to the bathroom, and the swinging doors into the kitchen.

No matter which side of the table he sat at, he couldn't keep an eye on every door. That inconvenient habit from his early training days at the police academy couldn't be shaken, no matter if he worked in a bustling city like Boston or a sleepy town like Goldcrest Cove.

So, he picked the lesser of two evils and tossed his jacket over the back of the chair that faced the front door. Tammi placed their menus, informed them that their waitress would be over shortly, and left to seat another family of four that just came in.

Krystal was about to sit down, but Devin moved too quickly.

"May I?" he said, gesturing to her coat. He had seen the way she appraised him after he shed his own jacket and it was unfair that he hadn't gotten to see what was under her coat too.

She nodded, and he gently took the collar between his hands to slip it off. Suddenly, he felt severely underdressed. He had looked up the restaurant online and thought it was casual enough for a blue button-down shirt tucked into a pair of dark jeans.

The black dress she wore with the long, off-shoulder sleeves was far more formal, but he absolutely loved the way the fabric clung to her skin and showed off that thin, but curvy figure. Now, he was sure that no matter what she wore, she'd be a knockout.

As he helped shed her coat, he noticed the black tattoo on her shoulder. The symbol was completely foreign to him. The center looked to be an upside V with one line crossing over it from the top left to the bottom right. Each end of this dividing line had a curved end and a circle toward the concave side of that curve. It was like nothing he had ever seen before, and even tilting his head, he couldn't figure out it's meaning.

Devin hung the coat over the back of her chair and pulled it out for her to sit. "Quite the gentleman, you are," she teased with a simpering grin.

"I try. Nice tattoo."

She glanced over her right shoulder where it was just barely visible above the lacy edge of the dress. "Oh, thanks."

"Does it mean anything?" he asked as he sat down next to her.

Krystal shrugged. "It's just an inside thing between some of the girls in town."

He smiled. "Like a secret handshake between friends?"

"Something like that."

Devin had to fight back his cop instincts to probe further and find out what exactly it was. If Krystal wasn't the only girl in the town to have one, was it some secret club or gang? Looking at her, and knowing what kind of business she ran, it was unlikely. He had to remind himself that she didn't fit the profile of a gang member. It was just a silly tattoo between friends. There was nothing sinister in this town.

He saw out of his peripheral as Tammi gave the family of four the booth setup he had coveted when they walked in. It would have served as an excellent vantage point to watch the room. If only he could stop being a cop for just a few minutes, so he could enjoy this date.

A couple of seconds of looking over the menu in silence, a young man, probably closer to their age compared to the waitress, came over wearing the typical uniform of the wait staff.

"Hey, Krystal!" he said, placing his hand on the back of her chair. "How are you this evening?"

Something in the way he looked at her, though friendly enough, set off red flags. Is this waiter just an old friend or something more? He mentally shook it off. He had no reason to be jealous. Not yet, anyway. This was only their first date.

"I'm doing fine, Mark. How's Kathy and the baby?"

Devin breathed a little easier as he glanced down to the back of the menu for the drink selections, knowing Mark would be asking about those soon.

"They're doing great. The doctor had some good things to report during our last appointment, so we think we're in the clear now."

"I'm so glad to hear it," Krystal said, and he could nearly taste the compassion in her words.

"What can I get you two to drink?" the waiter finally asked. "Wine, beer, soda?"

Devin looked up to Krystal and opened his mouth to ask if she'd mind sharing a bottle of wine, but she was already telling Mark that she just wanted a glass of water.

"And for you, sir?"

It was a strange feeling, to be the one that no one knew. It was as if Krystal was the rock star of the town and he was just another guy, no one important or worth getting a name from. For the moment, he pushed his ego aside and ordered water as well.

Mark nodded and hurried away to get their drinks.

"You seem to know a lot of people in this town," he remarked.

Krystal nodded as she looked over the menu. "Yeah, it's kind of hard not to get to know people when all of them have passed through the coffee shop at least twice. I'm sure you'll get to know everyone too, after a while."

He was fairly confident of that, but how long would it take before waiters and hostesses knew his name by heart? "Have you lived in Goldcrest Cove for long?"

"All my life," she said with pride. "My ancestors were some of the founding members of the town."

"Not many people can say that."

She shrugged, as if it wasn't anything special. To him, it was a big deal. He wanted to know everything about her, from her childhood memories to her fears and everything in between. Why did he care so much? This went way beyond sexual attraction and skyrocketed him straight into obsession, but it just seemed so right to feel this way about her. Being next to her was like returning to something he had lost. Like coming home, almost. But home had never been a great place for him. Krystal was better than home.

"What about you?" she asked, breaking through his stupor. He had been watching her for the better part of a few minutes instead of picking out what he wanted to eat for dinner. "Were you born and raised in Boston?"

Mark came to the table and dropped off their drinks before Devin could answer. As soon as they were alone again, he replied, "I was born in Worchester, but my dad moved us to Boston for his job when I was a kid."

"And you lived there ever since?" she asked before taking a sip of her water. Devin unconsciously copied her and took a swig himself.

"Up until a couple of weeks ago when I moved here."

"So, Boston's been the only home you've ever really known." There wasn't necessarily a question there, but Devin felt he needed to correct her.

"I never tried to attach myself to the idea of 'home'. Boston was great, don't get me wrong, but it was just a place I lived for a long time."

Krystal frowned. "Sounds like something a military kid would say, not a cop."

Devin had to admit that it did. It sounded insanely cynical, but she didn't know the kind of "home" he grew up in. Without understanding why, he decided to tell her just what he meant. "When I was growing up, home wasn't exactly home. It wasn't a great place to be. My mom died when I was too young to really remember her, and my dad didn't win any parenting awards."

A few beats of silence passed between them and Krystal cast her gaze down to the table. "I'm sorry to hear that." She looked back up to him. "You still turned out to be a pretty decent guy from what I can tell. I mean, you're a cop, so something must have gone right."

It did. Devin's father showed him that someone needed to defend the underdog, the powerless, the weak. He knew from a young age that he wanted to be that defender. He wanted to be there for the ones who had no voice, who might have felt that they didn't have any choices in life. He had been there. He knew what it was like.

"I became a cop, because I wanted to help people," Devin said as he lightly gripped the water glass, letting the cool condensation wet his fingertips. "I know it sounds pretty corny, but I knew I wanted to be a cop since the day the chief of police came into my third grade class. He talked about his job and what the department does to keep the city safe. My life kind of revolved around that goal. I went to police academy and jumped straight onto the force when I graduated."

Krystal leaned her elbows on the table and he watched the way the light from the votive candle centerpiece flickered across the smooth skin of her shoulders and neck. "I don't think that's corny at all. It's an admirable dream and I'd say you've achieved it."

He smiled through the hurtful memories that had resurfaced and nodded. "Thank you. What about you? Did you always want to own a coffee shop?" If they could avoid talking too much about him this evening, this date might actually go well.

Krystal leaned back and giggled. "No, not always." Her eyes flitted to something behind him and he knew Mark must have been making his way back to the table.

"Have you two decided?" the waiter asked as he pulled out the notepad from his apron pocket.

Krystal's gaze shifted between Devin and the menu, and it was clear she hadn't been thinking about food either. "Oh, uh... Just a plate of spaghetti with meat sauce."

Devin quickly looked down to his menu and randomly picked one. "I'll have the lasagna."

"Excellent choices." Mark took the menus away and they were alone again.

"The lasagna is really good," Krystal said. "Mrs. Pazzini has this special recipe for the sauce that I can never figure out. You'll like it."

Devin leaned forward and crossed his arms over the table. "I'm sure I will. Now, back to my question."

Krystal blinked. "What question?"

Was she just trying to dance around him, or did she really forget? Criminals did something similar when they were brought into questioning. "The coffee shop?"

"Oh, that. It was just something I thought of in high school. I told my friends about it and they were game, so we just worked hard at making it a reality."

Devin's eyes narrowed. "Right, but what started it? I mean, what was your motive? Do you love coffee that much?"

Krystal pursed her lips in thought. Such beautiful lips. "We all loved coffee and we saw a need in the community. I remember there was a coffee shop near the grocery store, but it didn't do so well and closed down when I was a freshman in high school."

"So, you just saw a need and decided to do something about it?" he asked, taking another gulp of cool water.

She nodded. "Pretty much."

"How did your family feel about you starting your own business like that?"

Devin could recall the very day he told his dad that he was planning on entering the police academy. He laughed and said he'd never make ends meet. Cops didn't get paid nearly enough for the kind of hell they were put through. He had been right, but Devin wasn't about to let him win. If anything, his rebuke propelled him forward to do even better, to earn high commendations, and prove him wrong. In the end, just one accident had validated so much of what his father said.

A sort of wistful look twinkled in Krystal's eyes at the mention of her family. "My parents have been really supportive. They probably would have wanted me to go into the family business, but my sister followed my lead and she's got her own salon on Johnson Avenue too. My mom says she brags about us to their friends in New York, but we don't get to talk to dad that much. He's always busy with his work."

"And what's that?"

There was a hesitance in Krystal, just like when he tried to revert the conversation back to her. "What's what?"

She did it again. Devin smiled, and he could see the faint color rising to her cheeks. He loved it when she blushed. "What does your dad do for work?" he asked slowly.

"Oh," she breathed. "He's... sort of like a people manager for a big company. He took over when my grandfather passed away. That's the family business. It's this nationwide conglomerate, I guess. It's hard to explain."

Devin stared, studying the way she anxiously fingered her drinking glass the way he had just a moment ago. There was something she wasn't telling him, and he could feel his guts twist. It wasn't a lie. He knew the exact moment when he was being lied to, but what she spoke were half-truths.

Maybe there was something about her father's work that she didn't want him to know? Krystal understood that he appreciated honesty above all else. She knew that since the moment he ordered black coffee that morning.

Instead of interrogating her like he would a suspect, he let it drop for now. "Fair enough. I hope one day, you'll be able to tell me all about it."

Krystal nodded. "I'm sure I will."

Chapter 4

The evening got off to a rocky start.

First, there was the question about her tattoo. Donning the dress, she had completely forgotten about it. The scalloped collar didn't quite cover up the moon glyph as her other clothes did.

It represented balance, something she prided herself in. The other witches in town had their own glyphs, including Alexa, Valerie, and her sister. It wasn't quite a global or cultural thing among witches. Sierra had started it with Amber and Taylor when they were friends in school, and the younger trio thought it was a neat idea. They all chose the moon glyph they felt best represented them and their goals as witches. But she wasn't about to tell Devin any of that.

Then, she narrowly skirted around some awkward conversation about her family. He seemed to accept that she didn't want to talk about them tonight.

Imagine how utterly confusing it would have been if she tried to explain that her father was the head warlock of the witch council in Albany, New York, who personally oversaw the entire north-eastern part of the country. There was no way to explain his laundry list of duties and responsibilities, including managing the Warlock Enforcer Units that were in charge of policing out of control witches, and settling minor disputes between covens.

Her mother's job would have been a lot easier to explain after that. She was his partner in the council, as was her maternal grandmother before her. That's when they had to move away from Goldcrest Cove, leaving Sierra and Krystal behind to start their own lives. Their parents met through their connections in the council and that's how they envisioned their daughters to meet their future husbands. They wanted her to marry a nice, influential warlock, whether he be on the council or maybe a son of a council member. Their greatest hope was that someone on the council would be the Twin Flame for one of their daughters, but neither were holding their breath.

Krystal had other plans. She had told her parents that she wasn't ready for marriage. She had to break the news to them after her mom tried to match her up with that boring warlock from Springfield years back. Since then, they had eased off. If they found out she was on a date with a non-magic, they would have some choice words for her.

After they avoided that conversation disaster, the evening went surprisingly well. Though Devin did mention a bit of a troubled childhood, nothing about his adult life seemed out of the ordinary. He was just an ordinary cop, dedicated to his job. There was some apprehension on his part when she asked why he decided to leave Boston and work in a tiny town like Goldcrest Cove, but his answer seemed justifiable.

"I just wanted a change of pace," he answered. "Boston is such a big city and there's a lot of crime. I needed a break from it."

To Krystal, it made perfect sense to want a slower pace. She had never personally been to Boston, but she could only imagine the kind of stress a cop would have been under. However, his reason didn't make sense with his motives for joining the force in the first place.

If he wanted to protect the innocence and uphold justice, he wouldn't get that kind of action in Goldcrest Cove. She couldn't remember the last time they had a major crime. Traffic stops and fender benders were going to be his bread and butter here. She was sure there hadn't even been a home invasion incident in years.

Just like she was hiding the truth about her family, Devin wasn't telling her the truth about his decision to move to Goldcrest Cove. She hoped that, in time, they would both be able to come clean.

The thought of telling Devin her secret made her palms sweat, but whenever he gave her that million-dollar smile, she was jelly again. After a while, she could feel his foot tap against hers under the table while they talked. But, he didn't withdraw or apologize. In fact, as their conversation turned to funny anecdotes about their jobs, she found the tip of her boots trailing up and down his calf.

The smoldering look in his eyes told her that he was enjoying it just as much as she was. From the moment he took off his jacket, she could feel that familiar heat spread from the crown of her head to the tops of her toes. He got her more hot and bothered than any man ever could and she loved it.

She adored everything about him, from the way his blue eyes appeared even brighter by candlelight to how his shirt accentuated those muscles he must have built up during his time at the police academy. He had to work out on a regular basis. There was no other way he could maintain such a body.

When there was a lull in conversation, her mind wandered to the idea of him, shirtless and sweating as he pumped iron. Thrilling.

"So," he began, "what do you do when you're not working your coffee shop and going out to dinner with cops? Do you just garden?"

Krystal giggled. "Well, for starters, I don't go out with cops. When I'm not at the coffee shop, I do garden some, but when I have the time, I love to cook."

Devin's brows shot up. "Cook?"

She nodded. "Yep. It's kind of a side-passion, next to coffee. When I was little, I'd help my mom make dinner. Sometimes, when she was too tired, she'd just shoo me into the kitchen and tell me to make us something. My dad thought that was a little demanding, but I loved it. I just think it's amazing how you can follow a recipe exactly to the letter, using the correct measurements every time, and come out with something that will taste amazing every time. Cooking is... it's reliable, exact, balanced. It gives me a thrill."

"So, why didn't you start your own restaurant instead?" he asked as he pushed around a bit of extra sauce on his plate with the flat end of his fork.

"There are plenty of restaurants in Goldcrest Cove."

"And you didn't see the demand for it."

She grinned at his wonderful memory. Few people got her the way that he did. "Exactly."

Devin stopped playing with his food and set his fork down. "So, what's your specialty dish, then?"

Krystal thought for a moment. "It's hard to pick, but I think my garlic mashed potatoes are my best. They're always requested at our gatherings."

"Gatherings?"

She tried not to let her surprise show, but he certainly would have picked up on the few seconds of silence as she scrambled for an explanation. No, she couldn't tell him about their witch gatherings held eight times a year on the wiccan calendar. Though she wasn't as devout as Alexa, she couldn't begin to go into describing all the intricate rituals and practices that the witches of their town shared. More often than not, it was just the six of them hanging out at someone's house on those given days.

"Our family reunions," she explained. "Whenever our family comes into town, we usually meet at our house and hold a pot luck. It happens more often than you'd think."

He seemed to accept that and nodded. "Well, I hope I'll get to try some of your famous mashed potatoes. They sound pretty good already."

Did that imply that he wanted to be invited to one of their gatherings? Did she just talk herself into a corner? What if, months down the road, he found out that her family was in town and became offended that he wasn't invited? She tried not to panic. They would cross that bridge when they came to it.

"And you?" she questioned as she folded up her napkin and placed it over her empty plate. "What do you do when you're not chasing bad guys or going out with baristas?"

It then occurred to her that they were nearly alone in the restaurant. How long had they been talking?

Devin didn't seem to notice the way she looked around at the empty booths and the busboys washing down the tables. "I'll admit that you're the first barista I've ever gone out with, but in my off hours, I like to go fishing."

Krystal smiled and scrunched up her nose at how silly that sounded. It sounded so Andy Griffith. "Fishing?"

He laughed at the face she made. "Yeah, my uncle owned a big fishing pond outside of Boston and I took every chance I got to go out and cast the line with him. He was a great guy, but he died when I was in high school. When I got my driver's license, I traveled all over to find the best fishing spots. I guess that's partly why I chose Goldcrest Cove. The town's right on the coast and I heard the fishing out here is great."

"You heard right. That and sailing are the big attractions for tourists."

"I guess that helps you and your shop stay in business too?"

Krystal nodded and huffed. "For the most part, yes. We're actually going to be getting really busy soon because of the holidays. Families will be in town and if they can't get coffee with their relatives, they're going to come to Perfect Books and Brews."

As if he had a startling thought, Devin sat back in his chair. "That's right, you sell books too. No doubt, you saw the need for a bookstore, right?"

Krystal grinned. "I'm very practical."

"I can tell. You know what you want, too. I can respect that."

She leaned forward on her arms, being careful not to let her long hair fall into the bits of leftover sauce on her plate. "I could say the same for you. It looks like we both know what we want, and we don't mess around when it comes to getting it either."

A hungry look glinted in his eyes, and it racketed up the heat level across her skin.

"Is that another personality quirk of someone who drinks black coffee?" Devin asked. His voice dropped so low that little sparks skittered through her core and straight between her legs.

"Maybe," she replied with a flirty smile that she hoped would drive him just as crazy.

Suddenly, the soft Italian opera music that had been playing for the last hour or so was cut short. Krystal looked up toward the hostess desk and she saw Tammi flip the closed sign.

"Oh, shit," she muttered. "Is it really nine o'clock?"

Devin pulled out his phone from his jeans pocket. "It's actually ten."

Krystal groaned and looked around for Mark. "I don't even remember him bringing the check."

"I have it," he said, slipping the receipt for their meal out from under his napkin near the edge of the table.

She laughed. "I didn't even notice."

"He brought it when you were telling me about the time Alexa cleaned the espresso machine and forgot to put a part back in. You thought it was broken for days before you found the missing part."

Krystal covered her mouth to suppress her laugh, mostly out of embarrassment that the rest of the world really did fade away when she was talking with Devin. She always thought that was such a cheesy love thing that was the stuff of movie scripts, but it really happened.

They stood from the table after she helped to stack their plates and trash, so the busboy's job would be a little easier. She grabbed the beautiful single rose he had gifted her, and they moved toward the front desk where Tammi was ready to take their payment. Krystal saw Devin leave a hefty tip on the table for Mark and she couldn't help but admire him a little more for it.

The waiter and his family had certainly been through a lot this year with the cancer diagnosis. It took forever for Krystal and the girls to convince Mark to bring his wife in for a cup of coffee, so they could covertly help in what little way they could.

They stepped out into the night air and Devin helped her shrug into her coat to block out some of the chill. Though, Krystal would have been glad for a little cold breeze to blow up her dress and cool her off. She would stand by what she told Alexa and Valerie. She would not invite any man to her home.

Not even if he was a hot, devoted cop who loved to fish.

"Can I drive you home? Or at least walk you there?"

In any other circumstance, she would have turned him down. She loved her solo walks between her home and work every day, but she wanted to spend as much time with Devin as she possibly could. That, and part of her wanted to share the experience with him, to let him see another piece of her secret world. It was the least she could do, as long as she couldn't tell him the whole truth.

"Let's walk," she offered. "It's such a short distance that it'd be a waste of gas for you." Devin agreed, and they set off toward Kellie Drive at a slow, ambling pace.

"I take it you don't have any siblings?" Krystal said, thinking of her own sister that would be looking through the window curtain when she came walking up with her date. She told her not to wait up, but it was very likely that Sierra would, just so she could ask how the date went. "You didn't mention any during dinner."

Devin's hands were safely tucked away in his coat pockets while she twirled the rose between her fingers. "I have a younger sister, actually."

Krystal waited for more. Nothing but crickets. Literally. Crickets and the tapping of their shoes on the cement sidewalk. "Okay? Is she still in Boston?"

"Yep."

She blinked back her confusion. He hadn't been monosyllabic up until now, so what changed?

"You two don't get along, I assume."

He let out a heavy sigh and she could see the mist stream out between his lips. "She's made some bad life choices, that's all. I assume you and your sister are close since you two live together?"

Krystal stepped a little closer and she could smell his cologne even better than when they were across the table from one another. "It's mostly out of necessity, but we get along really well. We always have. Contrary to anything I've said tonight, my family's a pretty tight-knit bunch. We have our fights sometimes, but it's nothing we can't resolve."

It occurred to her how perfect her life sounded compared to his. Devin wasn't damaged goods, but she couldn't imagine going through the kind of trials that he did. Her family had always been supportive and loving. A lot of magical families were. Big fights never ended well, so they learned how to compromise. Devin, being non-magical, didn't have such conveniences. The worst that could come out of his drama was a broken family or a broken heart. If Krystal and her sister really went at it, they could easily destroy this whole town.

Somehow, she wished she could tell Devin that not everything was so rosy. She wanted to lie and tell him something that would tarnish the image that her life was so unblemished and uncomplicated. It would need to be something so mundane, but nothing about her world was ordinary. If only he knew how truly chaotic things could be at times, how close she came to being discovered as a witch while working at the coffee shop alone.

Her secret rested just on the tip of her tongue, waiting to spill out and ruin everything, but Krystal couldn't utter a word.

"It definitely sounds like I won't be making any domestic violence calls to your place, then."

Krystal had been stuck in her own thoughts that she almost forgot who she was walking beside.

"Believe me, you can come make a house call anytime you want."

The way the words spilled out over her lips, it might have sounded like she really was inviting him in. Or at least giving him permission to come knock on her door whenever he felt like it. The very thought of him standing on her front porch at some late hour, dressed down in his civilian clothes and wanting nothing more than to be with her, did exciting things to her body.

Despite her suggestive blunder, Krystal smiled at the sidewalk as they turned onto Pinkerton Avenue.

"I might just take you up on that. Now, I'll know where you live without having to look at your driver's license or look you up in the department database."

"Yep, you'll know exactly where I'm at any time of the day," she said. "That's not completely fair, though."

She noticed how he veered closer to her. "How's that?"

"I don't even know where you live, and since you patrol all over town, I'll have no way to track you down."

He seemed to have gotten an idea and pulled out his cellphone. "Here," he said. "Add your phone into my contacts and I'll add mine into yours."

It sounded so high school to exchange phone numbers like that, but Krystal heartily agreed. She handed him her phone and hoped he wouldn't say anything about her lock screen wallpaper.

"Is this your cat?"

Yep, he noticed. "It is. His name's Artemis."

"Cute," was all he said before programing his number in. She wanted to be nosy with his phone, but saw it still had the manufacturer-set wallpaper and nothing clearly personalized. Maybe that was his style, or maybe it was a new phone and he hadn't had a chance to customize it yet. He also had very few contacts, and none of them read "Dad" or "Sister" when she surreptitiously scrolled for a bit.

Krystal handed his phone back to him and they continued walking.

"There, now you can reach me whenever you need me."

"I could probably just call 911 for that, too," she teased.

Devin made a face. "Yeah, but then you'll have to get through dispatch first. I want you to be able to get a hold of me without the whole department knowing about it."

Krystal shot him a smirk. "Oh, don't want everyone knowing that you dated the girl from the coffee shop?"

He shrugged. "Well, you know... I wouldn't want them to think I was dating you just to get free coffee or something."

She giggled. "I said you could try a chai tea latte on the house way before you asked me out, so they can't throw that in your face."

Devin shrugged his brows. "True. Do you have any problems with this small town knowing that you went out with a cop?"

She shook her head confidently. "Not at all. What could I possibly gain or lose from dating you?"

"Free rides in the squad car maybe?"

Krystal bit her lip, imagining her and Devin getting hot and heavy in the back seat. Didn't matter what car, as long as they were fogging up the windows. "Maybe robbers would think twice about targeting my shop."

Devin chuckled. "Something tells me there's not that much crime here."

"And you'd be right. You're going to be pretty bored. Goldcrest Cove is nothing like Boston."

Now, he was so close that their elbows were constantly brushing, each touch sending little shocks of pleasure that threatened to buckle her knees.

"It's definitely nothing like Boston, for quite a few reasons. One of the most important being that Boston doesn't have you."

Krystal grinned and she could feel her cheeks ache. She hadn't smiled this much in so long that her face wasn't quite used to it. "You really are a flatterer."

"I'm totally serious," he contested. "You're pretty amazing, you know that?"

She didn't know what to say, so she didn't say anything. She didn't think herself any more impressive than the next girl. No man had ever complimented her like that, anyway.

There were a million things she could point out about herself that made her less than amazing. She slurped her coffee, she always put the toilet paper back on the roll the wrong way – sometimes not at all. She still felt like she was stumbling through this business thing with her coffee shop. And she still had a long way to go before she reached her true potential as a witch. She wasn't even thirty yet and was still a child in her parent's eyes.

If anyone was amazing, it was Devin. He had a rough life and came out of it with a good career at least, even if his family was dysfunctional. He made something of himself and still turned into an upstanding citizen and a gentleman.

"Historic landmark?" he questioned.

Krystal looked up and realized they had almost passed her house. She turned and saw him reading the plaque next to the walkway that led up to her front porch. The low brick retaining wall between them and her lawn was just as old as the house itself, but made for an excellent place to sit if she wanted. Instead, she leaned against the square pillar next to the entrance to the walkway. Perched on top, sat an antique oil lamp that had been fashioned with solar lighting a couple of years ago.

"Yeah, remember how I said my family helped found this town? This was one of the first homes built."

"And you live here?" he asked, sounding rather surprised as his gaze diverted to the old two-story house behind the sign.

"Yep. Believe me, it's not that glamorous."

"You've kept it up very well."

Krystal peered around the pillar, wondering which window Sierra was peeking through to spy on her. Only one light appeared on in one of the upstairs bedrooms. "Thanks. We try."

Devin stepped closer and Krystal realized she had her back to the pillar still, trapped and utterly vulnerable. She liked the feeling. Maybe Alexa was onto something when she talked about those handcuffs. Too bad he didn't have any now.

"I had a great time tonight," she said, breaking the building silence between them.

"I did too," he replied, his voice dropping into a soft whisper. Even in the dim light of the lamp above her head, she could see his eyes dart between her mouth and eyes, as if he were debating whether to kiss her or not.

She licked her lips, readying herself for what she had wanted since the moment they met in the coffee shop.

"I think you've ruined me for any other dinner date I'll ever have," she teased.

"What if we have another dinner date? Do you think I could top tonight's?"

"Depends what you follow it up with."

Damn that sounded so suggestive, but Krystal didn't care. She'd suggest all she wanted as long as it would plant that idea into his head that she definitely wouldn't mind another date. She wouldn't mind a hundred dates after tonight. Being with him felt so right, so perfect.

"Well, I guess I better set a precedent then," he said before slipping his hand in her hair and pulling her up to meet his soft, silky lips.

Krystal sighed against him and wrapped her arms around his neck, ignoring the way her heavy purse resisted against her shoulder. Devin's free hand wrapped around her waist to steady her.

Her whole body came alive with a fiery passion that she had never felt before. She didn't just want to keep kissing Devin, she wanted to be consumed by him, heart and soul. Her muscles trembled as the pleasure mounted in her core.

His lips parted, and his tongue slipped into her mouth, playing and toying with her own. She had kissed guys before, but never like this. Krystal wove her fingers through his hair, gripping to keep him there for as long as possible. She was drowning in his scent and kiss, and she didn't want to come up for air.

Slowly, Devin eased away and lightly pecked at her lips, both of them breathless and yearning for more. If there was anything comparable to this, Krystal didn't know it. Earth-quaking, world-shattering, utterly flawless. Was this really happening?

"You should probably go inside," he whispered.

Krystal leaned forward in his embrace to kiss him again, but he denied her.

What had she done? She opened her eyes, but the sight that met her told her that she had done nothing wrong. He wanted her too. That hunger she had seen after dinner had reemerged and it made her even more feverish.

At least one of them had enough sense to pull away before it got too serious. She certainly wasn't the kind of girl to have sex with a man on the first date and he didn't seem like the kind of guy to push her into it, even if it was consensual.

Krystal nodded and let her hands fall onto his thick, muscled chest. "I'll see you tomorrow?" She absolutely hated the way her voice quivered and how the rose hung so loosely in her hands that she might drop it.

"Without a doubt," he promised, then gave her one last kiss to help her along.

Krystal smiled and turned to start up the walkway, only occasionally looking over her shoulder as she went, to see if Devin was watching her. He stood by the brick terrace, his hands thrown back into his pockets and waited for her to step inside before he finally strode back in the direction of Johnston Avenue.

Once the door was shut, she let out a contented sigh and slumped against the wood panels. The rest of the house was dark and quiet. She half expected for Sierra to come bounding down the stairs, begging for details, but she heard nothing. It was likely that her sister was still awake. The reason she hated getting up early in the morning was because she was always up late at night watching makeup and hair tutorials on YouTube.

At the moment, Krystal didn't care if her sister was sleeping or not. She dropped her purse by the door and flipped the rose in her hand like a music composer would as he prepared his orchestra for a phenomenal performance.

All the lights in the downstairs turned on.

With a grin, she pointed toward the family room through the wide, cased doorway to the right of the foyer.

The stereo system whirled to life and the volume cranked up as loud as it could go without blowing out the speakers. Poppy Latino music with its quick drumbeats, trumpets, and guitar blared across the house. She could feel the vibration of the rhythm through the floorboards. She saw a flash of tan and black skitter across the floor and straight up the stairs. Artemis never liked the loud music.

Krystal danced with each step she took down the foyer, shaking her hips and shoulders like she always did when she was ridiculously happy. That didn't happen often, but Devin made her this incredibly, absolutely, and stupendously joyful. If she wasn't careful, she would start levitating. She was that happy.

She slipped off her coat and tossed it toward the hall butler. It floated through the air for a couple of feet before finding its home on the hook. Krystal belted along with the Spanish words that she didn't even understand as she salsa-ed her way into the kitchen. She treated herself to some well deserved chocolate truffles that she had been saving for a special occasion. With the taste of Devin's kiss still on her lips, this was cause for a celebration.

This just might have been the best night of her life, and there were many more to come. Devin was everything she secretly hoped he would be. Perfect, charming, and an expert panty-soiler if there ever was one. And he wanted her, which made it all the better.

Krystal lifted the rose and box of candies into the air as she danced the conga around the kitchen island, smiling and singing like an imbecile.

She was vaguely aware that Sierra was making her way down the stairs and into the foyer, but Krystal refused to let her sister ruin this for her. She'd come in and probably yell at her about waking the dead with her crazy music.

Suddenly, the music died down and she looked to the entryway of the kitchen. Sierra was standing there, still in her pajamas and hair a little mussed. Obviously, she had been sleeping – or at least trying to.

"I take it the date went well."

Krystal plucked a white chocolate drizzle delight from the packaging and popped it in her mouth.

"Better than well!" she said with her mouth full. "It was amazing!"

Sierra laughed. "I can tell. You haven't come home that happy since you aced your math finals in college."

Krystal offered out the box to her. "This is way better than acing my finals." She waited until Sierra took her own coconut cream filled favorite before going into every detail of how absolutely wonderful the date had been.

"I mean, there were some things I had to fudge a little, like about mom and dad, but otherwise, it was so great to be with someone that I could be honest and candid with without having to worry about him blowing up." She showed Sierra the rose he had given her when they met outside the restaurant. "I even blatantly told him that I didn't like cut flowers and he took it so well. Do you know how many guys would have thrown a fit and had their egos bruised for that?"

Sierra looked to the rose, eyes wide. "Wow. I'm surprised you even called him out like that."

"Well," she said as she slipped another morsel into her mouth. "I did it tastefully, you know. I explained to him why I didn't like it, and I told him that next time, he can just get me seeds."

Sierra gave her a look. "Next time?"

Krystal's smile waivered. "Yeah, next time. Haven't you been listening? This guy is a dream! A prince straight out of a storybook and you ask me if there will be a next time?"

Sierra made a twirling motion in the air and the music turned completely off. "Krystal, he's non-magic. What if mom and dad find out?"

Krystal dropped the box to the kitchen counter, but held tightly onto her rose. "So what if they find out? This is the twenty-first century. If I love him, they shouldn't have a problem with it."

"Do you? Love him, I mean."

She snorted. "It's only been one date. How am I supposed to know if I love him? I'm only saying, 'if I love him'. Besides, mom and dad aren't going to find out about him until I want them to." Krystal pointed a harsh finger at her sister. "Right?"

Sierra propped her hand on her hip. "What am I supposed to do if they call and ask for you and you're out on a date?"

"Just tell them I'm out with friends. It's not that hard."

"Lying to mom is impossible, you know that," Sierra said. "She's got the second-sight, remember?"

Krystal rolled her eyes. That had to be one of the most useful, passive specialties any witch could have. Some could levitate, some could conjure storms, and some could see through time and space like their mother. She could tell if someone was lying just by searching their hearts. Krystal and Sierra could get away with nothing when they were children.

"Fine, then tell her I'm having dinner with a guy. It's telling the truth, but it's not giving any details."

Sierra nodded. "And then she starts asking for details and the shit will hit the fan. You know they want us to marry warlocks. Wealthy, notable, influential warlocks."

Krystal's mood might have been officially killed. "No one said I would marry Devin."

"What if it goes that far?"

She couldn't believe that her sister was thoroughly tainting this night for her. "Why didn't you say anything about this before I left? I was being Miss Downer and you were trying to pep me up. What changed?"

Sierra was quiet for a long moment and Krystal could sense the heaviness settle in the kitchen. "Mom called asking if everything was all right."

A twinge of fear snaked around Krystal's heart and squeezed. Another thing she could do was sense when something wasn't quite right in the universe, especially with her daughters. When Krystal got turned down for her business loan the first time, her mom was there in an instant to pick up the pieces and encourage her to keep trying, though she wasn't all that thrilled about the idea of her daughter being a businesswoman in the first place.

"What did you tell her?"

"I told her that you had an important thing tonight that you had been stressing about, but not to worry."

Krystal let out a tight breath and moved toward one of the cupboards to find a tall glass for the rose. "Did she pry?"

"No, but she certainly sounded like she wanted more details. I danced around the truth as best as I could, but I don't know if I could cover for you a second time."

She found an old glass soda bottle and ran some water into it. "Thank you anyway. Next time, just tell her to call my cellphone and I'll try to lie to her myself, so you won't get in trouble."

Since that catastrophe was taken care of, Krystal spun her finger toward the living room again to rekindle the peppy Latino music again. "For now, I'm going to enjoy Devin while I can."

She found her rhythm again and bobbed to the beat. Sierra, probably knowing that she wasn't going to win this battle, simply threw up her hands and danced with her sister. She might not have known the words, but she could be happy that Krystal was happy, even if they narrowly avoided getting busted by their mother.

Devin was in their lives now, for better or for worse, and though they still had a long way to go before love could even be a possibility, Krystal somehow knew nothing would ever be the same for her again.

Chapter 5

"I'm not telling you shit," Devin replied when his partner tried to winkle out the details about last night's date with Krystal.

"Come on, man!" he exclaimed as they managed to find a parking spot just across the street from the coffee shop. "You go on a date with someone as straight-laced as Krystal Hayden and you expect me to just drop it?"

Devin's heart was pounding a mile a minute, knowing he was about to see Krystal again. The night before had been nothing short of fantastic. Despite the way she passed him half-truths about certain things, he thought they really hit it off. And that kiss in front of her house... there were no words to describe how absolutely perfect it was. He didn't make a practice of kissing a girl on the first date, but Krystal's lips had been calling out to him all night long. When the opportunity presented itself, he couldn't pass it up.

Though Devin wasn't going to tell Aaron any of that, his comment about being straight-laced made him wonder.

"What do you mean someone as 'straight-laced' as Krystal? She seemed pretty laid back to me at the restaurant."

Aaron checked his mirrors as he parallel parked between a hunter green mini-van and a blue Nissan. "Ever since I've known Krystal, she's been pretty... how can I say it without being mean..."

Devin shot him a wicked glare. "If you're going to be mean, I'd rather you not say anything at all."

Aaron waved him off and angled his wheels before turning off the engine. "No, it's not a bad thing. She's just cares a lot about her business and she can be a little anal about it, I guess. Like, obsessively dedicated. I'm surprised she even agreed to go on a date with you when she could have been working. I've driven by the place long after closing and I see her inside with the lights on, working on paperwork at a table or cleaning something. She's just pretty one-minded when it comes to running that coffee shop. That's all."

Devin shrugged. He already knew all of that. The way she had talked about her business the night before, he would have expected nothing less. "So, the shop's like her baby. She's just trying to do a good job."

"Right," Aaron said as he slid out of the driver's seat. "Which is why it doesn't make any sense that she would take time off from her business to go out on a date with you. No offense."

He had to smile. "None taken. I can't help it if she's into me."

Into him was an understatement. Krystal seemed just as entranced as he was, maybe more. All night long, he replayed their long, open conversations and the way she responded to his kiss. There was no doubt in his mind that she wanted more and if he hadn't pulled away, they might have taken it inside. The only reason he did pull away was because he didn't want the evening to end awkwardly. They both had work in the morning, and he was sure Krystal wouldn't have appreciated her sister being in the next room while they had wild sex all night long.

The coffee shop wasn't quite as crowded as it had been the day before, which he counted as a blessing. Now, he could stand at the counter and chat with Krystal without the reminder that there were other customers waiting in line to place their order. Maybe there was an advantage to coming a little later in the morning, rather than right after they opened for the day. Though, the wait to see her again had been killing him slowly.

Krystal was working one of the espresso machines instead of manning the register. Her back was turned to him, but he savored the view. She wore a gray, lightweight sweater that hung off one of her shoulders and he could just spy a tiny piece of the tattoo he had seen the night before. The tank top she wore underneath covered up most of it.

He followed Aaron to the front counter, though his eyes were glued to Krystal as he watched her pour grounds in and work the handles on the machine like a pro.

"Hey Aaron," Valerie greeted as they approached. Immediately, Devin saw Krystal go still and she slowly turned her head. Her black ponytail swayed with the movement and he caught sight of her lovely brown eyes looking at him.

If he didn't have any sense at all, he would have moved around the end of the counter, took her hair in his hand and kissed down her neck until she begged them to go into the back room for some privacy.

"Good morning, Valerie," Aaron replied. "And how is your mood today?"

From the corner of his eye, he saw the sassy barista flip him the bird, and there was a completely black ring on her finger that she didn't have a problem showing off. "I don't know. You tell me."

"Looks like you're not happy."

Devin turned his attention away just for a second to watch the show. Aaron had a crafty smirk on his face, but Valerie was in no mood to play along. Was she wearing a darker eyeshadow than the day before?

"Bingo," she snarked with a sneer.

"What do I win?" he laughed.

"Play nice, Valerie," Alexa scolded as she made her way around the counter with a tray of dirty mugs.

The other owner of Perfect Books and Brews wiped the frown off her face and pretended like she was glad to be working that day. Wonder what got shoved up her ass.

"The usual?" she asked.

"Yes, ma'am."

Valerie's eyes narrowed, though she kept the smile on her face for her business partner's sake.

"Call me 'ma'am' one more time and I swear I'll spit in your coffee."

Aaron held up his hands in surrender. "No need to threaten my life," he laughed.

"I'll have coffee. Black," Devin told her.

She rang up their orders, but Krystal was already there with his cup, ready to go. "I expected you two to come in a lot earlier," she commented as Valerie stepped away to prepare Aaron's drink with his special mug.

"We got held up at the station for a morning meeting," Devin said. He didn't realize how much he missed the sound of her voice until she was actually speaking to him again.

"In that case," she said softly, leaning forward, "I hate morning meetings."

"Me too, especially when I'd rather be elsewhere."

It didn't occur to him that Aaron was still standing there until his partner slapped him on the back. "I'll let you two talk," he said before walking away.

Seconds ticked by, but Devin hardly noticed as they gazed at one another, silent and publicly unacceptable feelings communicated with just a single look.

"Did you sleep well?" he asked.

Krystal smiled and he almost forgot to breathe. Damn she had a way with him. "Yeah, I did. Why? Do I look tired?"

Devin shook his head. "No, not at all. We just got back to your place pretty late last night."

She giggled. "It wasn't that late. Besides, I can go to bed at midnight and still wake up at five in the morning. Silly biological clock."

"That's good to know," he said with a furtive grin.

Krystal leaned forward onto her elbows, the collar of her sweater dipping just enough that he could see the smooth skin of her chest. "Why is that?"

He copied her movement, their noses just inches away. What he would have given for them to be alone right then. "Now I know that if I keep you up all night, you won't suffer for it in the morning."

That slight rosy shade plumed in her cheeks. "And what about you? Are you a night owl?"

Suddenly, it felt as if the air in the coffee shop jumped ten degrees hotter. "I can certainly last all night, if that's what you're asking."

Krystal moved away a little and bowed her head to her forearms before letting out a string of giggles. Her black hair fell over her shoulder and Devin couldn't resist the urge to reach out and toy with the tips of the strands.

Just like the morning before, Valerie interrupted them and delivered Aaron's drink across the counter. Before he had a chance to apologize for breaking her friend, Valerie moved away to leave Krystal with her laughter.

"I'm sorry," she said after she composed herself. "It's just been a really long morning and you're making it so much better."

Devin grinned. "I'm glad I could be of service." A devilish idea popped in his mind and he lowered his voice to a whisper. "But my services come with a price."

"Is it affordable?" she asked in a hushed tone. "Because I don't pay myself until next week."

"I think it's a reasonable price. And don't worry, you don't have to pay a dime out of your pocket. What are you doing tonight?"

Krystal grimaced. "I'm working. See, yesterday I switched the evening shift with Valerie, so we could go out last night. That's why she's not exactly giddy this morning."

Devin nodded in understanding. "You did blame me, right? I would hate that your friend was upset with you."

She waved it off. "Oh, don't worry. I totally blamed you and Alexa."

"Why Alexa?"

"It was her car that had the brake light out."

Devin chuckled. "I should thank her, then. That brake light gave me an excuse to see you again... So there's no way I can get you alone tonight?" he asked again.

Krystal frowned and it might as well have been like someone broke her favorite toy. "Not tonight anyway."

"Tomorrow then? Are you working in the evening tomorrow?"

It sounded desperate, but Devin was. He enjoyed her company more than what was logical and he had been bashing his brains in trying to figure out why. Maybe a few more dates and he would come to understand.

"Tomorrow is Goldcrest Cove's annual Fall Harvest Festival. It starts at ten in the morning and goes right on until nearly midnight."

Devin sighed and snapped his fingers. "Damn, I forgot. That's what this morning's meeting was about. Half of the department will be making rounds at the festival."

Krystal nodded. "Yeah, the police department sets up a booth every year and lets kids come by to pet the K-9 units. Are you going to be at the booth?"

That was one fortunate thing. He wouldn't be stuck with the dogs all day. "No. Aaron and I will be walking around as security and directing the parking."

Her smile returned. "Well, you can stop by our booth then. We'll be giving out our famous hot chocolate. It's always a big hit every year."

"Seeing you at your booth isn't exactly the same as getting you alone," he said as he made a face.

She shrugged and a bit of her knitted sweater slid down further on her arm. "It's the best I can do. Take it or leave it."

Devin eased forward. "I'll take what I can get. Including this."

He pressed his lips to hers and she didn't shy away as he might have expected. Instead, she eased into the kiss and let out a tiny moan that made his hard on press a little tighter against the front of his pants. If Krystal wasn't careful, it'd bust through the zipper just to get at her. Her lips were warm, smooth, and delicious, just like they had been last night. If only he could kiss her all day long, then maybe he would be satisfied. Then again, he enjoyed that aching need for more of her. He never wanted it to come to an end.

Then, as if someone had blown the whistle on them, she jerked back and straightened up behind the counter, leaving him a little dazed.

"Not here," she mouthed to him and Devin glanced behind him at some of the customers who had been watching the exchange.

He didn't really care what they saw, but she had a point. This was a small town and word about their little kiss would spread through every sewing circle and school study group before long. Oh well.

"So, I'll see you tomorrow then?" he asked as he pushed off from the counter and started to back away with his and Aaron's coffee. Though he would have loved to stay in their little fantasy bubble all day, Devin did have a job to do and reality wouldn't wait for a cop or a barista.

"As long as you don't pull me over again," she teased as she cast him one more simpering smile.

"I'll try not to," he said.

Just as he turned around, he caught sight of another woman walking right into him. She was too busy looking over her shoulder at her friend who was talking about something to do with the PTA meeting at the school that afternoon.

By the time he clicked his heels to a stop, it was too late. She collided right into him, jostling them both enough that he lost a grip on his two coffees and she dropped her own. All three cups went tumbling, their lids popping off and the hot contents spilling out.

"No!" he heard Krystal shout from the counter.

Devin and the girl stumbled backward away from the mess, and he had expected to feel the scalding coffee stain the front of his shirt and trousers. But, nothing. He looked down and the creamy, blended liquid seemed to be contained in one huge puddle on the floor. Not even the woman's white blouse looked to be soiled by the accident.

He looked back to Krystal. One hand was extended toward them, while the other covered her mouth. Valerie and Alexa didn't move behind the counter, but stared with wide eyes, their gazes shifting between their friend and the mess.

"I'm so sorry!" the woman exclaimed. "I'll buy you another coffee."

Devin turned back and gave her a reassuring look. "No, no. It's all right. That was my fault too." He hurried toward one of the café tables that had a napkin dispenser, though it was silly to think that a few napkins would clean up a mess like this. It was a miracle none of it even got on his shoes.

It just slipped out. Krystal didn't mean to use her magic, but it just happened. Almost like a reflex. She looked behind to her friends, terror and apologies in her eyes. Valerie snapped into action and ran toward the cleaning closet to fetch the mop and bucket.

Alexa came to her side, a kind and grounding presence. "Are you all right?"

Krystal could only nod as Valerie rushed around the counter toward the mess. Did anyone notice? Everyone seemed focused on the two involved in the accident, rather than on her. At least she had the sense just to make the liquid fall away from Devin and the other customer, rather than make the cups levitate in mid-air. It could have gone much worse.

Devin glanced to her again as he helped pick up the empty coffee cups and she realized that they would need new drinks. On the house, of course.

She and Alexa moved in unison toward the coffee machines and took out a fresh to-go cup to pour for Devin.

"You're shaking. Here." Alexa took the cup from Krystal and she held up her hand to see that it was, indeed, trembling.

"Do you think they saw anything?" she whispered as Alexa took the carafe of black coffee and poured that first.

"I doubt it," she replied. "It was smooth, but I'm surprised you did it. You get onto us just for using our magic to put the chairs up during closing time."

Krystal groaned and covered her face. "I know, I know. It just happened. I didn't mean to."

Alexa ribbed her. "We all make mistakes, sis. Now, take this to your man."

She let that comment slide. They didn't belong to each other. They only had one fantastic, amazing, life-changing date. Did that mean they were a couple, or dating? Yeah, they just kissed in front of the whole coffee shop, so maybe they were. Nothing had really been agreed on, that was for sure. If her nerves weren't so wracked, she might have tried to ask him for an answer.

She took a deep, steeling breath and turned to see Devin waiting at the counter.

"Are you okay?" he asked as she handed him his coffee. "You look pale all of the sudden."

Krystal nodded. "Yeah, I'm fine. I'm just sorry you lost your coffee and all."

He shrugged. "It happens."

"Alexa's making Aaron's espresso right now," she said as she gestured behind her and hoped that he didn't see the way her hands were still shivering. She hadn't been this shook since the time she almost got hit by a car out on Johnson Avenue. She never neglected to look both ways again.

Devin looked like he was about to say something and then his partner walked up to the counter to interrupt. "What happened?" he asked. "I was in the bathroom."

The way Krystal looked, he might have guessed someone was shot right there in her coffee shop.

"Just a little spill," Devin answered for her, then went into explaining what had happened.

They both looked toward Valerie who was mopping up the coffee while the other woman in the white blouse, Jessica, continued to apologize profusely for causing her so much trouble. Like a trooper, Valerie wasn't snapping at her like Krystal would have expected. Instead, she just patiently assured her that everything was all right. She made a mental note to charm the poor girl's coffee, so she would chill out. Hell, Krystal needed her own latte charmed for the same reason.

She turned to check on Alexa and saw she was already done and making her way around to deliver the drinks. So much for doing a charm on the sly. Aaron took his coffee and turned to head toward the door. "Let's run down to McRae's before they run out of donuts," he said to Devin before walking away.

Devin gave Krystal a look to convey that he really didn't care to follow, but he had to. "I'll see you tomorrow then?"

Krystal nodded and let out a long breath. "Tomorrow." She managed to muster up a smile just before he walked out the door. She hated to see him go, but loved to watch that fine piece of man swagger out the door and down the sidewalk.

Valerie waddled toward the back door with the bucket of murky, sudsy water sloshing with each step. "Next time you decide to use magic," she whispered to Krystal. "You can clean it up."

Krystal pushed back her bangs and propped her hands on her hips without a word. She wasn't about to get into it with her co-owner when another customer was walking through the door. As soon as she spotted his white collar and black jacket, she straightened a little behind the counter.

It wasn't every day that the town's preacher came walking into her shop. Mostly because he confessed that he didn't like to be dependent on any substance, even coffee. Understandable. If he was walking into Perfect Books and Brews, it must have been for a good reason.

"Good morning, Father Frank," Krystal greeted, putting on her best smile, so the man wouldn't see the emotional turmoil she had just gone through. If there was one thing Christians could pick up on, it was a person in need of prayer. Though she could definitely use some, she didn't care to burden others with her problems.

Though, by the way the preacher looked, he had problems of his own. Usually, there was a spry skip in his step that reminded her a lot of Alexa. Maybe that was something seriously religious people had in common. They were always so happy, so contented.

"Good morning, Krystal," he said, a slight downturn in his voice. "How are you?"

"I'm doing just fine," she lied. "Is everything okay?"

Krystal glanced to the chalkboard, knowing she hadn't been keeping track on this busy morning.

Fridays and Mondays were always crazy. There were two tick marks and it wasn't even noon yet.

Whoever decided to get dangerously close to their blessings quota would be hearing from her.

Father Frank rested his hands on the countertop and gave an unconvincing nod. "I'm doing all right. Though, to be honest, I am pretty tried." He combed back a bit of his dark blonde hair from his forehead and looked to her with calm, sincere brown eyes that were always so filled with emotion. "I've been struggling with Sunday's sermon all week."

"Oh?" she asked, guiding her ponytail over her shoulder to cover up some of the skin she had been reserving for Devin's eyes. "What exactly is the trouble?"

He pursed his lips and blew out his cheeks in a look of mild annoyance. "The good Lord gave us both parts of the Bible – the Old and the New Testament – because they are essential to one another. I've known that since seminary, but the Old Testament is so hard to base a sermon off of. Much of it is the history of the Jewish people, and a few books are reserved especially for old Jewish laws, so unless I take a story from one of the books of the prophets, it's almost impossible for me to form a cohesive message. I can reference the Old Testament all week long, but sermons always seem to be just out of reach."

Krystal nodded, though she had very little idea of what exactly he was talking about. All she needed to know was that he was struggling with coming up with his sermon. Sounded like he needed a good ole' fashioned enthusiasm charm mixed with a little dose of focus to get the creative juices flowing.

"I'm sorry you're having such a hard time. I can at least give you some coffee so you can have an extra zip of energy."

He smiled and nodded gratefully. "Which is exactly why I'm here. I'll have your house blend with some French vanilla cream."

Krystal narrowed her eyes and smiled sweetly. "If I recall right, you liked two sugars, right?"

Father Frank pointed at her, his brows arched in surprise. "Good memory."

"It's all that coffee," she said in a low voice as if it were some secret. In reality, she made a point of remembering everyone's coffee of choice, especially when they would prove to be regulars. Though Father Frank wasn't exactly a regular, she couldn't forget the way he always wanted exactly two pumps of the sweet syrup for his coffee.

She turned away to start making it as he pulled out his thin billfold from his pants pocket. "Don't you want me to pay you first?"

She waved him off. "It's on the house. You do so much for this community already."

Krystal was giving away coffee left and right this morning, but stroking the preacher's ego might improve his confidence. She approached Alexa who was already pouring the coffee and leaned in close.

"I'm going to trust you with this one," she whispered. "He needs help writing a sermon, so charm it with some enthusiasm and focus. Got it?"

Alexa seemed more than eager for the chance to practice and nodded. "Got it," she confirmed.

When Krystal turned around, she was met with another unexpected guest coming through the front door. A great gust of wind swept in with Amber as she came tripping over the threshold, a box tucked under her arm and other hand gripping the handles of a shopping bag.

Amber, another witch in Goldcrest Cove, operated one of the few bed and breakfasts in town.

Known for her exuberant personality and lively sense of humor, her guests instantly fell in love with her. Out of all the hotels and bed and breakfasts in town, she had the highest return guest rate of anyone.

Krystal wasn't so keen on the idea, but Alexa was convinced that she was a fairy or sprite in another life.

That would explain so much.

Her dark purple hair fell across her face and she mumbled out a few curses at the wind for messing with her. Like Alexa, she was far deeper into the wiccan religion than Krystal was willing to get, and she couldn't help but wonder how this visit would go with Father Frank standing right at the counter.

Amber let the coffee shop door close behind her. She bent down low before whipping her hair back up with a toss of her head to reveal her dark, almond shaped eyes. The preacher had already turned to regard her with amusement, but as soon as the inn keeper saw the Christian man, she put on a big smile as if she hadn't just let out a string of profanities.

"Good morning, Father Frank!" she exclaimed as she scuttled forward with her parcels. "I trust the church is doing well these days?"

Krystal pressed the heel of her palm between her eyes and winced. Not the brightest thing to say.

Father Frank laughed anyway and nodded. "Things are well, thank you. How's your bed and breakfast?"

Amber invited herself around the counter and plopped her box on the counter next to Krystal. "Never better. Rose House is still the best rated bed and breakfast in town. I know because I checked this morning."

Alexa joined them at the counter and presented Father Frank with his coffee as if she were giving him the keys to the city. "Here you go. One coffee, French vanilla creamer, and two sugars."

He gave his nod and lifted the cup to the three witches as if to toast them. "God bless you fine ladies, and thank you. Have a good rest of your day."

Amber made a silly gesture, touching her forehead with her fingertips and motioning to him like she were some Middle Eastern nobleman. "And you also."

When Father Frank was out of earshot, Krystal gave Amber a light jab in the ribs. "Why do you have to be so damn weird?" she hissed.

She held up her hands in a beseeching way. "What the hell am I supposed to say to him? May the force be with you too? I certainly can't come back with a 'blessed be' or he'll start in on some righteous Jesus talk."

Alexa butted her hip against the counter. "I did that by accident and he didn't seem to mind. He even smiled. Father Frank's not the kind to shove fire and brimstone down your throat, really."

Amber gave a helpless shrug. "Whatever. Listen, I need coffee. My guests this morning cleaned me out."

Krystal crossed her arms and gave her a sassy look. "Then go to the store and get some."

"I can get it cheaper from you. Besides, it's good business. I tell them it's your specialty house blend, they love it, and they come back to your place in the afternoon." Amber pointed between them.

"I get them addicted and you're the dealer. That's how it works."

She rolled her eyes and heard Valerie come struggling through the back door with her mop and bucket again. It was a chilly, windy day outside, but Krystal could see a light sheen of sweat on her forehead.

"Dumping out dirty water that difficult?" Alexa teased.

Valerie shot them daggers with her eyes. "No, but fighting off an army of cats to get through the alley is."

Amber gasped. "You didn't kick my babies, did you?"

Krystal's eyes went wide. "Your little pride of cats followed you here?"

She flipped her hand at her dramatically. "Listen, they follow if they want. I don't tell them to come with me. They just come."

"Well," Valerie growled, "tell your pride to migrate or I'm going to turn half of them into mice, so the other half will eat them." She stormed off to put away the mop.

"She's just cranky," Alexa soothed Amber. "You know she'd never hurt your fur-babies."

"Either way," Amber said, turning back to Krystal, "give me my coffee so I can leave before that black storm cloud gets close to carrying out her threat."

Krystal shook her head ruefully and filled the order, grabbing several pre-packaged bags of their house blend coffee grounds from the cabinets and dropping them in Amber's box. She had a point. It was good business to keep supplying her with their product. That's what the witches did. They supported one another, and just like Taylor cut her a good deal on the components for their famous hot chocolate, they would cut Amber a deal to keep her guests happy and peppy in the morning.

Thinking about the hot chocolate reminded her that she would get to see Devin again the next day at the festival. Even though she would have absolutely loved to have seen him sooner than that, she did have a shop to run and a favor to return for Valerie. It was only fair after she made her friend stay for the closing shift when she was obviously way too tired.

Yet, if she had a chance to do it all over again, she would have still traded shifts for the chance to spend time with Devin. She just couldn't press her luck too far.

Chapter 6

Devin, Aaron, and the other officers from the department spent most of their morning setting up barriers around Main Street and making sure that traffic would be smoothly redirected down Johnson Avenue and other surrounding streets so the community had their space for the day.

Main Street was much like Johnson Avenue, except wider and the older buildings were occupied by lawyer and doctor offices instead of restaurants and boutiques. Though it couldn't be considered the commercial side of town, it certainly had a different energy. The red brick sidewalks were lined with benches and short trees skirted with iron fences to keep anyone from trying to climb them. Almost twice the amount of traffic passed down Main Street compared to Johnson Avenue, but there were significantly less pedestrians to worry about.

Just beyond the overhangs in front of the offices, businesses, and organizations from all over town came together and set up their booths. A bouncy house had been blown up at one open end of the street and kids of all ages flocked in that direction. One overjoyed cop had the privilege of monitoring the play place for the entire day, and Devin didn't envy him.

Other booths had games set up and there was a stage where a local band performed at intervals throughout the day. When the sun went down, a costume contest would be held for the scariest, cutest, and most intricate getups. Many teenagers, kids, and even adults, were already in their costumes and it wasn't past noon.

A barbeque restaurant had moved their smoker to Main Street and was selling their pulled pork sandwiches while some booths were giving out canned sodas. Devin could smell the smoky, savory aroma of the cooking meats and he could hear his stomach rumble over the roar of the cars he was directing into designated parking spots. He and Aaron were just two of the cops on parking duty. The rest were on the south side of Main Street where all the food was.

Two things were making him extraordinarily grumpy. One, he didn't get his coffee that morning – at home or at Perfect Books and Brews. Two, he hadn't eaten since he and Aaron grabbed a donut from Mrs. McRae's on their way to start prepping for the event. He was tired, hungry, and eager to see Krystal at her booth. Instead he was stuck waving his arms at families packed into their SUVs and giggling high school girls who weren't paying attention to where they were going. Most people had the sense to walk to Main Street instead of drive, but the crowd of vehicles was becoming a little more than they could handle.

"Hey," Aaron said as he walked up. Devin was busy waving on a couple in a sedan. "Do you think you could run down and grab us a couple of sandwiches?" he asked, slipping a ten dollar bill to his partner.

This was just the excuse he was looking for. "You sure you've got this?"

"Yeah, I'm going to start directing them to Lola Lane now. I can't remember it being this insane last year."

Devin clapped him on the back. "If you're sure you've got it," he said, taking the ten from Aaron.

"I'll be right back."

"Take your time," Aaron called over his shoulder as Devin hustled toward the north opening onto Main Street. "I think Krystal's booth is set up in front of the dentist office."

Good to know. He couldn't exactly remember which brick office front that was, but he was sure to pass it on the way to the barbeque stand. He kept his eyes peeled, searching for Krystal's black bangs and listening for her bubbly laugh through the din of the crowd.

When he reached just about halfway down the street, he wondered if he had passed it. Devin couldn't even tell which office was which behind the fall decorations of hay bales, stuffed scarecrows, comical animated monster cutouts, and big business banners. The bobbing heads, some half concealed by ghoulish masks didn't help either. It was completely possible that the entire town had turned out for this evening. He had been to festivals and fairs in Boston, but it seemed that Goldcrest Cove took their community dedication to a whole new level.

Finally, he relented and decided to ask someone. Surely if he said Krystal's name, they'd know exactly who he was talking about. At the very least, he could ask where the Perfect Books and Brews booth was and they'd be able to point him in the right direction.

He found a colorfully decorated booth where children were picking out plump pumpkins from a massive mountain piled on the back of an old fashioned wagon cart. The booth for Green Man Nursery was covered in ivy vines – probably artificial – and what seemed like a thousand different kinds of flowers sticking out of stacked hay bales around the table where the owner of the nursery was sitting. With half a dozen bright pink orchid blossoms pinned in her short, messy brown braid, she smiled and watched the children and their families choose. He couldn't help but notice how her bright blue eyes contrasted so starkly with her hair.

"Excuse me, ma'am," he began. "Can you tell me where Krystal Hayden has her booth set up?"

The woman looked up and her eyes went wide. "She's not in any trouble, is she?" she asked, her voice so soft that he could barely hear her over the gleeful squeals of the children.

"No, not at all," he replied. "I just need to find her."

The woman pointed further down the street. "She's three booths down on the other side of the street."

Devin gave her a grateful nod and moved away. As if by pleasant chance, the crowd parted just enough for him to have a straight shot to where Krystal and Alexa were passing out cups of steaming hot chocolate. When his eyes locked on her, his footsteps quickened instinctively.

"Fancy meeting you here," he said with a grin as he stepped up to the booth. The two girls, who had been in the middle of a good laugh, looked up.

Alexa cast a furtive glance to her friend before moving away. "I'm going to go see about getting more water," she said before bending behind the table to pick up one of those bright orange water coolers that athletes used.

"Do you need help with that?"

But it was too late, she was already lifting it and waddling off down one of the alleys in between the stretches of old office buildings. This left him and Krystal alone to talk. Though, how alone could they possibly be on Main Street during one of the biggest community events of the year?

"Everyone really went all out on the decorations," he said, slipping his thumbs through his belt loops.

Krystal looked especially pretty that day in her dark green dress and beige sweater. She leaned against the table top between the tub of chocolate powder mix and stacks of cups. "Yeah, it really brings people together, you know?"

"I can see that," he laughed, looking around to the throngs of families. "I almost couldn't find you. Luckily, the lady at the Green man Nursery booth pointed me this way."

"Oh, that's Taylor. She's real sweet. She's big into helping everyone out. The church is using her pumpkins for the carving contest later, and she helped decorate some of the booths with her flowers. In fact, this is her hot chocolate mix."

She tapped on the tin container. "Well, a part of it anyway. She grows a lot of herbs, not just plants and flowers."

His naturally curious mind drove him to pop the lid of the container and take a sniff. It definitely smelled like powdered cocoa, but there was a distinct hint of something he couldn't quite name. "Smells great. I'll have to grab two cups on my way back from getting some barbeque."

Krystal groaned. "It's killing me not to go grab some. Have you had Mr. Coleman's barbeque before?" When he shook his head and smiled, totally entranced by her vivaciousness despite the long day they must have had already. She reached out and grabbed his arm excitedly. "You're going to love it. His wife still won't give me the secret recipe, but it's absolutely amazing."

"Is she as secret about her recipes as Mrs. Pazzini is about her lasagna sauce seasonings?" Krystal smiled. "Just about."

He took her hand in his, and just as he suspected, her skin was ice cold. "You should be wearing gloves. It's at least fifty-five degrees out here."

Then, as if his touch were the key ingredient to helping produce her own body heat, her hand grew instantly warmer. He didn't think he could transfer that much.

"Oh, I'm all right," she giggled. "Handling these hot cups all morning is helping me stay warm."

Despite the seemingly magical turn in her skin temperature, Devin sandwiched her hand between his and rubbed briskly to get more blood flowing to the surface. "So, when can I whisk you away from here?"

Krystal smiled that sexy, flirty smile she did just before returning his banter. "I think you may have to arrest me. That's the only way I can leave the booth with good reason."

He shot her a scheming look. "Well, it's a good thing I brought handcuffs then, huh?"

"You wouldn't," she said, her words laced with a challenge.

Devin chuckled. "No, I wouldn't. That's too much paperwork. I've been patient so far. I think I could wait a few hours. When is this wrapping up again?"

The smile faded and Krystal cast a glance toward the end of the street where the stage sat. Currently, it was empty of performers or announcers. "I don't know. When the sun goes down, it'll get even colder and we're going to be extra busy."

Devin thought so. He heard someone talk about the costume contests starting around nine or ten at night. Not to mention cleanup and hauling all her hot chocolate equipment back to the shop.

She'd be busy all night and probably in no mood for any company once she was done.

"What if I came over and helped you pack up?" he asked, taking up her other hand. It was just as warm to the touch as the other had been.

A slight panic streaked through her expression. "Oh, you don't have to do that. The three of us can get it."

Devin let out a long breath. "You know something I don't get?" He didn't wait for her to guess. "You three run the only coffee shop in town, you get plenty of business that would pay for a fourth or fifth employee, but you don't hire anyone. Why is that?"

That bit of distress returned and lingered. As if by instinct, the cop in him came out and he gave her a hard look, as if demanding the truth. He'd let little things slide, like about what her family business entailed and the secret meaning behind the tattoo on her shoulder blade, but if they were going to start anywhere, it might as well be here with the thing that meant the most to her; the coffee house.

"It's an agreement the three of us made when we started out," she said. "We're all in this together. I know it sounds silly, but it's kind of like this sisterhood pact, even though we're all just friends. I don't know if you can relate, but we've always been close. We grew up together. It happens when you're in a small town like Goldcrest Cove. We would never hire anyone else because... we just don't have a lot of other people we can trust to stick around and be dedicated to a dream that isn't theirs."

Suddenly, Devin felt foolish for even questioning her. He thought there was some other, perhaps more mysterious, reason for their seclusion. He was wrong and he could see it in her eyes that she spoke the truth. He nodded in acceptance.

"Well, I guess that means we'll just have to work around your schedule. What about tomorrow? It's Sunday. Do you think I can steal you away for the afternoon?"

She gave an affirming nod and immense relief was written in her smile. "Yes. We close the store early on Sundays. We only stay open until four. We did have the store closed for the whole day at one point, but there are too many churchgoers who like to come in for coffee after services."

He could understand that. Her talk of church reminded him that he had agreed almost a week ago that he would go with Aaron to the Catholic Mass the next morning. He wasn't a religious man, but he was being polite to his partner. It wouldn't hurt him to sit through Mass for an hour or two anyway. At the time, he didn't think he had anything better to do. Now, as long as Krystal was busy, he still had no reason to stay home, twiddle his thumbs, and wait for her to get off work.

"Great. Can I pick you up from your house or the coffee shop?"

Krystal debated for a moment. "Go ahead and meet me at my place around four-thirty."

He grinned. They were finally going to go on their second date, and he knew exactly what he wanted to do. "Great. The weatherman said it would be warmer tomorrow, so I met with one of the harbor masters and he agreed to let me borrow his boat for the day. Wear something warm, but maybe bring a change of clothes, just in case."

Devin gave her a sly wink that might as well have turned her into mush. She laughed out an agreement, though it seemed a little slurred behind the spell he had unwittingly cast over her. He'd have to use that wink more often.

"I'll stop by again to get that hot chocolate," he said as he released her hand. "I've got to run and get that barbeque. Do you want some?"

Krystal blinked and nodded. "Sure."

When she reached under the table, he waved her off. "No, no. My treat. I'll be right back."

"I'll be here."

Devin strutted away, proud that something was finally working out for him and Krystal now. Two evenings away from her company seemed like an eternity, but he would finally get his reprieve tomorrow. Out on the water, they'd be completely alone and free to talk, to kiss, and maybe something more.

For the last forty-eight hours, he searched his heart and mind for exactly why Krystal had knocked him senseless. He was happier than he had ever been, his mind free of the guilt and torment that had possessed him since the incident in Boston. Just knowing her had shone a light into his dim world and he couldn't imagine going a single day without seeing her. He'd willingly try every fancy coffee and tea combination they had, just so he would have an excuse to see her at the coffee shop.

More than anything, Krystal's presence began to feel like something Devin had always tried to avoid committing to.

Home.

She felt like the closest thing to home he had ever known. Boston was big, stressful, and held too many poisoned memories. The little house that he, his father, and sister were crowded into never felt like a place he could run to for safety and comfort. He wasn't even sure if the modest home he rented out on the north side of town could ever be home to him.

But with Krystal, he felt like he didn't have to be the one in need of protection, nor the one who was obligated to protect anyone else. He could relax with her. That might have been the only reason he didn't make a big deal out of being seated in the middle of the restaurant the other night. He was okay with not being in control. He could let his guard down for the first time in months.

"Did I just hear you agree to go sailing on a boat with Devin?" Alexa said as she returned with the filled water cooler.

Normally, the petite witch wouldn't have been able to carry that sloshing load on her own strength. With a touch of subtle magic, she could carry that cooler as easily as if she were carrying a feather pillow.

"What?" Krystal asked as she shook off the last of Devin's little mind-melting trick. As if his smile wasn't dangerous enough, now his eyes could make her a little wet too.

"Devin. Boat. Water…" Alexa leveled a look at her. "You're terrified of the open water, remember?"

Oh, goddess.

Krystal covered her mouth. "I didn't," she gasped.

"I heard it clear as day." Alexa crossed her arms. "At least you won't have to trade shifts with anyone. I would hate to have to cover for you like Valerie did."

Fear skittered through her and she could already feel her hands tremble. "What am I going to do?" she squeaked. "The last time I went out on a boat, I nearly fainted. You remember that trip to the marina when we were in elementary school?"

Alexa nodded. "Yep. You fainted and almost knocked your head on the railing, but you fell straight into Jimmy Linder and he broke your fall."

Krystal covered her face with her hands the way she had when she had accidentally used magic right in front of Devin. She still couldn't wish away that nervous niggling in the back of her head that someone saw her do it too. "I have to cancel on him."

Her friend took her shoulders in a firm grip and shook her. "Look at me, sis." Krystal did. "You are a strong daughter of Gaia, remember? The water is not your enemy. It has the power to destroy, but you are one with it and the rest of nature. It has no reason to hurt you. You can do this."

The logic behind her pep talk was compelling, but Krystal had never claimed that title of 'daughter of Gaia', even though her mother tried to drill that into her head as a child. She still believed in the goddess, but whether such an ancient deity would save her from drowning was another matter entirely.

Self-delivered pep talks would have to do.

"I can do this," she said to herself. "It's just water and boats have life jackets, right?"

Alexa grinned. "That's the spirit."

Maybe she should bring plenty of wine, so she could just get drunk and forget she was on a boat at all. Then again, what if she tried to walk while inebriated, and fell overboard? She didn't want to risk it, nor have Devin think she was an alcoholic or something.

She shouldn't have been so afraid. Being alone with Devin on a boat out on the open water should have been the best date idea in the world. The water was his element. After all, he loved to fish and this was a chance for her to immerse herself in something that he enjoyed. They could do so much out there and she felt that rush of heat through her body at just the thought of it.

"Hello, ladies," she heard from across the table.

Krystal turned and hoped her skin hadn't flushed a shade of red that was too noticeable for Father Frank.

The girls returned his greeting and she couldn't help but notice that he certainly looked better than he did the morning before when he walked into the coffee shop. The dark circles weren't hanging around his eyes, and there was a bit of that usual spring in his step. How much zeal did Alexa give him in that cup of coffee?

"The festival is a real hit this year, isn't it?" he said, smiling to one of the families passing by the booth. Yep, he got a pretty big dose.

"It is," Alexa replied. "Has the pumpkin carving contest started yet?"

"No," he said excitedly. "It will soon, though. I'm just waiting for the little ones to pick out their pumpkins. Taylor was so generous to donate this year."

Krystal slipped a cup from one of the stacks and prepared his hot chocolate. "She was. She knows how much your events like the pumpkin carving and Trunk-or-Treat help the kids in the town." Father Frank only shrugged. "I'm just doing what I can. My congregation is the life of this town, not me. If I didn't have their support and volunteer work, nothing would ever get done. I'm so grateful for them."

It wasn't hard to admire a figure like Father Frank. Though they might have disagreed on theistic theories, he had a kind and caring heart. In her book, he was aces for that alone. She wasn't about to go rub elbows with him or confess her sins, but she could certainly respect him.

"How's that sermon coming?" she asked as she sprinkled on the mini marshmallows for the final touch on his hot chocolate.

Father Frank clasped his hands together and if it were possible for his smile to get any bigger, his lips would tear open. "Excellent. That extra boost of coffee really helped me to focus, I think. I went home and the ideas just kept pouring out. I'd love for you ladies to attend Mass tomorrow, so you can hear it."

Krystal gave him a helpless look. "I'm sorry, but we open the shop early on Sundays, so your congregation can get their morning pick-me-up before they come to the church. I know you wouldn't want them falling asleep in the pews."

"True, true," he said with a nod. "Well, I'll just stop by and give you three a brief version after the service. Though, I'm sure I don't know how I'll be able to be brief when I'm so on-fire for this message."

Alexa capped his hot chocolate for him. "Sounds like it's going to be great," she said with the right amount of interest that would make her true indifference pass under the radar.

"It is. In fact, after I was done writing the sermon, something came over me and I just couldn't stay at home. The Lord told me I needed to go out. So, I did and do you know what happened?" Krystal smiled, though she couldn't imagine how much longer he was going to talk. "I ran into Elizabeth Thatchman." The two girls exchanged looks.

"Elizabeth Thatchman?" Krystal clarified.

"Yes," Father Frank continued. "She was at the grocery store getting some things and the Lord told me I needed to speak to her. So, I did. I didn't talk about what she does or anything, and she admitted that she had been meaning to come and see me."

Sliding a glance to Alexa, she saw her friend's brows wrinkle with confusion. "Elizabeth Thatchman wanted to come and see you?"

Father Frank leaned over the table to get closer, probably thinking that they weren't hearing him. They heard him perfectly well. They just couldn't believe it.

They had gone to school with Elizabeth Thatchman. She had her problems at home with her father and older brother, but at the time, they thought it was completely unrelated to the way she slept around with their senior class and even with some of the guys from the community college who came to visit for the summer.

Habits didn't die in high school and she had been working at The Torn Sails Bar and Grill to the south of town. She served drinks and offered other services on the side. Everyone knew about her and Krystal hated it when mothers would use her as an example to their daughters of what could happen if they made the wrong choices in life.

"Yes. In fact, I'm meeting with her here, at the festival. We agreed that meeting in private wouldn't be prudent, so we decided that a very public, crowded place was perfect for a nice conversation."

The preacher looked so proud and Krystal couldn't discredit that. There were plenty of stories about how sinners came to the Christian god and found salvation through forgiveness and Krystal respected those values and teachings. There was nothing wrong with them and there was nothing wrong with Father Frank's efforts to mend the brokenness that had consumed Elizabeth's life. With luck, maybe she could leave her job at the bar and go on to do something more respectable. Sierra did say she had a certain knack for styling her own hair, so maybe Krystal could put a good word in for Elizabeth.

"I'll admit that I haven't seen her," Alexa said. "If we do see her and she's looking for you, we'll send her your way."

Father Frank took the hot chocolate from her and gave her a quick nod. "God bless you both. I think today's going to be a great day."

"And hopefully there will be a party in heaven, right?" Alexa said.

"Lord willing – and I know He is, then yes. There will be a party in heaven."
With that, Father Frank walked away and disappeared into the crowd, though
Krystal could still hear him greeting people and shaking hands all the way.

"A party in heaven?" she questioned to her friend.

Alexa shrugged. "I was scrolling through the channels one night and heard an
evangelist come on, so I listened a bit and that was just something he said."

She hung her arms around her friend's shoulders. "At least you try," she
laughed.

Alexa returned the embrace and they enjoyed the lull in business. Everyone was
too preoccupied with getting their barbeque from Mr. Coleman's smoker to get
hot chocolate right then.

Traffic would pick up after lunch, and it was a good thing Alexa went to refill
the water barrel.

"You know, you've been a lot happier lately," Alexa said as they watched the
crowds amble by. Little kids tugged at their parents' hands to get them to move
faster toward the bouncy house, while laughing teenagers loitered in the middle
of the street.

Krystal had to nod to Alexa's statement. "You know what? I have been."

"I presume we have a certain cop to thank for that?" she wiggled her hips
suggestively. "Did you two do anything last night? I thought I heard you talking
about going out yesterday."

She let out a sigh. "No, we didn't go out. Not in the physical anyway." She
turned to face away from the crowds and leaned against the edge of their table. "I
couldn't stop dreaming about him, though."

Alexa mimicked her posture and a fresh giddiness flooded over her. "Dreams?
Oh, do tell."

"I'm not going to tell you what I dreamed about," Krystal laughed.

"You're blushing, so I guess it was something good." Alexa shot her a cunning
smile. "May all your dreams about Devin come true."

It was a simple wish, not a charm or even a premonition, but it meant the world
to Krystal that Alexa did want happiness for her and Devin. Valerie, who was

back at the coffee shop, didn't seem that enthusiastic. Though, Krystal could only guess that it was because she thought there would be more shift switches in the future, if Devin were to ask her out more often.

If she could help it, that wouldn't be an issue. Devin seemed to respect that fact that she was a working woman, and as long as she could keep her head on straight, Perfect Books and Brews wouldn't fall to ruin just because she was falling hard for the new cop in town.

Chapter 7

D evin had to admit that he wasn't sure what to expect when he and Aaron sat down in the hard pew next to other complete strangers in the church. Well, they were strangers to him, but not to Aaron. Dozens of people, men and women, young and old, came by to greet Aaron. Devin's handshaking habit came in handy when he was introduced to teachers, deacons, lawyers, and other members of the Goldcrest Cove community that he hadn't had a chance to meet previously.

They were a friendly bunch, and Devin expected nothing less. He hadn't seen a frowning face in days and Goldcrest Cove seemed to defy all the typical conventions of city life. There were bound to be a few sour faces, even in a town this small. Yet, when they walked down the sidewalks or when he stood in line at the grocery store, they were all eager to prove themselves friendlier than their neighbor. Devin couldn't figure it out.

This wasn't the only church in town, but every pew was filled from end to end with families, married and unmarried couples, single churchgoers, and elderly patrons who seemed to migrate to the first few rows.

Just when he thought he would have a little elbow room, a young man scooted his way past a single mom with her two daughters, bumping into their legs and feet as he went. For whatever reason, Devin felt compelled to study this guy. There was nothing in his mannerisms or his attitude that would suggest he was a threat, but something didn't feel quite right.

He sat down heavily and pulled down his vest that was fastened over a dress shirt. A colorful tie with a paisley print peeked out from his unbuttoned jacket. The stiffened strands of his gelled hair were smoothed back away from his face. There was nothing sinister in the way he watched the congregation. Yet, there was a slight nervous glint in his eyes that told Devin this might have been his first time in the cathedral too.

In a move that he didn't quite expect of himself, Devin offered out his hand to the man. "Good morning," he greeted.

The stranger appeared slightly startled, but recovered quickly and shook Devin's hand. "Good morning."

"You new too?" Devin asked, hoping he didn't come across as too pushy. At least with his uniform off, people could breathe easy around him. If he asked a lot of questions, they might have just thought he was inquisitive instead of interrogative. People were nervous around cops for some reason.

"How could you tell?"

Devin shrugged and laced his hands in his lap before casually leaning against the back of the pew. "You've got the same look I did when I first walked in, and no one is saying hello to you like they're old friends."

The stranger huffed and looked around with a slightly cynical grin. He must not have been into the religious scene either. "Yeah, it seems like everyone is really friendly around here. I just moved here. I met Father Frank the other day at the grocery store and he invited me. I thought about brushing it off, but I didn't have anything better to do. Plus, he was so insistent and excited in that weird, contagious way. Everyone in town seems to be."

"I've only been in Goldcrest Cove for a couple of weeks and I'm still not used to it." He ended on a bit of a laughing note. "I'm Devin Daniels, by the way."

The stranger nodded his acknowledgement. "Jacob Nathanson."

"Nice to meet you."

Devin was about to start in on asking if he was adjusting well enough, despite the effusive friendliness of the townspeople, but the procession of altar boys and the priest made their way down the center aisle toward the front. There would be plenty of time for talk afterward.

When the service started, the congregation hushed and listened to the words of Father Frank Sellers. If anyone had been careless enough to drop a pin, it could have been heard pinging against the stone floor from across the sanctuary. Devin was almost afraid to move, lest he break the sacred silence that descended.

Once the first opening welcomes were out of the way, the rest of Mass continued. Though there was plenty of ritual in the Mass, Devin found himself enjoying the music that echoed off the high rafters of the stone cathedral. He guessed this building had to be as old as Krystal's house. The stained-glass windows were a breathtaking piece of artwork alone, not to mention the carved statues of saints and crucifixes on the walls.

Devin had intermittently gone to church as a child. When his father wasn't hung over on Sunday mornings, he'd dress nice for a change and take him and his sister, Alana, to the nearest Methodist church. Each time they reunited with their dad after the service was over and Sunday School was let out, both Devin and Alana had the same thought. Would dad see the light and stop drinking? Would something in what the pastor said change him this time?

No such luck.

After a few days, he'd be right back into the same routine and they wouldn't get a chance to return to Sunday School the following weekend.

Devin didn't go to church much as an adult, and neither did Alana. That might have had something to do with the choices she made later in life, the decisions that drove a wedge between her and the rest of the family.

Sitting in the pew now, listening to Father Frank talk so animatedly about the Old Testament laws and former punishments for sins committed against the Lord, it was a wonder his father didn't repent the first time they attended a church service. Then again, they didn't have Father Frank for a preacher.

Even Devin, who never considered himself to be an unrighteous man, found himself moved by the message, and it wasn't even halfway through the service yet. He wasn't the only one. Women all across the sanctuary began to sniffle. Men's brows furrowed with concentration as they soaked up everything Father Frank spoke. The guy beside him that he had met before Mass began, Jacob, seemed to be deeply stirred by the sermon.

He leaned forward, propping his elbows on his knees and fingers laced in that prayer-like manner while he listened intently to the priest. Devin occasionally glanced his way and after a while, he could see silent, glistening tears wet the newcomer's face.

Beside him, Aaron nodded along to everything Father Frank said.

There was absolutely no doubt that a revival energy permeated through the congregation. Even the children, who would have been fidgeting and restless by now, found themselves sitting still and listening alongside their parents. Teenagers were no longer looking at their phones, but had their eyes fixed on the altar and reverent image of the crucified Christ behind Father Frank.

The priest paced across the carpeted platform, around the podium, and down the steps a few times as his speech became more animated, more lively, more convincing.

Those silent tears from Jacob turned into quiet sobs that mingled in with the other sounds and signs that he wasn't the only one whose soul had been touched.

Perhaps Devin was too jaded by his experiences as a youth to let Father Frank's charisma infect him, but he simply didn't feel the same way that the others did.

Much of what he said made sense, but he wasn't about to start shouting or praising as some did.

He checked the time on his phone. It had only been twenty minutes.

Suddenly, Jacob shot up from his seat at the pew and shuffled past the families. They hardly seemed to notice the interruption, but Devin watched the way the man nearly stumbled into the aisle and jogged out the back doors.

No one else was getting up to leave and there was still at least another forty or so minutes left of this sermon to listen to. Surely, Father Frank hadn't even reached the point of his message. What kind of emotional outpouring would occur when he did reach his climax?

Jacob Nathanson never came back into the sanctuary, and Devin somehow wished he could have left too. All this mawkish sentiment was making him slightly uncomfortable. But, out of respect for the priest and his partner next to him, he stayed glued in his seat.

With Valerie perched on top of the counter next to the espresso machine and Krystal sitting with her legs crossed in a chair she pulled in from the lobby, Alexa read off their daily horoscopes from her phone. Perfect Books and Brews was completely empty at ten o'clock in the morning, which was typical for a Sunday. And since Father Frank had spread the news about his amazing upcoming sermon, she was pretty sure the cathedral was packed that morning.

That was just fine for Krystal, because it meant they had some downtime before the big after church rush. They made a daily habit of reading each other's horoscopes before they flipped the open sign in the morning, but they had a line waiting for them even before Krystal unlocked the doors. It might have been warmer than the day before, but there was no reason to keep them standing on the sidewalk, shivering, and waiting for six-thirty to roll around when they opened the shop early for Sundays.

To Krystal, these horoscope readings were purely for amusement. Despite what Alexa, Amber, and her mother always told her, she didn't believe that the stars predicted one's future. There were only general coincidences. She was fairly confident that she could take any of the horoscopes from the astrological signs and twist it around to pertain to her or anyone else she knew. They were always written so ambiguously.

"Today is a fairly quiet day for you," Alexa read to Valerie, who was a Capricorn, "to keep your head down and get on with your work. You are developing your talents and building on your skills, and even if your progress is slow, it is always steady. It's likely that you value hard work and tangible results, and are very self-reliant."

Valerie sipped on her café mocha, the first she had drank all morning since they arrived. They had been far too busy serving the early-bird customers to fix their coffee earlier, so they took the time to do so now. "Well," she said, "I think they got the self-reliant part right."

Krystal set her cup on the counter after she downed the last drop of chai tea latte goodness.

"Then what skills are you developing that I don't know about?"

Her friend looked thoughtful for a while as she tapped the edges of her converse shoes together. "Well, I have been working on my stealth in the new video game Shane got. Don't tell him though. He doesn't know I've been playing it on the PS4 after he goes to bed."

Krystal gasped. "Shame on you," she jokingly rebuked. "Playing your roommate's game without his permission."

Valerie raked back her hair. "I'm sure he doesn't care, but he'd have a fit if he knew I was at a higher level than him on his own game."

Alexa cleared her throat. "May I continue?"

"Yes, do please continued with these fascinating predictions," Krystal teased.

The blonde stuck out her tongue at her and scrolled through the app. "For Aries... you are likely to be full of energy today, expanding to fill whatever platform you are given. Rather than demanding the attention of others or insisting on getting your own way, use your power to inspire others. Rather than rebelling for the sake of it, fight for a cause you believe in. You don't need to be forceful or dominating for others to be inspired by your actions."

Valerie pointed at her. "See! No dominating today! That counts for Devin, too."

"Yeah, let him dominate you a bit," Alexa joined.

"Make sure he brings handcuffs on that boat!"

Alexa rolled her eyes in feigned pleasure. "I'm sure there will be tons of places he can chain you to."

The two girls broke into riotous laughter, but Krystal only smirked. She quickly stood up and snatched Alexa's phone away. The girl jumped to get it back, but Krystal held it well out of reach. One advantage to being taller than her friend, she could mess with her so easily.

"Let's see what it says about Cancer," she mused, reading the phone at arm's length. After a while, Alexa admitted defeat. "The moon is very active today, connecting with every single planet at some point in the day, so you may find your moods ebbing and flowing even more than usual. Go with the flow of your feelings and don't worry if others get frustrated at your apparent moodiness, they are not as sensitive as you and experience the world differently."

"Oh, a warning to us all!" Valerie exclaimed.

Alexa made one last leap to claim what was hers and Krystal finally lowered the phone, so she could steal it back. "Warning to me too," she added. "At least now I'll know to keep my own emotions in check."

Krystal laughed and straightened out her V-neck blouse. "What emotions? You have moderate peppy, more peppy, and extra peppy."

Alexa shrugged. "I have my moments too, you know."

"We never see them," said Valerie as she took another long sip from her mug.

"Then I'm doing a good job, aren't I?" she replied as she thumbed through the app, reading the other horoscopes aloud.

Krystal wasn't listening, though. Her mind was trailing back to what the app said about being aggressive, demanding, and dominating. She had been accused of being those things frequently, but always passed it off that she was simply driven and competitive at times, especially when it came to her business.

Lately though, her mind had been consumed with lesser things that had nothing to do with her business. Knowing Devin and nearly obsessing over him had trumped a lot of things in her life. Instead of watching marketing podcasts or researching how to make her business better, she caught herself cooking in the evening with her mind brimming with lovely thoughts about Devin and the good times that were ahead. Her stomach was doing backflips whenever she thought about their date that evening. But that couldn't compare to the absolute bliss she felt when she knew she'd get to kiss those perfect lips again and feel his hands caress her one more time.

Just thinking about it now made her knees weak.

And as she predicted, what her horoscope couldn't exactly say, Perfect Books and Brews didn't go into a financial rut, because she didn't stay late to sort receipts or come up with final profit stats for the day. The espresso machines didn't burst into flames, because she didn't clean it that extra time when it didn't really need it. The tables didn't fall apart when she neglected to wipe them down one last time before leaving. The books didn't tumble off the shelves when she let a few get out of order.

Slowly, Krystal began to realize that her little extra measures, the things she did because she thought that if she didn't do them, everything would go to hell in a handbasket, didn't matter one bit when it came to the efficiency of the store. She could put things off for a day or two. She didn't have to scrub as hard or inspect everything with a magnifying glass – which she had been tempted to do sometimes.

The world was still spinning, and she could feel the tension ease from her shoulders. Krystal could breathe, and Devin was filling her lungs for her.

The brass bell over the front door jingled, throwing Krystal out of her thoughts. She turned and watched as a flood of people streamed into the coffee shop in a mass of smiles, laughs, and chattering voices.

The three girls put away their mugs and phones, and stepped into action to do what they did best. Brewing and charming coffees. Though, after the first few customers who came in to rave about Father Frank's sermon, it was clear that the single tick mark on the chalkboard might be lonely that afternoon. These people didn't have any problems, now that their religious shepherd had fed them with the spiritual encouragement they needed.

To Krystal, that was just fine. The people weren't there for charms or uplifting of any kind. Just coffee, and she could provide that in abundance without magic.

"I wish you could have been there, Krystal," Mrs. Thompson told her as she and her husband ordered their usual lattes. "Father Frank's message was so... so... I can't even begin to describe it."

"It was eloquent and so poignant," Mr. Thompson added.

That was the kind of endearments she heard for the rest of the morning and well into the afternoon. Those who heard Father Frank were so stirred that they just couldn't stop talking about it. The coffee shop buzzed with conversations about the sermon for hours, as couples and groups of clustered people pushed tables together, so they could all talk and discuss the points of his religious argument, things Krystal wasn't remotely curious about. Everyone else was fired up, though.

Three-forty-five came and though no new customers were coming in, some had stayed for hours to socialize in the shop. She turned to her friends behind the counter and Krystal could tell they were already beat. After the hard work with the festival booth the day before, and the after-church rush, they were both probably eager to head home.

In any other situation, Krystal would have told them to go ahead and take off early and she would take over the task of closing up once the last of their customer's left. However, in less than an hour, Devin would be showing up on her doorstep and she wasn't even ready to go on their little open water excursion. She fought the urge to be terrified about going out on a boat, reminding herself that as long as she was spending time with Devin, it was well worth it all.

Valerie looked up and must have seen the torn, dejected look in her friend's eye, because she adamantly shook her head. "Nope," she declared. "I'm not doing it. I already covered for you once and I've got a videogame calling my name."

This caught Alexa's attention and she lifted her gaze from her phone. "What?"

Krystal glanced over her shoulder to the group of customers still gabbing it up. Realization dawned in Alexa's eyes and she let out a long, tired breath. "I guess I can stay. Mr. Fish can wait a little longer for his dinner."

Mr. Fish was Alexa's dark blue and black betta fish. Living in the apartment space over Miss Macy's Antique Shop came with restrictions. One of which was that she couldn't own any pets that had a potential to make a mess on the carpet. So, dogs and cats were out of the question. Fish, however, were perfectly acceptable.

Krystal came forward and hugged her. "Thank you!" she cried and then stooped down to retrieve her purse from under the counter, so she could rush out the door. If she hurried, she could make it home in time to pack that extra change of clothes and feed Artemis, if Sierra hadn't fed him twice already.

Devin stepped onto Krystal's front porch at exactly four-thirty, just as they agreed. With the tiny packet of assorted vegetable and flower seeds in hand, he rang the doorbell and waited. Inside, he could hear the swift trampling of light feet upon wood flooring and the harried, hushed words of two girls arguing on who should answer the door.

His thumb stroked over the ribbon that bound his modest offering together and waited, his heart pounding faster than it should have. Just like on their first date, he was nervous. This time, he wasn't so much nervous for the fact that Krystal would be standing in front of him at any moment. This time, he was excited. This would be the second time they were completely alone. No waiters, no customers, nobody in Goldcrest Cove would be there to watch over them. Out on that boat, it would be just them.

The heavy front door swung open, but it wasn't Krystal standing there to greet him. This must be her sister. She gave him a friendly smile and her dark eyes roved over him from head to foot. Feeling like he was under inspection, he squared his shoulders.

"You must be Krystal's sister," he said and offered out his hand that had been shaken at least a hundred times that day already.

"And you must be Devin," she said, taking his hand in hers. She gave just as firm a handshake as Krystal did and he guessed it must have been a family trait. "My name's Sierra."

"Nice to finally meet you."

It wasn't quite like meeting the parents, but close. If Sierra felt the same way about Krystal, like Devin did about his little sister, he knew he was in for a string of probing questions and every word he said would be under intense scrutiny while he was there.

"Come in," she quickly said, waving him on. "Krystal's still getting ready. The coffee shop was pretty busy just before she left."

He stepped inside and looked around the foyer and staircase up ahead that led to the second floor. Somehow, he had expected a sort of Addams Family interior with a towering stuffed grizzly bear and suits of armor everywhere. The outside of the house was aesthetically pleasing enough, but he always wondered how these antique homes were decorated on the inside.

Krystal's home was tastefully designed with just the right vintage touch of artificial potted plants, antique furniture, and family portraits that hung on the walls. The trim and detailed accents harkened back to an age when master craftsmen were easy to come by.

Apart from the stunning architecture and fascinating accents to the décor, there was a certain energy about the house that he recognized. It felt just the way the sanctuary in the church did earlier that day. A spiritual essence seemed to pervade the air and seep into his blood. It was calming, tranquil, just the way he felt when he was around Krystal. Whatever it was about her and the house, he definitely didn't fight it like he had during Mass. He didn't feel like he could be free to experience that kind of liberating peace, but here, he knew that he could.

The tiny baying of a cat met his ears and he searched for the source.

Padding from one of the rooms to the right of the foyer, a beautiful, long-haired Siamese cat looked up at him with such striking blue eyes. They stared at one another for a moment as its long, bushy tail swished from one side to the other, silently judging him just the way Sierra must have.

"That's Artemis," Sierra said. "He's not big on being petted, just as a warning."

Devin remembered seeing that cat on Krystal's phone. He nodded in acknowledgement to the sophisticated, almost regal-looking cat. "I'll be sure to keep my distance then, won't I?"

The cat, as if satisfied with his greeting, turned and sauntered back into what appeared to be something like a living room. He heard the tiny jingle of Artemis' collar and tag as it deftly pounced up onto the couch cushion.

"Krystal told me you're the new cop in town, right?"

Devin nodded to Sierra. "I am. Aaron Wright is my partner."

She smiled and nodded as she moved toward the left of the foyer and into the kitchen. "Oh, Aaron's a pretty cool guy. I went to high school with him. Quite a character, as you probably know already. Do you want anything to drink while you wait?"

"No thanks," he said just as he heard the soft tap of footsteps coming from upstairs. He didn't move from his spot as Krystal came into view and hurried down the steps.

"I'm so sorry," she groaned. "I didn't think getting changed would take me so long."

Devin smiled a toothy grin when he saw what she had changed into. Her hunter green tank top paired well with the off-white skirt embroidered with cream flowers and leaves that weaved all across the surface. In her hand was a matching sweater and a small tote bag that must have contained that extra change of clothes he requested her to pack.

"It's totally fine," he assured. "Worth the wait."

Krystal finally looked up to him and brushed back a bit of a stray bang that was in her eyes. She smiled at his sly compliment and there was a definite shift in the air around them. That calm remained, but it was joined by the urgent need that came whenever he let himself daydream about Krystal. It was that same, fiery yearning that came when he allowed the thought of her to devour his very being. He had never let a woman affect him like that before.

He hadn't expected to get stiff this soon, but at least he wore comfortable jeans. If he didn't settle down, he might take this date too far, too soon. He still respected Krystal and wanted to take this nice and easy. No reason to ruin it all on the second date.

Sierra came back with a glass of water in her hands. "Ready to go?" she asked them. "I've got someplace to be too, so don't worry about me being here when you get back."

He would have been considered blind if he didn't see that wink. At least he wasn't the only one thinking about what would happen after they came back to shore.

Krystal passed her sister a look before joining Devin at the door. "I'm ready," she told him. Then, her eyes fell to the tiny parcel in his hand.

Devin felt awkward presenting her with another gift, but by the way her eyes lit up, he knew he had done right.

"Oh, how sweet!" she exclaimed and gently took the seed packets from his hand to admire them. "Sierra, he got us seeds."

Not technically for both of them, but since it was for the garden they shared, Devin accepted it.

Her elder sister came over and looked at each of the labels as Krystal tore off the ribbon and flipped through them. "And he got the good brand." Sierra threw him a covert thumbs up. At least he had won her over. Would Krystal's parents be just as easy?

She passed off the packets to her sister and stood on her tip toes to plant a sweet kiss on Devin's cheek. "Thank you."

"You're very welcome." He wanted to say that he would buy her the hardware store's entire stock of every kind of seed they had, just so she would give him more kisses. He knew saying something like that in front of Sierra might have upset the balance out of his favor.

"You two go on and have fun."

With Sierra's blessing, they left the house and walked out to Devin's black Dodge Charger sitting at the curb.

"What are we going to do when it gets dark?" Krystal asked as he opened the passenger side door for her. The days were getting shorter now and the sun would completely set in about an hour or so, but he planned for them to be out on the water to watch it. Maybe there was an advantage to waiting for her to get off work so late in the afternoon.

"The boat has some lights." And when he said "some", he really meant one lantern fixed at the helm. When he slid into the driver's seat, he continued, "The boat isn't exactly what I had bargained for. I thought we were going to get something a little bigger, but the harbormaster could only set me up with a bow rider. Maybe in the future, we can get a fishing boat like I wanted." Krystal tossed her bag onto the floorboard at her feet and that reminded him. "Also, you probably won't need that change of clothes like I suggested."

"Huh?" Krystal questioned as he pulled away onto Pinkerton Drive and made a quick U-turn to head toward the harbor. The radio began to play some rock music that he promptly turned down. He didn't know what she liked to listen to, but he didn't want to offend her, just in case she wasn't one for heavy metal or punk music.

"Like I said, I wanted a bigger boat, but he didn't come through. There's no place for you to change if you wanted to."

She nodded in understanding, but there was a note of hesitance in what she said next. "Well, I guess that's good then. Why would I need a change of clothes anyway?"

Devin shrugged. "In case you got too wet from the spray that came off the bow or fell in." Beside him, Krystal shifted uncomfortably in her seat, but said nothing.

"You all right?" he asked as he made a right turn onto Lavender Lane.

"I have a confession to make," she began, her face twisted in a grimace. "I'm a little nervous... Okay, I'm a lot nervous. I haven't been out on a boat in a really long time."

He smirked. "Nothing to be nervous about. It has a few life jackets and I'm an excellent swimmer, in case you do take a spill."

Krystal didn't seem convinced, but he was sure that once they got out onto the water, they would be fine. If she really had a problem with going out on a boat, then she would have said so when he first offered it. At least, he hoped that she would have. So far, she had been fairly honest with him, so she had no reason to lie to him about this, right?

Even as they neared the harbor, Devin hoped that her anxiety wouldn't get in the way of her having a good time. He so wanted to give her a good time. After all the hard work she put into the booth at the festival and the effort she puts into the coffee shop every day, she needed a break from reality just as much as he did. He hoped that he could be her fantasy just as much as she was for him.

Now that she was close, sitting in the seat next to him and her wonderful perfume filling the inside of his car, he felt all the stress from the previous week melt away to the floorboard beneath his feet. Being with her was so easy, so natural. Nothing on earth could possibly replicate the effect she had on him. He hoped it would last.

Chapter 8

Krystal kept her eyes fixed on the planks of the dock ahead of her, being careful to walk right over the parts that were nailed into the framing below. The irrational fear that any one of these sturdy boards would splinter and cave in beneath her was too convincing to push aside. She also hated the way the platform seemed to tilt to one side, rather than remain perfectly level.

The only thing that kept her moving forward was Devin's hand in hers as he guided them toward the boat moored to one of the pylons. The salty breeze teased her long black hair that she had let down after she had gotten home, and her bangs were tossed to one side or the other as they ventured further out on the dock.

Everything in her screamed that this was a terrible idea. Twilight would settle in soon and she saw that Devin had overstated the amount of lights on the boat. That one light would have to guide their steps across the deck and somehow get them back to shore well after the sun had set. The moon was just barely in its waxing gibbous phase, which was preferred over a crescent or even a first quarter phase, but Krystal couldn't help but wish that it were full. So many wonderful things could happen on a full moon and it would have given them more light to see by.

She could hear the waves slapping against the side of the boat as it bobbed and swayed with the tide. All across the harbor, she could hear the fishermen and other mariners tie up their vessels for the night, yet she and Devin were going out anyway. What was Devin thinking when he set up this little arrangement? He had already told her that he had planned to come out long before he met her, but why go out on the open water at such an hour?

Maybe the two fishing poles and tackle box in his free hand had something to do with that.

"Here we are," he said, presenting the boat to her as if she were supposed to be impressed. The railings were practically nonexistent, but it was better than she had envisioned. Somehow, she thought he would take her out on a huge sailboat and she would have to learn something. With this, at least he could drive and operate the boat while she hung on for dear life. She could just barely see the bright orange lifejacket peeking out from behind the driver's seat near the helm. There were two seats to the front of the helm on the bow, but Krystal knew for a fact that she wouldn't be climbing up there this evening.

She nodded and hoped that her apprehension wasn't too evident. She desperately wanted this to go well. Not just because she needed to get over this pesky fear of drowning, but because it was unlikely that they would get another chance for a date until her next day off, which seemed like a lifetime away.

"Nice," she said with a weak nod.

Then, without even asking, Devin led her onto the deck behind the helm. With her feet straddling the edge of the dock, she watched the boat sway and she hardly knew where to step first. Seeing her hesitation, Devin set down his fishing gear and leaned up to slip his hands around her waist.

"I've got you."

In one fluid, graceful move, Devin lifted her up and over the gap between dock and boat, then lowered her to her feet just beside him. His hands lingered there and Krystal grinned, despite the unease she felt as the boat seemed to oscillate beneath her. That tight, fluttering feeling sparked low in her belly and she gripped his forearms for stability.

"So far so good, right?" he said.

Though her eyes were roaming for something to hang onto as soon as he let go, she nodded.

"Yep. So far so good."

Devin released her to snatch up one of the lifejackets and offered it to her. Krystal shuffled slowly toward the helm and held onto the little barrier between the steering wheel and the rest of the deck. The fiberglass was cold beneath her skin and a little damp from a previous trip out onto the water.

Was the rest of the boat that way? Was it just as slippery under her feet?

She wordlessly took the lifejacket from Devin as he began to explain his plan to take them out to the mouth of the bay and float there.

"If we're lucky, we'll be able to catch our dinner."

"Dinner?" Krystal questioned as she alternately braced herself against the barrier and tried to strap the lifejacket over her chest and torso. It was bulky, awkward, and definitely unattractive, but Krystal was taking no chances. Devin could just make love to her wearing this and he'd have to like it, but she couldn't see herself taking it off anytime soon.

"Yep," he proclaimed. "That's the plan. We'll catch at least three, maybe four fish, go back to my place and cook them up."

Krystal shot him a sassy look. "Do you have a well-equipped kitchen for something like that?"

Devin saw her struggle and came forward help her get the nylon straps straight. "Well, would you prefer to cook at your place?"

His fingertips grazed across the middle of her back as he fixed the one waist cinch and buckled it in the front. In one swift jerk, he tightened the strap and pulled her close to him. A breath escaped between Krystal's lips and she let herself fall against him. Her hands flattened against the soft fabric of his long-sleeved shirt and she could feel his taut muscles beneath. If the damned lifejacket wasn't in the way, their chests would have been flush together. It was totally killing the romantic mood and might as well have been the best cock-blocker in the world.

"I think cooking at my place might be easier," she replied after she regained her balance and pushed herself off of him.

Devin seemed amused. "Are you sure you want to wear that all evening?"

Krystal adjusted the lifejacket. "It's either that or you tether me to the helm. Take your pick."

"Having you tied up might prove interesting," he offered with a shrug of his brows that suggested so much.

She giggled. "Well, I don't know. What if we hit something and the ship sinks, but you can't untie me fast enough?"

Devin gave her a look, as if to say that she was being silly, but slipped out a sheathed pocket knife from his jean pocket. "That's where these come in handy."

"And if you're knocked unconscious?"

Instead of telling her that she was over thinking everything, which was all completely true, Devin leaned down and kissed her lips. The first kiss in two days and it still felt as electrifying as the first. Would it always be that way? Would he always get her panties a little wet when he demonstrated his claim on her so sensuously? It was such an easy, simple thing to do, but it made the world stop spinning for a few seconds.

He pulled away, leaving her wanting more, as usual. "Nothing like that will happen." And for one crazy, clarifying moment, Krystal believed him.

Before she knew it, Devin had revved up the engine and they were making their way out into the bay, the dock just a tiny speck on the water. Krystal refused to sit. She kept hanging onto that safe spot right next to the helm where Devin skillfully navigated them to a spot so far from the shore. One where Krystal could only see the twinkling lights of Goldcrest Cove as twilight set in.

Tiny sprinkles of seawater chilled her warm cheeks and all she could hear was the roar of the motor that sped them farther into the middle of nowhere. Once they reached that indeterminate spot that Devin must have had in mind, he slowed the boat down to a stop and they drifted a bit. Once again, the boat resumed its gentle rocking and Krystal gripped tighter as she felt the little nauseous tickle in her stomach.

The winter clouds had rolled in, casting the sky in an ethereal light blue with darker blotches. To the west, the last streaks of ochre and gold stretched out across the horizon, framing the strip of mainland against the dark water. The ocean acted as a mirror to reflect back the beauty of the waning light, yet not completely duplicating the sunset as the ever-moving waves fractured the image.

All at once, her parents' teachings came back to her. The water, receptive and healing, represented so much to witches. Just like Alexa said, it had the power to destroy through floods, storms, and typhoons. Yet, it was the life force of all living things. Plants needed water to survive, as did all of the creatures that inhabited the earth. The water was eternally tied to the moon, something else that they couldn't live without. The moon's sway over the water was just another bit of proof that all life was connected. Linked and woven together in a magical, yet completely natural way.

Through the splotches of clouds above, she could see bits of twinkling stars and the glowing moon. She tilted back her head, ignoring the way her body bobbed with the ebb and flow of the waves, and tried to see if she could spot the constellations she and her sister had to discern when they were little girls.

"What's on your mind?" Devin asked from the stern of the boat, seated upon one of the benches. His hands were occupied as he baited a hook with a wriggling worm that he had dug out of a Styrofoam box full of soil.

Krystal watched him and sweetly smiled, finally feeling what Alexa had said the day before at the festival. She was one with nature, part of it and yet a completely separate entity from it. It had been a long time since she had felt so attuned with that magical essence within her that bound all witches to the earth.

"Just how pretty it is out here," she replied. "You can see for miles around."

Devin smiled up at her. "See, it's not so bad."

Krystal took one step, then another and gradually let go of the ship. It took a moment for her to get into a steady rhythm with her arms extended out from her body to balance herself. But she managed to make it over to Devin and sat beside him.

"No, it's not bad at all," she said, feeling completely silly for how she had behaved earlier. Not only was it insensible, but also completely un-witch. If Krystal's mother had seen her like that, the old witch would have thrown a fit and scolded her. She still wouldn't dare look over the edge of the boat into the dark, shadowy water they floated on.

"So, why were you so nervous in the first place?" he asked as he passed her the fishing rod.

Krystal took it and watched how the now skewered worm and hook spun around the pole. She took a deep breath. "When I was little," she began, "I used to love coming out onto the docks with my family on the weekends. One day, I leaned too far over, because I thought I saw a fish and I fell in. I must have been two or three years old and I didn't know how to swim. My dad dove in and got me, but I almost drowned that day."

She looked to Devin, whose hands had stilled over the hook, a thoughtful and considerate look in his eyes as he listened.

"I was afraid to even take a bath for months. My mom had to sponge bathe me until I figured out how to take showers instead. I've avoided big bodies of water ever since. No pool parties, no fishing... I wouldn't even go near Jackson Creek where all the kids at school hung out."

Devin nodded. "I can see how that would be traumatizing for a kid."

Krystal lifted one of her shoulders in a half-shrug and she realized, once more, how clunky the life jacket was. In a daring, slightly frustrated decision, Krystal unbuckled the one thing that would keep her from drowning and tossed it to the deck. She still didn't know how to swim, but Devin definitely would.

She met Devin's proud gaze and he continued to bait the hook. "So, I guess I won't regret bringing you all the way out here after all?"

Krystal felt slightly naked now without the lifejacket, but it was for the best. She needed to conquer this fear. If things got serious with Devin, she wanted to be with him when he came out here to fish. If she was constantly terrified of the water, she never would and then where would they be? If she couldn't compromise even a little, they might never spend time together unless it was on her terms. After seeing the kind of model her parents presented to her at a young age, she knew that wasn't the way a healthy relationship worked.

Then again, honesty and open communication played a vital role too. Baby steps.

"No, you won't regret it," she replied as he slipped the last of the slippery worm securely on his hook and looked to her as if he were ready to take on the world instead of a few fish.

"So, I'll take it that you never fished before, right?"

"Unless the little toy rods with magnets for hooks counts."

Devin laughed. "No, that doesn't count."

Taking a firm hold on her hand, he led her toward the very stern of the boat where the motor sat silent. Krystal widened her stance a bit as she swayed and rolled with the motion of the boat beneath her. Devin set his own reel down and stood behind her. If she looked down, she'd see the water rolling against the hull, so she kept her eyes level with the horizon.

"All right, you'll want to reel up the slack a bit."

Krystal looked up to the tip of her pole and saw the hook and worm had gotten tangled with the rest of the line that fed through the hoops. "Might have a problem with that," she giggled.

He took the pole from her and with nimble hands, untangled the line and spun the reel handle until the hook tapped against the top hoop. Then, he briefly tapped the release button to give it the slack she needed.

He handed the pole back to her, but he repositioned his hand over hers as she gripped the handle.

"All right, you're going to ease the rod back to cast it. Are you left or right handed?"

"Right," she said, but had a hard time focusing on her lesson while Devin stood so near behind her, the front of his pants just barely grazing against her bottom and his strong arms blocking out the cool sea breeze around her.

"Okay, so you're going to pull it back to your left at an angle. Not directly over your head like you've seen in the movies."

Devin's hand guided her to pull the rod back to her left, her right arm crossing over her midline just enough that when she threw the line, it would have the right momentum to travel pretty far. Krystal could feel that warmth spiral through her as she realized that so much of their bodies were touching.

Now, she was so glad she had ditched the lifejacket.

"Just when you're ready to cast, press the release button and fling it out. Don't let go of the rod though."

Krystal laughed. "Oh? Why not? That would make things more interesting, wouldn't it?"

Devin chuckled and the vibrations rumbled across her shoulder blades. "These rods aren't cheap, that's why. If you throw one of them out, I'll have to throw you in to get it."

She cast him a challenging, but playful glare, just like she had at the festival when he threatened to arrest her. "Don't you dare."

"I wouldn't throw you in," he said. "But I would be very upset. Ready?"

Krystal nodded and did exactly like he said. Together, they cast the line and she felt the reel whirl just above her hand as the poor worm flew through the air, still attached to the hook. Then, she heard the light plop.

"Not bad," he said with a nod. "Now, you'll let it sink for a bit. Then, you'll want to reel it in, nice and slow."

Devin bent his head a little and his hot breath splashed against her neck. She wasn't cold by any means, but she felt her whole body erupt in goosebumps as he angled his other arm around to guide her hand to the reel handle.

Krystal pinched one of the knobs and Devin's hand laid on top of hers again. He set the pace for her as she gently pulled the worm back in.

"This isn't so hard," she remarked. Though, she could feel something else that was getting pretty hard and he wasn't afraid to let her know it. They might have had layers of clothes between them, but his hard on pressed against her with boldness.

"One thing about fishing," he whispered in her ear, "you have to be very quiet or you'll scare the fish away."

He could whisper all he wanted as long as it was to her. Krystal stifled the sigh and closed her eyes as the heat descended from her core to straight between her legs. She kept reeling in the line, but her brain was entirely focused on Devin and the way his body felt against hers, solid, sturdy, and one hundred percent enticing.

There was a certain element of complete and utter safety in his arms, like she had been cocooned from the rest of the world, untouchable, unreachable. Here, there was only Krystal and Devin. They weren't on the water or even fishing. To her, they were floating in an ethereal bubble of absolute, tantalizing pleasure. It continued to mount as each breath he breathed on her neck opened up a world of feeling for her. She could have stayed like that forever, basking in his presence and calming energy that set her soul on fire.

A slight tug on her line made her heartbeat quicken even more. She jolted out of her erotic daze. Devin must have felt it too, because he quickly jerked the reel backward and then let it go slack, feeling for any change. Nothing.

"What was that?" she asked.

"Might have been something nibbling on the line."

They reeled it in quickly and saw the worm was completely gone. Krystal let out a tiny sound of disbelief, still mindful to keep her voice to a minimum.

Devin let out a sigh. "It happens. Take the other line while I rebait this one." He leaned down to take the other rod and handed it to her. "I trust you remember how to cast it?"

Though she so wanted Devin to show her again, she nodded and checked him out as he walked back toward the tackle box and set to work. He could be totally and unerringly sexy without even trying.

She cleared her throat and did exactly as Devin had showed her before.

"You're a natural," he commented from the seat behind her.

She began slowly twirling the reel handle, mimicking his pace as before. "I have a good teacher."

He smirked up at her and she wondered if he could tell how absolutely turned on she was by the whole experience.

Even if Krystal wasn't afraid of the water, she never understood why so many people loved fishing. By all accounts, fishing was supposed to be a completely boring pastime. There was no mentally challenging aspect about it. It wasn't like cooking, where Krystal could always have her hands busy doing something with a recipe. It wasn't like fixing a special espresso that required concentration and focus.

But, if she was fishing with Devin, she knew she could grow to love it. She was already loving it and they hadn't even caught anything yet.

The sun dipped lower and lower on the horizon, its light and warmth receding from the earth. But to her, Krystal was more than just warm; she was even sweating a bit. In that moment, she wished she hadn't left her bag in the car that had her body spray and deodorant. Even though there was probably no way to apply any without Devin noticing.

Devin stood and moved toward the other side of the stern, just a couple of feet from her. When he cast his line, it didn't take her long to notice that his line buzzed a lot longer before the reel finally stopped turning. She didn't even hear the sound of impact as the hook sank below the waves.

"That was pretty far," she whispered.

He shrugged nonchalantly. "Lots of practice." Damn he was hot. She was in way over her head.

"So, why do guys like fishing so much? It's a pretty mindless sport, isn't it?"

He nodded. "And that's the point," he replied. "I can come out here after a hard day at work and just relax. I don't have to think."

Krystal tilted her head. "And that's something that guys like to do? Not think?"

He slid her a frisky glance. "Believe it or not, we need to shut off our brains every once and while, so they don't overheat."

"I can't imagine a moment when I'm not thinking or feeling something."

He shrugged. "We're all made differently. And there are plenty of other mindless things men can do to unwind."

Krystal smiled. "Valerie's roommate, Shawn, plays videogames all the time."

Devin paused in reeling in his hook to gesture to her. "See? That's probably his outlet, while my outlet is fishing."

What she couldn't understand was why Devin would need an outlet in the first place. Did it have to do with his job as a cop, or that nameless past childhood drama involving his father? What about the obviously strained relationship with his sister? Why should a man such as him, ever need an escape from life? He was in Goldcrest Cove now, far away from Boston and whatever troubles he left there. Wasn't that enough? Or was there something else he wasn't telling her?

"Are there any other mindless activities I should know about?" she asked, adding a certain feathering of suggestion in her words. "Any other way you like to unwind?"

She saw the slow smile spread across Devin's face and she knew exactly what he had in mind.

"Well, maybe you'll find out."

Then, Krystal felt that tug on her line again. She jerked the rod back, just like Devin had. But the line didn't go slack again. Whatever was on the other end must have snagged itself on the hook, because it was not letting go.

She let out a soft cry and pulled until the rod began to bow and bend.

Devin set his rod down in one of the holders on the edge of the boat and came to her side. "I think you got something."

The utter elation almost rivaled the thrill of Devin's touch as he gripped the handle with her and held it back, so she could keep reeling it in. The battle ensued for what seemed like forever before her catch finally surfaced.

The fish squirmed and thrashed about as Devin grabbed the line and pulled it over the deck. It had to be at least a foot long, but Krystal was never a good judge of size.

"You got a bluefish!" he announced. "It's a snapper, but still, it'll make for a nice dinner." Devin gripped the fish and worked the hook loose.

"That's the first fish I've ever caught," Krystal laughed, still in disbelief that she was actually here, with Devin, doing the one thing she had never thought she would do. The reality hit her that she was out on the open water, unafraid of the consequences, and having the time of her life.

Devin was right. She might have just been starting out, but fishing did take her mind off of the stresses of reality. She wasn't thinking about the coffee shop and the fact that she would be taking Devin back to a house that wasn't entirely cleaned to her liking. She didn't think about the fact that he didn't know her secret, or the fact that he probably had a few of his own.

For just a little while, she was blissfully unaware that anything could possibly ruin this date.

Chapter 9

As soon as the door was open, Krystal scampered inside. The buzz from catching, not only her first fish, but three fish, hadn't worn off.

"I'll preheat the oven!" she cried excitedly as she left Devin in the foyer. He could only smile and listen to her scurry around the kitchen, pulling out whatever supplies she needed.

In one hand, he carried the small foam cooler, filled with ice and the bluefish fillets he had skinned on the docks after they moored the bow rider to one of the pylons where the harbormaster directed him. Krystal didn't care to watch as he sliced up the fillets, but she sure seemed eager on the ride home as she babbled about how exactly she would cook them once they arrived back to her house.

He stepped into the kitchen and whistled at its size. Somehow, he expected a house this old to be small, inefficient for modern needs. Krystal and her family must have renovated, because he had only seen kitchens like this on the cooking channel. Stretches of counter space lined the walls with tall, beige overhead cabinets above them. The backsplash was a charming wallpaper design of herbs, flowers, and vines. The granite countertops were a dazzling green with speckles of gold and silver throughout.

Krystal didn't skimp on the appliances either. A gas range was installed in the kitchen island that served as somewhat of a focal point for the kitchen. The refrigerator looked new and boasted one of those deep freezer drawers to free up the upper cold storage. Devin was even impressed by the double oven setup, one of which was already preheating.

Strewn out across the counter was a deep baking pan, a roll of tin foil, and a bag of vegetables.

Krystal had her head in the refrigerator, moving contents around.

"Sierra always moves the butter whenever she makes toast in the morning," she mumbled. "I swear, she puts it in a different spot every time."

Devin watched her, his gaze sliding over her. She had already shed the sweater she had been wearing out on the boat and her tank top hugged her form just right, so he could see all of her lovey, perfect curves.

In the excitement of catching fish and discovering Krystal's fear of the water, Devin had to give up on any errant thought about getting cozy on the boat. Though his manhood was a little disappointed, the evening was far from over.

Krystal must have found the butter and then began grabbing for other things, like a green bottle of lemon juice. She bumped the refrigerator door shut with her hip and fled back to her cooking station. He could have watched her like that all night, but she turned and regarded him with a slight look of impatience.

"Are you going to help me?" she asked as she pulled the elastic tie from her wrist to pull her hair back into a ponytail.

Devin set the cooler on the kitchen island and his eyes went wide. "Oh, I can't cook. Ask anyone."

"Nonsense," she said with a flip of her hand. She obviously didn't notice the way he appraised her chest and flat stomach while her arms stretched above her head. "Everyone can cook. You just follow the recipe."

Somehow knowing that he wasn't going to win this argument, he popped the lid off and let the odor of dead fish fill the kitchen. "What first, chef?"

Krystal tore off pieces of foil. "Bring the fillets over here and we're going to wrap them in tin foil for baking.

Sounded simple enough. He found the paper towel roll and grabbed a few, so he could carry the fish to her without getting his hands or the counter messy. Devin waited for Krystal to drizzle the olive oil over the foil before slapping the fillets down.

"No, no. Skin side down," she instructed, then corrected the two he had placed.

"And you said cooking was easy," he muttered.

She giggled as she reached across him to pinch the end of a couple of fillets to bring them to her spreads of foil. "It is. I'm sorry I wasn't clear."

And they continued like that until they had all the fillets laid out in the pans. Krystal handed him the pepper shaker and she took the salt, so they could season them just right.

"Not so much pepper, though," she added. "I don't like the kick."

Devin slid three fillets to his side of the counter. "Well, these will be mine then." And he loaded them down with pepper, just like he did with everything else he ate.

"And you can keep them too," she giggled. "I can't stand a lot of hot spice. Nice and subtle for me."

Devin let a fiendish grin spread over his lips and he slid a glance her way. Nope, she didn't even realize what she just said could be taken in an entirely different way. "I'll have to remember that."

Krystal slid down a cutting board from a fixed rack on the other counter and pulled a few lemons out of one of the vegetable bags. "Can you hand me a knife from the block over there?"

"Should I ask which one?" Devin reached for a couple of the steak knives first.

"No, you've got it right. The lemon skins are hard to cut into so I just use those."

He handed her the knife and it took a little bit of careful maneuvering, but they managed to share the same cutting board as they sliced into the lemons. Krystal took the slices and evenly distributed them across the fillets. "Now for the butter."

The oven beeped to let them know it was done preheating as Krystal took up the sticks of butter and used the same knife to cut thin squares. Devin picked up the shavings and positioned them between the lemon slices just as she directed. He hadn't done anything like this before, cooking with a woman in her own kitchen. Even before his mom passed away, he didn't dare step in her way when she was making dinner. She preferred it that way, but it seemed Krystal was eager to have a sous-chef work alongside her.

"Can you fold up the tin foil to make boats while I go grab the herbs?" she asked as she rinsed off her hands in the wide, deep sink behind them.

"Boats?"

"Yeah, so the juices won't spill out."

Devin shrugged and watched her disappear through a swinging door at the other end of the kitchen, but not before plucking a white-handled knife hanging upon a peg next to the door. While he bent and formed the foil into the boats, just as she asked, Devin couldn't help but acknowledge to himself how completely head-over-heels he was for Krystal. He knew he was attracted to her, not just for her beauty, but her soul. But their trip out onto the water opened up something new within him.

All his life, he had run from almost every relationship. His family had let him down, his friends were practically nonexistent because of his demanding job, and just in the last year, he learned the hard truth that getting attached to anyone was a big mistake.

He was making that same mistake with Aaron and Krystal as he made with Paul.

Yet, somehow, he didn't care. He wanted to feel that fellowship, that fondness for someone's company again, like he had when he was a kid. In this town, he couldn't afford to be detached. Everyone knew everyone, and it was going to be impossible not to feel something for the people he served and protected every day.

It was equally impossible not to be drawn to Krystal. He couldn't put his finger on what exactly it was that made her so damned irresistible, but he felt he was getting closer to learning the truth. A little longer, a few more kisses, and maybe he would figure it out. And what happened if he did? Would it reveal her soul to such a degree that he would lose interest? No, never.

Krystal came back in, a fistful of savory smelling sprigs of herbs.

"Thyme, tarragon, and parsley," she explained as she arranged the fresh herbs over the fillets.

"Straight from your garden, I presume?" he asked as he moved behind her, his focus on anything but the fish.

"You got it," she replied.

Devin reached up and ran his palm beneath her long, silky black ponytail. He saw the way tiny bumps rippled across her shoulders and upper arms.

"What are you doing?" she asked coyly. He didn't have to see her face to know she was smiling.

"Nothing," he whispered before planting a tiny kiss just below her ear.

Krystal squirmed and giggled as she reached over to grab the bottle of white wine near the back of the counter. He let his hand drift down her slender side to rest on her hip, right at the edge of her tank top. Just one slip of his fingers and he could be touching her soft skin and make that gooseflesh spread a little farther south.

She either didn't pay any attention, or she was too focused on the task of getting these fillets in the oven.

"Do you want anything to go with the fish? Rice? Broccoli?"

"You," he mumbled, his lips grazing over her neck.

Krystal laughed again. "I'm serious. These fish will take about twenty minutes, so if we want something else to go with them, we need to fix it."

Devin knew he had to get her attention someway, so he let his hand tuck under the fabric of her tank top. His fingertips slide across the smooth skin on her hips, just above the loose waistband of her skirt. "No," he breathed. "Just fish is fine."

Then, he remembered the hot chocolate from the festival the day before and how absolutely addictive it was. He also remembered spotting a wood burning fireplace in the living room as he passed it just moments ago.

"Actually, do you have any more of that hot chocolate mix? Maybe we can spend that twenty minutes by the fireplace?"

It was a risky move. He hadn't been anywhere near a fire since the incident. He even hated it when someone on the street struck their lighter to start smoking a cigarette. And that was just a tiny flame. He had no idea if he'd relapse in the presence of a bigger fire. Why did he even suggest it? Krystal was doing so much more to him than just giving him a hard on.

Yet, something about being in Krystal's company made him forget about that. He didn't hear the screams or smell the burning flesh as he did whenever he even thought about fire. Maybe the weeks of therapy in Boston did the trick. Only one way to find out.

Krystal sighed and he could see the way her hands trembled a bit as she crimpled the edges of the tinfoil boats to seal the fillets. "That sounds like a good plan to me. Do you want to go start the fire?

There should be plenty of wood and kindling on the hearth, and the matches are on the mantle."

Yep, he was about to get a full immersion test to see if he could function like a normal person again. Devin gripped her hair and gently pulled her head to the side, so he could steal a kiss on her lips. The skin on her hips grew warm and he hoped she wasn't catching a fever after spending all that time out in the cold night air.

Krystal leaned against him until he could feel her back pressed against the front of his body, dependent and pleading as she eased into his kiss. A bit of her own heat transferred to him and he felt his face flush. That never happened.

Devin pulled away and tapped her hip as he pulled down her tank top. "Better get those in the oven."

Krystal's eyes popped open and once more, she was the chef in the kitchen and began placing the foil packets in the wide baking pan. "You are so distracting, you know that?"

Devin only laughed as he left the kitchen and walked into the living room. He swallowed hard when he picked up the box of matches. There was nothing to be afraid of. The fire would stay contained in the fireplace and she even had one of those fireplace screens, so the embers would bounce off the iron if the logs shifted.

He set to work, placing the logs like he used to when he was younger. His dad's house had a fireplace too and both Devin and Alana used to roast marshmallows when their dad wasn't home or was passed out in his recliner. Those were the only times they had a moment's peace, and fireplaces used to be one of those things that served as a reminder of what happiness he did have growing up.

He wadded up the old newspaper, shoved it under the rack that the logs sat on, and took up the matches one more time. Just a tiny flame, completely controlled.

He struck it and watched as the red tip sizzled and sputtered to life. He felt the moderate heat on his face as the flame burned at the end of the match. He stared at it, facing the fear head on, just like Krystal did. If she could be strong, then so could he.

Devin lowered the match under one of the balled up newspapers and soon it caught fire, which spread to the rest of the kindling. He set the screen in place and stepped away as the fire grew and ignited the logs rather quickly. The stones in the firebox would keep it contained.

In the kitchen, he could hear Krystal start to take down a pair of mugs from the cabinet and it hadn't been more than a few minutes, but the lemony, fishy fragrance of their dinner wafted all the way to the living room. Krystal had told him that bluefish was delicious when cooked right, and it certainly smelled like she was doing it right. It beat frozen dinners anyway.

A long, relieved breath escaped him and he turned his attention to the framed pictures on the mantle to distract himself. There were a few pictures of Krystal and her sister when they were little girls in school. Krystal had the same black bangs masking her forehead, but her smile was missing a tooth or two. Other pictures appeared more recent. A family portrait of Krystal, Sierra, and whom he assumed were their parents, posing in front of a large tree.

Their father was tall, and it seemed that Sierra took after him more as far as facial features went, while Krystal had her mother's dazzling brown eyes. They all looked so happy, smiling at the camera with those genuine smiles that crinkled the outer edges of their eyes like they had just been laughing about something.

Devin didn't have any photos of his family like that. Not after his mom died, anyway. There was one picture he remembered of when Alana was just a baby and they posed for a picture. They were happy then, but the sickly look in his mother's countenance tainted the shot for him. He both loved and hated that photo. It was the only one he had of his family before it fell apart, but it served as a constant remembrance of why it fell apart in the first place.

Yet, he couldn't be sad for his own past. Not when Krystal's was so unlike that. Somehow, her happiness made up for all the trouble he went through, because her happy childhood meant that he could enjoy her that much more now. No doubt, it was the stable family unit that made her into the woman she was today. For that, he could only be grateful.

Krystal walked into the living room, the two steaming cups of hot chocolate in her hands. Devin seemed to be thoughtfully gazing at one of the photos perched on the mantle and she winced.

"Oh, please don't look at my fourth-grade school picture," she grimaced. "I didn't want to even go to school that day, but my mom made me."

He turned and took one of her cream-colored mugs from her. "I think it's cute," he said with a chuckle.

"The only reason I was smiling was because Sierra stood behind the camera guy making faces to get me to laugh."

"She did a good job, then," he stated before looking back up to the family photos. She wondered if he was silently comparing her picture-perfect family to his own.

The one he appeared to be admiring the most was actually a total farce. They had all been arguing about something earlier that day, and they really didn't want to take the picture, but her mother insisted. They didn't have a good, recent family portrait after Krystal and Sierra grew up. She couldn't even remember what the argument had been about, but her father cast a charm that made them laugh hysterically for no reason, just so they would look good for the picture.

The picture was taken, and they continued to laugh until Sierra couldn't take a breath anymore and then her father cut off the charm. Looking at it now, no one would have ever guessed that they were anything but one big, happy family. They had their squabbles, but Krystal couldn't tell Devin any of that story. She wouldn't tell him about their little traditions, their family huddles, their beliefs, and how grounded they were in their witchy culture that deviating from it had become something of a chore and taboo thing over the years. He would never know how estranged she wished she could be from all of it some days, and how on others she craved the connectedness and stability of those traditions. Not yet anyway.

She sat down on the sofa and curled up her legs after she kicked off the ankle boots she had been wearing. "That fire got going pretty quick," she remarked, looking toward the fireplace that had roared to life within such a short span of time. "It takes me forever to get one log to catch fire."

Whenever the fireplace was being particularly frustrating, she just used some of her magic to get it going. Either that, or she called on her sister who seemed to be a whizz with fire. She was no pyro, but she was a Leo, and their mother always said they were her fire babies. Both instilled with the energy, love, and passion of the element according to their astrological signs. Krystal just rolled her eyes at the time, especially since she was quite the dunce when it came to setting anything on fire. Perhaps that was a good thing. She never burned a meal.

Devin didn't respond to her comment, but moved around the marble-inlaid coffee table to sit next to her on the sofa. He sipped his hot chocolate and stared at the fireplace, a blank and yet completely telling look on his face.

"Are you okay?" she asked, sliding her feet off the sofa, so he could scoot closer if he wanted.

Devin didn't move.

He only nodded. "Yeah, I'm fine. Did you need help cleaning up?"

"No," she replied. "I put everything away while the water was heating up." Making hot chocolate at home was probably a lot easier than at the festival. She tasted the thick brew and grinned.

"I always thought hot chocolate tastes so much better in a mug than in a Styrofoam cup."

Once more, Devin didn't reply. Right about now, she wished she had her mother's scrying gifts, so she could see exactly what it was that troubled him. He didn't seem so bothered when he was feeling up her shirt. He wasn't troubled at all when he was driving her utterly and completely insane with his nearness when they were in the kitchen. If the recipe had been any more complicated, she probably would have screwed it up. The trip outside into the garden to get the herbs gave her a little time to cool off, but when he whispered in her ear again, she was right back to feeling like her blood was boiling over.

Now, in front of the fire, she could feel that heat magnify, her body drawing on its energy. In every vein, every bone, she felt her need for him to speak, to look at her with those entrancing blue eyes, to caress her skin the way he had earlier. She bit her lip, waiting and wondering if she had done something wrong to make him clam up like this.

Slowly, she decided to try something. Krystal slowly swung her legs up to fill the space between them, her bare toes just barely touching the outside of his thigh. Her skirt hung over her legs and knees, draping down and over the edge of the cushion. He wouldn't be able to see anything from where he sat, but with just one move, she could easily open up for him. All it took was one word, one push and Krystal was ready to give into him completely.

Krystal curled and flexed her toes, teasing the fabric of his jeans until he finally snapped out of his stupor and looked to her. She smiled, trying to hide the fact that she was a little irritated with the way he just distanced himself without realizing it. "Where did you go?" she asked, letting her head list to the side until it came to rest on the back sofa cushion.

Devin's chest expanded as he took a deep breath. "Somewhere I don't need to be." She hated the way he had to actually put effort into that smile to try and reassure her that he was all right.

"I'd much rather you were here... with me."

She watched his eyes flit toward her propped up knees. "I'd much rather be here too."

Krystal smoothly eased one of her feet to rest on his thigh. "Then, please stay here for a while. I enjoy your company."

Devin put his mug on the coffee table, and she didn't protest when he took hers as well to set it beside his. In that one move she had anticipated, Krystal parted her legs and let Devin slide over her. His mouth seized hers and her arms found their way around his shoulders. The hem of her skirt slid up and she could feel his coarse jeans rub against the inside of her thigh.

She let out a tiny moan of encouragement as he pressed himself against her. This felt so totally right. Everything from the way his strong arms trapped her there on the couch to the way she could taste the hot chocolate on his tongue as it slipped between her lips.

His hand found its way beneath her tank top again, roaming higher up her sides until the tips of his fingers played with the edge of her bra. Krystal arched her back as the fire and energy poured through her at the command of his touch. They were just kissing, but she was already getting hot and wet.

She hung onto him tighter as he peppered kisses down her jaw, around her ear and along the tender skin of her neck. Before she realized it, the tank top was off and dropped to the floor beside the couch. Krystal reached down and tugged up his own shirt, demanding that it come off too, but Devin was too busy to comply. His attention drifted down her chest, his teasing lips trailing along the edges of her bra. Now, she wished she had worn something a little sexier than the plain satin bra she had pulled on earlier that morning.

Devin's hand drifted down her side, over her hip and slid up her skirt to caress her thigh. Krystal let out a long sigh and tilted her head back against the throw pillow behind her. The heat consumed her, spreading and centering around the point of pleasure between her legs. If Devin explored any further, he just might get his fingers singed.

Her fingers wove through his dark hair, keeping him there at her chest as his tongue played with the soft flesh. He nipped at precisely where her nipples would be beneath her bra and she cried out as they hardened into peaks.

Her eyes rolled into the back of her head as he stayed there, tantalizing her to the fullest extent while his hands played with the edge of her panties. Just when she felt his other hand reach beneath her to unclip her bra, Krystal became vaguely aware of something else.

She turned her head and opened her eyes just enough to see the fireplace. The flames, usually a dancing mix of orange and gold, had turned into a hot blue and purple as the logs slowly disintegrated into ash. The tips of the flames themselves couldn't be seen, but rose higher up the chimney.

Her eyes went wide and another sense broke through the high Devin was sending her on.

Something was burning.

As if the thought had reminded the world that there was something else going on besides Krystal and Devin making out, the fire alarm trilled its loud, obnoxious warning in the kitchen.

Devin flinched and moved off of her. Without a second thought, Krystal cursed, hopped off the couch and ran to the kitchen. The fish had only been in for less than ten minutes and there was already a trail of smoking coming from the oven.

She grabbed her mittens and a towel and threw open the oven door to begin fanning. Devin moved into action too and opened the window over the sink.

"Do you have a fire extinguisher?" he asked.

Krystal waved off the last bit of smoke and peeked inside. The outer edges of the tin foil were blackened and the heating elements glowed white hot. "There's no fire," she shouted over the fire alarm.

She knew she had set the oven for three-hundred and fifty degrees, but the internal thermometer read nearly six hundred. Could her oven even get that hot? It was a miracle the elements hadn't blown.

Devin grabbed the cutting board from the sink and began fanning the fire alarm, so it would stop tormenting their ears. Krystal carefully pulled the pan out and set it on the set of pot holders, though she wondered if they would combust under the heat. Thankfully, everything seemed to be cooling down. Even the fire in the fireplace lessened to normal again.

Krystal leaned against the kitchen island, staring at the pan of charred bluefish fillets and wiped the sweat from her forehead. She had been sweating, but for how long? As soon as they started making out? Or just before the alarm went off?

Her hands began to tremble as the shock settled in. Something wasn't right and she knew it had to do with her magic. The fire growing out of control and the strange oven malfunction weren't separate coincidences. They were linked. They had to be. Why hadn't she realized this before? "Are you all right?"

Devin was in front of her, his hands lightly settled on her shaking shoulders. There was no way she could tell him what she suspected. He'd think she was insane.

"Yeah... Yeah, I'm fine," she said with a hasty nod. She was standing in the middle of her kitchen with her shirt off and they nearly burned the house down just by kissing and getting hot on the couch.

Of course she wasn't fine.

"How do you feel about ordering pizza?" he asked, a faint but apologetic smile on his lips. She was so thankful that he didn't ask how any of this could have happened, that she started laughing.

"Pizza sounds great. I think they'll deliver this late."

Krystal jumped when Devin's phone went off in his pocket. A heavy guitar solo rang out through the deathly still kitchen. He pulled it out of his pocket and she saw the caller ID read Aaron's name.

"Go ahead," she told him as she moved back toward the living room. There was no way they could continue what they started after all that just happened anyway.

She picked up her tank top and slid it over her warm, slightly sticky body and thought about dousing the fireplace before it got out of hand again. Devin's conversation floated into the living room, undeterred by the foyer and walls between them. There were no secrets kept in a house like this.

"What?" he snapped. A moment of silence passed before he let out a long sigh and Krystal was too curious. She came back into the kitchen with their hot chocolate mugs that had been reheated somehow by just sitting on the coffee table. Whether by her or the fire, she wasn't sure.

Devin had his back turned to her, his hand stilled in his hair as if he were raking his fingers through in frustration. Every line of his hard, chiseled back screamed that something was wrong. Krystal watched and waited, her chest tight with two completely separate fears that seemed to meld and amalgamate together into one huge knot.

"All right. I'll be there in a minute." He hung up his phone and turned to meet her curious, frightened stare. "I need to go down to the station," he said, severity dripping from his words like a foreboding sludge. "Stay inside and don't open the door for anyone unless it's me or your sister."

He hurried out of the kitchen and grabbed the empty foam cooler sitting on the counter.

"Devin, you're scaring me," she admitted as she followed him into the hall. "What happened? What did Aaron want?"

Devin's lips tightened together as if he were debating on telling her at all. He looked heavenward, then stepped closer to her. "Please, don't panic. There's been a homicide on the north side of town. I need you to stay inside and don't tell anyone about this. Call your friends if you want, but don't tell them anything, okay? The department doesn't even have all of the information yet, so I don't want anything being spread around."

Murder? In Goldcrest Cove? It was unthinkable. All Krystal could do was stand there with her jaw slack and lips parted in horror. "Please tell me you're joking?"

Devin cupped his free hand under her chin and kissed her lips, as if that would make this sudden nightmare float away. "I wish I was. Promise me you'll stay inside?"

Krystal closed her eyes and nodded her agreement. He was a cop. He knew what he was doing, and he probably saw this all the time in Boston. This was nothing new to him, but Krystal's mind pulled up the faces of those friends and customers who lived on that side of town. Who was it? Whose life had been snuffed out? Better yet, who committed this act? Now, more than ever, Krystal wished she could see through time and space like her mother, so she could help them catch the criminal who did this.

Devin kissed her one last time, and then left her in the foyer. The front door closed behind him and a sudden rush of cold descended over the house. Everything went still, the only sound coming from the crackling fireplace in the living room.

Krystal's happy world felt as if it were crumbling around her like the tiny pieces of shattered glass from a mirror after it had been struck. One by one, the shards hit the ground as her heart continued to beat. There was a murderer on the loose in Goldcrest Cove and the unthinkable might have been finally happening with her powers. The dark, uncontrollable magic that matured as a witch became older, seemed to be finally manifesting itself in her.

Chapter 10

D evin followed the hasty directions Aaron had given over the phone. Really all he had to do was follow the flashing red and blue police lights from the squad cars that surrounded the scene on Jackson Creek Road. Tape that the department probably never thought they would have to use, was being woven around the area where the woman was found.

Aaron wouldn't give many details over the phone. The cop was too dazed to talk much anyway. Chief Nickels wanted Devin on the scene as soon as possible. That was all he really knew. Thanks to his long resume of dealing with crime scenes, he proved to be somewhat of a rare asset for Goldcrest Cove. He thought – and he was sure that everyone else did too – that there would never be a crime on this scale in such a small town.

He spotted Chief Nickels' shock of white hair against the darkness, facing toward the murder victim. Aaron was some distance away, scanning over the crowd of the other officers who were talking amongst themselves. Thankfully, a crowd of civilians hadn't formed. The last thing they needed in this town was a panic.

Devin steeled himself, pushing aside any thought of Krystal and the amazing evening they had together. If it hadn't been for the smoke detector, it might have been even better. But, he knew if he thought about her, his mind would slip into that dark place that yelled at him to run back and protect her at all costs. He couldn't do that. Not when he had a job to do and a responsibility to the department.

Aaron spotted him coming forward and ran to meet him. Before he could even begin to go into the details, Devin asked his questions first. There was a certain order in what he needed to know and what he didn't. Hopefully his partner would understand that.

"When did they find her?" he asked.

Aaron walked alongside him as he charged toward the scene and ducked under the yellow police tape that stretched between two trees near the side of the road. He could already smell the strong, coppery odor of the blood before he even saw the body. "Mr. and Mrs. Hollington were driving down the road and they saw her with their headlights. They came back, thinking it was a drunk teenager passed out on the side of the road. They called us as soon as they realized she was dead."

There was nothing but woods along Jackson Creek Road. It was the perfect spot to dump a body, but if the murderer had any idea what they were doing, they wouldn't have left her so close to the road where they could find her. Not only that, but it would have been a lot easier to toss the body in the creek that wasn't too far away. No one would have found it there for days, maybe longer. Maybe never.

"Did you call the medical examiner to come and determine the time of death?"

Aaron stammered a bit and then said, "Yeah, I think Chief Nickels called them in, but he hasn't shown up yet."

"What about CSI from Boston?"

His partner looked nonplussed. "Devin, we just found her. No one is here yet."

Devin should have expected that much. In Boston, everyone would be there within mere minutes. It was his job as a cop to secure the scene and make sure nothing was tampered with. He had listened over the shoulders of plenty of investigators to piece together crime scenes, but he was still no expert.

Chief Nickels came forward, his expression full of righteous indignation. "About time you got here."

"I can't do much, Chief," he admitted, trying not to let himself get riled over his boss's tone. He was just as stressed as any of them. "But I can take a look." Even from a distance, he had an eyeful. The torso of the body was mutilated rather methodically. "Did anyone touch anything?"

"We ain't that stupid, son," Chief Nickels spat out in his rather thick southern accent. If he remembered correctly, the senior officer was from Tennessee originally. And he had the country temper to boot. These first couple of weeks on the job were almost as tough as his time at the academy. Chief James Nickels could have been a great cadet trainer.

"Good. Can we tell if the body was moved at all?" Devin's eyes deviated from the corpse for just a moment to inspect the grass and dried leaves that had been trampled in the wake of the hysteria.

"How can we tell?" Aaron asked, following his partner as he walked all around the body, but didn't go near it just yet.

"Drag marks in the grass or on the pavement. If the killer dropped her off at the road, there would be blood on the curb."

"I'll have a team check," Nickels said. Now it was like this was Devin's case and it felt odd to be giving orders or suggestions. He wasn't an investigator by any means, and he wasn't trained as one. The chief put a lot of stock in him, apparently.

Nickels rounded up two of the other officers who weren't occupied and told them to look up and down the road.

From what Devin could see, there were no obvious signs that the body had been moved before the department arrived. He'd have to check deeper into the tree line for any other clues. For now, he needed to turn his focus back to the body.

He stayed a good yard away from the victim, not wanting to step into the puddle of blood that was slowly seeping into the soil around the corpse. She wore high heels and a moderate knee-length skirt, but the shirt was too torn open to identify it as anything but sleeveless. Her purse, spattered with blood, lay beside her, which might have suggested that the murderer wasn't after her money.

By the way her torso was carved open, Devin guessed she must have been either knocked unconscious before the deed was done, or the slit in her throat was what killed her first. He couldn't imagine anyone sitting still long enough for a giant cross to be carved into their chest that way.

That was all he could determine at a glance. He asked for Aaron's flashlight and he squatted down to take a closer inspection.

"No bruising or cuts on the fingers indicate that she struggled... But the bruising on her wrists means that she might have been tied up while she was still alive." He checked around her neck and, though the blood had poured out from the gash in her throat, he could just barely see the deep purple blotches. "And she was strangled at some point."

Her face, blankly staring into the night sky, was unfamiliar to him, but that didn't mean a whole lot. He still had a difficult time remembering the names of his fellow officers. "I'm assuming she's been IDed?"

Behind him, Aaron replied, his voice thick with emotion, "Yeah. Her name's Elizabeth Thatchman. She worked at Torn Sails Bar."

Devin skimmed his light over the body, searching for any other hint he could go on. "Did she have any enemies?" It might have been a better question for a friend or family member. But by the way Aaron sounded, his partner must have known Elizabeth. Not surprising.

"I wouldn't say enemies," Aaron said warily. "I don't think anyone openly hated her. I doubt anyone would wish this on her, anyway."

Devin sighed. Yeah, people may not openly admit they hate someone until they decided to pop them off one day. But this... This was something else. Even after being on the force for a number of years, being the first on crime scenes similar to this one where victims had their heads bashed in, arms severed, intestines spilling onto the pavement, his stomach still churned at the sight of so much blood and carnage.

"Since you know her, do you think you can come up with a list of names and associates? We can give the investigator the list once he gets here."

"Investigator?"

Devin looked up to his partner and squinted. "We don't have an investigator on staff, do we?"

Aaron slowly shook his head. "Not really. You'll find out we all have to fill different shoes here in Goldcrest Cove. Investigator isn't one we've really needed in a while."

With a helpless shrug, Devin looked back to Miss Thatchman's body. "I guess I'll have to do it then, unless you have any better ideas."

"Just don't expect a raise from Nickels." Aaron paused and they both stared down at the lifeless, mangled corpse with her arms and legs set at odd, contorted angles. "I still can't believe anyone would do this."

Devin stood up. "People are capable of a lot." He knew from experience that was true. And though he would have never wished this kind of death upon anyone, maybe it would be a good chance to give this town a taste of how imperfect and nasty the world could be. "I want that list made up," he continued. "Coworkers, her boss, any known friends or family members. I want to know if she was working or if she was on a date tonight. By the way she's dressed, I would assume the later."

Aaron smacked his forehead. "Damn it, I totally forgot you had that date with Krystal tonight. Man, I'm sorry."

He closed his eyes and tried to not picture Krystal's face right then. He couldn't linger on the fact that someone had been killed in her hometown and they hadn't caught the killer yet. He couldn't think about the idea that she might be in danger, even though it was a longshot. He didn't know for sure, but this appeared to be a crime of passion. Someone hated this girl enough to kill her, but no one hated Krystal. She was well liked by everyone in town and they all knew her name. He took consolation in that.

There was no reason for anyone to kill her.

Then again, was there any reason for someone to kill Elizabeth Thatchman?

"It's fine," Devin said. "She understood I had to go."

Aaron seemed relieved. Or, as relieved as he could be in a situation like this. "That's good. Did you tell her why you had to leave?"

"I told her to stay inside and I said someone had been murdered, but that was all."

Devin handed the flashlight back to Aaron, satisfied that he got all he needed to know for now. When CSI arrived from Boston, they would take any DNA or forensic evidence off the body to be sent to the labs. From there, it could take days, maybe weeks to get the results back. Hopefully, by then, Devin would have a list of suspects to pull from. All they needed was a good match and they could put the murderer behind bars.

"If you want to go check on her or finish out your date, I think Nickels would understand. It's your night off anyway."

There was no way he could go back and finish what they started after something like this. It would take a lot of brain bleaching to get him to forget about Elizabeth Thatchman. It might be physically impossible for him to get a boner for a day or two – even if Krystal stripped down naked for him.

"No," he said. "I'll stay here and see this through. She'll be all right."

He and Aaron walked away and ducked back under the yellow tape. "How did it go anyway? I'd much rather be talking about your budding love life than this right now."

There was weird mix of humor and melancholy in his statement that made Devin pity him. For such a small town, this was going to be a big blow. They were probably thinking the same thing. Once the news leaked out, the citizens would surely react. They would come banging on the police station doors, demanding answers and action. They could only do so much.

"The date went fine. Did you know she was afraid of going out on the water?"

Aaron made a sound like he wanted to laugh. "Yeah, I did. She didn't say anything about it?"

"Not a word," Devin replied with a bit of bitterness. "But, I don't know if she's afraid anymore. We took the boat out and she seemed to have a good time, though she was pretty nervous at first."

It might have been a dangerous thing, but the farther they walked away from the body to go check on Chief Nickel's progress with the curb search, he found himself relaxing a bit. Maybe thinking about Krystal was what he needed to block out the harsh reality of what this town was about to experience. Its first murder case in probably decades, if not longer. He didn't envy them. Not one bit.

Krystal kicked her legs in the air behind her as she lay on her stomach across her bed. She watched her two friends' faces on the screen as she three-way FaceTimed them. Artemis laid at the foot of the bed, his tail curled around his body and unconcerned with the drama that had unfolded earlier that evening. When she hurried upstairs to call her friends, she found him sprawled out across her comforter, asleep. She had wondered where the pudgy cat had run off to while she and Devin were getting hot and heavy in front of the fireplace.

"And then he left?" Alexa asked, her blonde hair in damp ringlets on her shoulders.

"Yep," Krystal replied as she laid her head down on her forearm and tilted the phone just right, so they could still see her. "I haven't heard from him since he left."

"Have you tried to call him back?" Valerie asked. Krystal could see the light blue light from a television screen dancing across her face in the darkened room. She must have been winding down for bed, because her eyes were free of the usual black eyeliner and thick, matte eyeshadow.

"Nope. I'm letting him do his job."

"I still can't believe someone was murdered in Goldcrest Cove," Alexa whispered, as if it were some taboo thing to even say the word "murder" in this town.

"Me neither."

Krystal narrowed her eyes. "Was that Shawn?" The deep masculine voice was what gave him away, and the fact that no other pairs of lips were moving.

Valerie's wry expression confirmed it. "I told you to hush or I'd take it into the other room," she scolded the teacher who must have been watching television beside her on the couch. Then again, maybe he was playing a videogame.

"Hi, Shawn!" Alexa shrieked.

Valerie made a face and turned the phone, so they could see him with a controller between his hands. He took his blue eyes off the television long enough to say a greeting, and then Valerie angled the phone back to her face. "Sorry, girls. I wanted to watch him get through this level."

"Well, can you do me a favor and go to your room, so we can talk about something privately?" Krystal asked, itching to ask for her friends' advice on this new development in her powers. It was a good thing she decided to get the business of this murder out of the way. Otherwise that might have been a rather awkward conversation with Shawn later. He still didn't know he was living with a witch.

The two girls waited as Valerie got off the couch, walked down the hall, and into her darkened room. She paused, only to call to her big black lab, Thor, to come join her. The tinkling of the dog's tags on his collar verified that he was going to be their second eavesdropper for the evening. At least dogs could keep secrets. Only when Krystal heard the door shut did she blurt it out. "Something's going on with my powers."

"What's going on?" Alexa asked, her eyes wide.

Krystal then went on to explain how ever since she first came into contact with Devin, she had felt these weird hot flashes that steadily got worse after they kissed.

She didn't give them a ton of details about how they ended up on the couch, but she told her friends about the way they treated the poor bluefish like a sacrificial offering and charred up the fireplace chimney.

Valerie, not usually one for hysterics, began to freak out more than Krystal had. "Oh, my goddess! Are you coming into your dark magic? I mean, it makes sense since you're a little older, but do you think Devin really has something to do with it?"

Krystal shrugged helplessly and sat up on her bed, crossing her legs underneath her. "I don't know. I mean, I am an Aries, and fire is supposed to be my element, but I've always had trouble with fire rituals. It's probably one of the things I'm terrible at as a witch, and now it's just blown up."

For witches and warlocks, their dark magic normally began to develop in their later adult years. Krystal's parents didn't get their dark magic until shortly before they were married. She suspected that she still had a few more years of uncomplicated magic to deal with before anything like this would happen to her. It was much like puberty, only more inconvenient and highly dangerous if not mastered quickly.

Alexa bit at her nail. "Fire represents passion, love, and change too. None of that really describes you."

Krystal nodded in agreement with that. She might have been the most placid Aries in existence. She prided herself on keeping a cool and level head when it came to making decisions or dealing with people. Never prone to angry outbursts or mad flings of emotion.

"Up until she met Devin," Valerie corrected.

She nodded to that as well. "And I only get heated like that when I think about him."

Krystal had plenty of time to stew about this in between the time that Devin left and when she called her friends. She had to think through it before she ever called them, or she'd be a mess of confusion.

"That must be it, then," Alexa said excitedly as if they had just solved the mystery of the universe. "So, your special witch power is fire manipulation."

"That's just it, though. There is no manipulation here," she said with blatant frustration. "There's no control, no focus. I get hot and I get everything else hot too, like the fireplace and the oven, which were both putting off heat."

Valerie nodded and a weird smile spread over her face. "It's like you just intensify any kind of heat source around you. That's so cool! You're a real-life pyro."

Not in all the years Krystal had been a witch, had she ever met someone who could genuinely control fire as their dark magic, or specialty. Some witches preferred to call their focus of dark magic as their special magic, whereas some still called it dark magic. Mostly that was because whatever new ability that happened to be, there was a destructive force behind it that took years, maybe decades of training to harness.

That thought alone made Krystal's guts meld into one big knot. If Devin was the catalyst for her dark fire magic, then she would have to distance herself from him. If she dwelled on that idea too much, Sierra would come home to a heartbroken sister. Krystal refused to allow herself to fall to pieces like that. They could figure something out, so she could be with Devin and still embrace this dark magic she was coming into.

"Right, so what do I do about it?" she asked.

Both of the girls gave her blank stares. This might have been the first time she was ever asking for help from the two witches she had practically trained since they were kids. She was always the one to answer their questions and solve their magic problems. Now, she was coming to them for ideas, because Sierra wasn't answering her phone and calling her mother was out of the question. If she asked too many questions, the truth would leak out about Devin and she'd have a real shit show on her hands.

"Hell, if I know," Valerie replied. "Aren't there charms to suppress fire?"

"There are," Alexa answered, "but this isn't a case of suppressing a physical, open fire like a camp fire. This is suppressing passion itself."

It sounded so unnecessarily poetic, but Krystal didn't correct her. She might have been right.

"Okay, I think there's a charm for that, but I'd have to check our catalogue."

Some witches had their books, some had a digital database for their spells, charms, and potions. Krystal's family had a catalogue, almost like a rolodex of flash cards containing every spell passed down through the generations. Sierra and Krystal would someday add their own personally crafted charms into the catalogue, but it would be many more years before they could manage to create spells from scratch. Maybe, with her friends' help, Krystal could make one to stave off her dark magic. To her knowledge, it had never been done. But there was a first time for everything.

"Do you really want to block out all that passion you feel for Devin?" Alexa questioned, her face twisting. "You two are so into each other and if he's the one that brings out this power in you, don't you think he's worth keeping?"

"Of course, he's worth keeping, but I can't set the furniture on fire every time we start making out. What if I hurt someone? What if I hurt him?"

This time, neither of them had an answer. They knew perfectly well what could happen when a witch's powers got out of hand.

"I hate to admit it," Alexa started, "but maybe you should call your mom or dad and ask them. Have you talked to Sierra yet?"

Krystal held back her bangs for a moment. "No, she hasn't come home yet, but she's probably thinking that Devin and I are having sex right about now, so she may not come back for a while."

"Have you called her?" Valerie asked.

"She's not answering her phone."

"Do you think she's all right? There is a murderer on the loose after all," stated Alexa, then she let out a cry that rang in Krystal's ears for a solid few seconds. "Oh, dear Gaia! What if she was the one murdered and that's why Devin didn't tell you any details?"

The thought had occurred to her, and even though she had discredited such an idea, it still made her lungs seize. "No, Devin would have told me. Family members are the first that get called."

"I sure hope you're right," Valerie said as Thor leapt onto her bed to sit with her. Krystal could see the flash of black fur as he roamed behind his owner. "I wouldn't want someone keeping information from me like that, especially if they knew."

The image of Devin staring into space and his comment about mentally going to some place he shouldn't have gone, came to Krystal's mind. He was definitely keeping a dark truth from her, just like she wasn't telling him everything.

"Maybe I should call him, just in case."

Alexa jostled her phone a bit, making the camera blur her image for a minute. "Hold on a second!" she said. "You said you didn't want to call him, because he was busy working. Now, it sounds like you really didn't trust him to tell you if Sierra was dead. What's going on? You're never this wishy washy."

It wouldn't have been surprising if they found out Alexa's dark power was to see straight through lies like Krystal's mother. She rolled her eyes and thought about how to tactfully word it all. "Okay, so I think there's something Devin isn't telling me, but I don't know what it is. We've established that we both like honesty from one another, but there's just these little hints he keeps dropping that makes me thing he's hiding something."

Valerie's eyes narrowed. "Do you think he's done something or maybe he *is* something?"

"That's what Sierra suggested, but I know he's not a warlock, and I know he's not anything magical or supernatural. I just think there's something about his past that he doesn't want me to know about, that's all."

"Girl," Alexa joined in with a shake of her head, her curls tumbling around her cheeks, "you need to find out what that is. If you two can't be open, this relationship isn't going to work."

Krystal no longer had to wonder if she and Devin were in a relationship. The way he felt up her skirt was enough evidence that they were more than friends anyway. No doubt about it.

"In all fairness, I haven't exactly come out of the 'broom closet' either, so he has the right to keep that secret from me if I have to keep secrets from him."

Back in high school, they had come up with a saying that caught on amongst the other witches in town. Whenever they talked about revealing what they really were to non-magic folk, they referred to it as "coming out of the broom closet". It was cute at the time, and proved to be a nice code phrase for them if they talked about magic in public.

Alexa and Valerie both nodded in agreement.

"Okay, you've got me there," Alexa conceded. "Still, I do agree that you should call him. Just to make sure he's okay and that Sierra is all right too."

Krystal nodded and fell back on her pile of feather pillows at the head of her bed. "What about this whole dark magic business? I mean, I'm really torn about this. I like Devin a lot and I don't want to ruin things by breaking up with him, but I also want to learn to control this now that it's here to stay. I want to have my cake and eat it too."

Once a witch earned her dark magic, there was no way to give it up. If this magic held any semblance to the element of fire, it would rear its ugly face every time Krystal became emotionally charged about anything. Whether she was mad, sad, or in Devin's case, madly turned on, she'd feel that same raging heat within her and it could get out of control.

"I say you get out your catalogue and look for something to keep your emotions in check. Maybe not totally suppress them, but just put a dampener on them, you know?" Valerie offered.

"And in the meantime," Alexa added, "I'll look through the copy I have of my dad's book and Valerie can look through her parent's book, right?"

Valerie made a face. "That may be a little hard for me. I've been trying to transfer it all onto my computer and it's been a really slow process. Nothing's in order anymore." She angled the phone around to show her friends the disorganized stack of old parchment beside her desktop. "But, I'll definitely try to find something."

Krystal gave a strained smile. "Thanks, guys. I owe you one."

"Can I get tomorrow off then?" Valerie asked. "It'll take me that long to go through this shit anyway."

She shot her friend a look. "Mondays are super busy for us. You know that." Krystal froze when she heard a car door slam close to the house. "I think someone's coming, hold on."

"Did you lock the door?" Alexa whispered.

Krystal only nodded. Not only did she lock it, but she charmed it too. No non-magic folk was going to step over her threshold. If the door handle jiggled without a doorbell ring or a knock, she knew it was someone she definitely didn't want in the house. If they did try to ring the doorbell, Krystal would just ignore it. However, if the door swung open without any effort, she knew it was Sierra.

She let out the breath she had been holding when Sierra came traipsing through the foyer. Artemis perked his head up and looked toward the stairs. Yeah, now he wakes up, but the sharp beeping of the smoke alarm didn't faze him. "It's Sierra. Got to go."

She promptly ended the three-way video call and ran to see her sister in the kitchen. It was nearly ten o'clock and she was fixing herself a pot of tea. She spotted the green and yellow package on the counter and knew Sierra was about to brew up some lemon and ginger tea.

"Hey," she greeted halfheartedly. "I drove by and didn't see Devin's car so I just assumed – "

She didn't have time to finish her sentence as Krystal ran up and hugged Sierra around the neck. Her sister had the tea bag in one hand and the sloshing kettle in the other. Krystal let the relief wash over her, knowing that her sister was still alive. At least now, one crisis was averted.

When Krystal pulled back, she stamped her bare foot on the kitchen tiles. "Why didn't you answer the phone?"

Sierra blinked at the sudden turn of emotion and pulled out her phone to check the notifications. "I'm sorry, I put it on silent. Is everything okay?" Then, she sniffed the air. "Did you burn something? You never burn while cooking."

It was hard to miss the smell of charbroiled fish that was sitting in the trash can. Artemis came bounding in and went straight for said garbage can to see if there was some way he could get to the burnt offerings.

"I did tonight," Krystal sighed. "It's a long story. I might need some of that tea. It's caffeinated right? And is the spell catalogue where you last left it? I need to look through it."

Sierra turned up the range dial after she set the kettle down and shot her sister a perturbed look. "One, you never drink caffeine this late, and two, why do you need the catalogue?"

"Like I said, it's a long story."

Chapter 11

Aaron was reading back the list of individuals they would need to interview that day, all of them associated with Elizabeth Thatchman in some way. Devin wasn't listening as they ambled down the sidewalk toward Perfect Books and Brews. His eyes burned, and his muscles ached with the need to jump in the squad car, leave Aaron to the investigative work, and go home for some much needed rest.

Last night, he neglected to do that. He stayed at the crime scene with Chief Nickels until CSI and the medical examiner showed up. He relayed as much information as he could since half of the other officers had gone home for the night, including Aaron. They were smart. Now Aaron was fresh and ready to tackle the job of visiting these homes and businesses to get to the bottom of what happened.

"And that's it," he said as they passed McRae Morsels.

Devin looked up and opened his mouth to reply, but a yawn came out instead. When he was done nearly popping his jaw out of place, he said, "How many does that make?"

"Weren't you listening?"

Even though Devin had already downed two cups of coffee earlier that morning before meeting up with Aaron at the station, he was still exhausted. Up to a certain point, he just couldn't function on so few hours of sleep. After all the excitement with Krystal, the murder, and paperwork that needed to be done before too much time had passed, Devin felt like he hadn't slept in days. Not even the prospect of seeing Krystal again could revive him at this point. But, maybe a cup of their famous house blend coffee could.

"Not really. How many?" he asked again.

"Just ten. Most of them are her coworkers." He folded up the paper loaded with addresses and phone numbers and shoved it into his pocket.

Devin nodded as they stood in the line that stretched out the door and a little down the sidewalk, just like it had last week when he came here for the first time. That seemed like a lifetime ago. It occurred to Devin that he and Krystal almost crossed a delicate line last night, and they hadn't known each other for a full week. Yet, it felt so natural, so right to be with her in that way. If he wasn't so tired, he might have gotten another hard on just thinking about how soft and addictive her skin felt in his hands.

Many of the other customers in line looked just as dead tired as he was. As soon as they saw the two cops come forward, they turned to their neighbors and start whispering. One woman got out of her place in line to come up to him.

"Is it true there was a murder last night?" she asked as she tightened her scarf around her neck.

Luckily, Aaron spoke first. If he hadn't, Devin might have snapped at the woman. When he was tired, he could get downright grumpy too.

"I don't know what you heard, ma'am, but we're not allowed to disclose anything like that to the public."

Her eyes went wide. "So, it's true?"

"I didn't say that," Aaron replied, and Devin could hear his words laden with repressed impatience.

"So who was murdered?" the next older woman in line asked, her grey and silver hair fluttering in the wind.

"No one said that anyone was murdered," Devin piped in.

"Officer Aaron just implied it," the first woman said.

Aaron crossed his arms. "I said, in a manner of words, that if there was a murder, I wouldn't be able to tell you anyway."

Now the second woman's husband was joining in. "That's not what I heard."

"We don't care what you've heard," Devin said. "If there was a murder, you'll hear about it from the newspapers, not from us."

And no doubt, the news would be all in the papers by the following morning. The head reporter for Goldcrest Cove Chronicles was at the crime scene the night before and asking far too many questions that could not be answered. Chief Nickels requested that he not cause a panic in the community with the article. That might as well have been like asking a hummingbird to flap its wings a little slower. It just wasn't going to happen.

The nosy citizens seemed to accept that and went back to whispering and speculating amongst themselves. What he didn't understand was how anyone could have found out about the murder so soon. It was only last night, and everyone was told to keep their mouths shut. Granted, he did tell Krystal, but he knew that she wouldn't have gone blabbing about it all over town.

Once they were in the warm coffee shop, the air suffused with the pungent aroma of coffee, Devin almost felt a little more awake. Since they were limited on how much they could say about the murder case, they were restricted to silence as they shuffled their way up to the counter.

Krystal stood behind the register, and his heart sank when he saw the weary look on her face. She didn't have dark circles around her eyes like he must have, but there was a sluggish quality in her movements as if she were moving through water.

It did occur to him that he left her in a state the night before. She was obviously shocked and in need of consoling when he told her there had been a murder in Goldcrest Cove. He was sure that plenty more people would react in the same way once the papers printed the story. Perhaps he should have called or stopped by, even if it was three in the morning by the time he left Jackson Creek Road.

She must have been scared out of her mind, waiting alone in that big house. Devin passed a hand over his face and rubbed at his cheek, wishing he could have gone back and done things over again. At least now, he could talk to her.

They came to the front counter and Krystal gave them a sleepy smile. "Good morning," she said.

"The usual?"

Devin was taken aback by her formalness. This wasn't the greeting he expected, tired or not.

Aaron nodded. "Yep, the usual for me."

"Can we talk in private?" Devin asked softly, ignoring the way his partner looked at him as if he had grown a second head.

Krystal blinked and seemed confused at first, but then nodded. She turned and asked Alexa to take over. The two walked into the back office off to the left of the front counter, past the bathrooms.

When she shut the door behind her, Devin stepped forward to wrap her in a tight hug. Holding her again was like taking in a breath of fresh air, clean and cool. Devin was liable to fall asleep on his feet, he was so comfortable with her.

"Is everything okay?" she mumbled against his chest.

He pulled away and lifted her chin up so he could take his fill of her gorgeous, expressive brown eyes. In them, he saw a late night plagued by worry. Damn, he should have called.

"Are you okay?" he countered.

She nodded and her eyelids drooped a bit. "Yeah, I'm fine. I just... I had trouble sleeping, that's
all."

"I should have called you," he apologized.

Krystal waved him off. "No, it's fine. I know you were working and I've watched plenty of crime shows. I know it's an involved process."

Devin cracked a smile. It wasn't exactly like in the movies, but he appreciated her understanding.

"So, who was it? Or am I allowed to know?"

Taking a breath, he said, "I'll tell you, but you have to keep it to yourself. It was Elizabeth Thatchman. Did you know her?"

That was a stupid question. Krystal knew everyone.

By the renewed shock in her face, he had all the answers he needed. Maybe she could be the first one he interviewed about the case. He guided her toward one of the armchairs near the desk that was littered with receipts and printed reports. Evidently, Krystal hadn't had a chance to do a lot of organizing lately.

"Can you tell me if she had any enemies? Anyone who might have wanted to hurt her?" Devin leaned against the edge of the desk and watched her eyes dart as she scrambled for the answer.

"Well, no, not really. I mean, she wasn't hated or anything. She was actually pretty nice. We went to school together and..." She paused, as if debating whether to tell him the next bit or not. "She slept around a lot. I know it's not right to talk about her like that, but she did. Elizabeth was in a bad place at home from what I knew."

"Does she have any family in town?" he asked, crossing his arms and willing himself to listen closely, despite the fact that he teetered on the line between grabbing her to pin her to the desk and finish what he started last night, and falling asleep where he stood.

"Her dad's been in prison for a few years and her brother's a drug addict. I don't think anyone's seen him since he left town maybe... six years ago? I can't remember exactly. No one really knows where her mom is."

Damn. He was hoping that Elizabeth's family would be the first he could contact. If he had been listening to Aaron's report, he might have known that family wasn't really an option.

Devin rubbed at his bloodshot eyes. "Did you tell anyone about what happened last night?"

She donned a sheepish look. "Well, I told Alexa and Valerie, but only because I wanted them to understand why I was telling them to not leave the house. And Shawn Stokes, Valerie's roommate was listening in on the conversation, but I didn't know it until after the fact."

"Would they have told anyone?"

"I told them not to tell anyone and I trust that they wouldn't."

His eyes narrowed. "What about Shawn?"

Krystal smirked. "He's a teacher, so I doubt he would tell anyone. He definitely wouldn't want his students freaking out."

She had a point. "I've already been asked about the murder by some of your customers. If you didn't tell them, then who did? None of the other officers are dumb enough to let this leak out and the papers haven't run the story yet. The only other people I can think of are Mr. and Mrs. Hollington who found the body, but we debriefed them and – "

Krystal let out a laugh. "You really expect Mrs. Hollington to keep herself from gossiping about this?"

There was his answer. "She would have told people?"

"I'm surprised the entire town doesn't know already," Krystal remarked. "If she gets a hold of a juicy secret, everyone knows it within a few hours."

He made a face. "Well, at least we know she hasn't found out about us yet."

She smiled, the first real smile he had seen all morning and he basked in its beauty while it lasted.

"Can I see you tonight?" he asked, his heart running away with his mouth before his brain could stop him.

The smile gave a slight downturn and he knew he would do just about anything to get it back, even if it meant pinning her to the filing cabinet and doing her right there in her own office while the coffee shop was packed with customers.

"I work late tonight, and I really need to get back on track with all this stuff." She motioned toward the mess on her desk. "I haven't had a chance to sort out anything and that puts Alexa behind on getting financial reports to me too."

"I'm sorry if I'm the one that's been holding you up."

She shook her head frantically. "No, it's not you. I could have done it on Saturday night, but with the festival and all, I was too tired afterward to think straight. And I could have on Friday, but I... I just didn't feel like it."

His brows shot up. "You didn't feel like taking care of your business?"

Krystal rolled her pretty eyes. "Yeah, I know, but I swear an alien hasn't abducted me or anything. A lot has been going on in the past few days."

"I'd have to agree with that," he replied with a smile. "A lot of amazing things, though."

A slight blush rose to her cheeks and he wondered if the heater kicked on, because the temperature in the room must have spiked. He might need to take his jacket off. He pushed himself off the desk and leaned over the chair, his weight supported on the arms to trap her there. Devin kissed her, letting himself drown in her perfume and the electrifying energy that was so signature to every touch they exchanged.

"What about tomorrow night?" he asked after he eased out of the kiss. "Are you doing anything special for Halloween?"

Krystal sighed and he could see her body tensed a bit. "Sort of. Sierra's going to a costume party and I had thought about meeting with Alexa and Valerie after they closed up the shop. I get off early tomorrow."

Devin grinned. He loved it when she got off early. "Maybe dinner at my place? Or your place? We won't burn the meal this time. We can answer the door for trick-or-treaters, too."

"I'm not too sure about that," she said, a sliver of apprehension in her voice that he couldn't quite make sense of. Did that apprehension have something to do with how her muscles went rigid when he kissed her?

"About burning the dinner, coming over to my place, or the trick-or-treaters?"

She pulled away and the solemnness in her expression sent a spark of fear through him. "None

of it."

"Dare I ask, why?" he said, hoping this didn't have anything to do with the murders. If she was afraid to go out, he would gladly come to her place. He'd stay there all night, sex or no sex, and stand guard over her home as long as it meant he could be with her.

"I... I just need some time to think."

Just like that, Devin's world went into a spiral. He knew those words well. It was the same thing his previous girlfriends had told him when they learned about his troubled childhood, or about the demands of his job as a cop in a big city.

He never expected to hear this from Krystal. She knew about his past. Perhaps not all of it, but there was plenty of time to gently tell her about those things. Or, was there time? Was she going to drop him now, after they had already experienced so much together? Was the chemistry he felt not reciprocated?

He blinked for a long couple of seconds, but he refused to release her from the chair or let that mind numbing dread take hold. "What is there to think about? Did I – "

She reached up and slipped her fingers through his hair in that way that drove him crazy with desire. "No, no!" she cried. "It's not you. None of it is you. I just need to get some personal things sorted out, that's all. I promise it won't take long." She kissed him, long and hard as if to prove that she was still interested in having him, all of him. "As soon as it's all worked out, I'll let you know."

Devin wasn't sure how long she needed. Days, weeks, months? He would wait as long as she needed, but he hoped that it wouldn't change the way she felt for him. There were two adages he couldn't forget. Absence makes the heart grow fonder, and out of sight out of mind. He'd go to the coffee shop twice a day if it meant he could keep the bond between them fresh and alive.

He nodded in mock understanding and left it at that. He desperately wanted to know what it was that made her so hesitant now. What it was that she needed to work through exactly, but he was sure that she would tell him when the time was right. She had to, or he was going to lose his mind.

"You look exhausted," she said, her gaze drinking in the mess he must have looked like.

He chuckled. "I was up all night."

Krystal patted his shoulder. "Come on. I'll get your usual coffee and pump a shot of espresso in it to wake you up."

He could think of plenty of other things that could wake him up. Coffee would be the most convenient at a time like this.

"Maybe make that two espresso shots," he said as he straightened and let her stand. "I've got a laundry list of people to see today about Elizabeth before I'm off duty." Krystal stiffened when he spoke the murder victim's name and he regretted his blunder. "Are you going to be all right?"

She nodded. "Yeah, I'll be fine. I wasn't that close to her, but it's still hard to think that someone would kill another human being. She didn't do anything to deserve that."

That seemed to be the general consensus, but there had to be a motive behind the murder and Devin was determined to find it out. Even if it meant coming back to get more espresso shots until he could think straight enough to find an answer.

There was no way Krystal was going to tell the girls about the extra charm she put in Devin's drink. Not only because they had two tick marks on the chalkboard and it wasn't even ten o'clock yet, but because she didn't want to get into the conversation about the murder that took place last night.

It was already unsettling enough that Elizabeth Thatchman, a woman who had done no real wrong to anyone, had been murdered in cold blood. She hoped, despite her initial reactions to the news, that Devin would tell her more in time.

She also hoped that she could get her shit together before he started to give up on having a relationship with her.

When she told him that she needed time to think, she might as well have driven a stake through his chest. His eyes, tired as they were, couldn't hide the pain he felt when she said those words. She wanted to take them all back, say to hell with safety, and jump him right there on her desk. The papers strewn across the desktop would ignite, and they would all burn to ashes, but at least she wouldn't have put him through such emotional pain again.

Krystal and Sierra had stayed up half the night, leafing through the rolodex catalogue for anything that might help. They looked under passions spells, emotion spells, fire rituals, fire suppressants, emotion suppressants, everything. Not one spell or charm seemed to fit what she needed. They either came at such a high cost to the recipient – such as no emotions at all, the unending feeling of cold, etcetera – or they wouldn't do the job exactly as she needed.

Sierra hadn't come into her own full dark magic yet, so she was clueless on how to contain or control it. They had thought to call Amber, who had come into her dark magic long ago. Like Krystal's mother, she had the ability to scry, or see things that weren't in the physical or present time.

But her ability was much more passive, indirect. Her abilities weren't harmful in any way but to herself. Krystal remembered the day when she came in, talking about all the weird stuff she had seen like ancient battles and futuristic space discoveries. After a while, she learned to focus her abilities, but it wasn't elemental magic like Krystal was dealing with.

Taylor, just like the rest of them, hadn't come into her dark magic, so she was of no help either.

Their last resort was to call her parents, but Krystal was still determined to figure this out for herself. That's why she needed time to think. Time to search through other family spell books to see if there was something, anything, that would help her get a handle on the fire that burned inside of her for Devin.

When the two cops left, Krystal still felt no more at ease than when he had come in. She was too tired and there was the strong temptation to charm her own coffee like she had for Devin. Hopefully, he wouldn't be bouncing off the walls with the extra spritz of energy and focus she had put in his coffee. It might have been risky mixing espresso with that kind of charm, but she did it anyway.

She let Alexa take over the front counter for the rest of the morning and banished herself to the coffee machines, turning out drink after drink. She needed something to distract herself, and she didn't look her best for the customers anyway. The only reason she had put herself on the register at all was in the hopes that Devin and Aaron would come in.

Just when she thought the flow of customers was slowing down, the brass bell over the door jingled again and Valerie let out a groan before she even turned around. Krystal didn't have to look when she heard her sister bounding across the floor in her high heel boots.

"Krystal! Oh, my goddess! Krystal!"

She turned and saw Sierra scrambling around the counter.

"Get back over there!" Krystal hissed, pointing toward the lobby.

"No, no, no." Sierra grabbed her arm that was holding a peppermint latte and nearly spilled it.

"No, I'm coming to warn you."

"Warn me?" Krystal carefully pried her sister's fingers from her and went to deliver the drink to the customer who was waiting off to the side of the front counter.

"I was getting out of my car to go to the salon and I saw her."

Krystal shot Sierra a look. "Her, who?"

"Mom," she whispered. "She was talking with Mrs. Macy outside the antique shop on the corner."

Alexa took the next drink order as Krystal was faced with this new emergency. "Did you call her?"

"No, I swear, I didn't. She must have seen or felt or whatever it is she experiences when there's trouble and now she's here to check it out."

Not two seconds later, the brass bell jingled, and their heads swiveled toward the door. A woman, just old enough to have earned a few splashes of silver in her dark hair, stepped into the lobby. Her brown eyes searched for her daughters, but she didn't have to look for long. Her smile, warm and radiant, made the coffee shop ten times more welcoming than it was before. Just having her there improved the atmosphere somehow. Their mother had that effect everywhere she went.

She strutted forward, the flaps of her long white coat opening to show her bell-bottom jeans and black turtleneck. "There are my girls!" she exclaimed with her arms wide open.

Krystal loved her mother, and enjoyed her visits, but now was not the best time. With a murderer in Goldcrest Cove and her dark magic busting loose, she wanted her mother, Catherine, as far away as possible.

Instead of telling her to turn around and drive right back to Albany, Krystal came forward and embraced her mother. "What are you doing here?" she asked with a laugh, hoping to hide her irritation.

"I came as soon as I knew something wasn't right." Catherine cast a derisive glance to Sierra.

"You told me everything was fine when we talked on the phone last week."

Now it was Sierra's turn to hug her mother. "Everything was fine and still is fine," she replied.

Catherine gave her girls the look. The same look that told them she didn't believe anything they just said. "Let's talk in private."

"Mom, I've got a coffee shop to run," Krystal whined.

All Catherine had to do was give her the *other* look. This look was the one all mothers gave when their child was being unruly or unreasonable.

The sisters exchanged glances, and then walked straight toward the back office, admitting defeat. Krystal mouthed a quick apology to Alexa and Valerie who watched on in mild amusement. They were probably glad Catherine was there, because now it meant Krystal would get the help she really needed. So much for trying to be a grownup witch and do everything herself.

For the second time that morning, Krystal closed the door to her office for another private meeting. This one wouldn't be so pleasant.

"So, tell me," Catherine began as she shed her coat and made herself comfortable in one of the chairs, "what's going on with my girls."

Sierra tried to step in and save the day. "Well, the salon is doing great. I had to take on another hairdresser to pick up more appointments."

Catherine nodded. "That's great, dear. But, I'm talking about bad news. I know something is going on with one of you, and if you won't come out and tell me, I'll have to use magic to figure it out. And you know how I hate to do that."

Krystal didn't have to know how to scry to know that her mother just told a fib. She loved to use her magic when it came to raising her daughters. She used it every chance she got. It was completely possible that Catherine already knew what was going on, but wanted the girls to tell her on their own. Just like when they were little and had done something naughty.

With a pinched face, Krystal took a deep breath and let it out. "I've started my dark magic."

The way it sounded, anyone might have guessed it was a code word for when a young girl started her first menstrual cycle. Dark magic was way more problematic than that though.

Catherine's face lit up. "This is wonderful, honey!" She stood up and embraced Krystal once more, a little tighter this time. She pulled back and cupped Krystal's face in her hands. "My little baby is growing up."

Krystal wondered if her mother was going to start crying.

"Tell me what it is," Catherine said, taking a step back. "Is it scrying? Oh, I hope it is. It's such a useful magic, after all."

Krystal shook her head.

"Flying? Green thumb? Dream magic? Time travel?"

She shook her head to each of them. "It's fire, mom."

Catherine's face opened up with delight. "Elemental magic! Oh, that's wonderful!"

"Nothing gets you down, does it?" Sierra asked as she moved to lean against the file cabinet.

Krystal cracked a tiny smile and tried to hold in her giggles. Her sister had a point. Her mother was probably way too excited about this. This was far from exciting for Krystal.

"My dear," Catherine said with a certain flair of crossness in her tone, "when you have daughters and they come into their dark magic, then maybe you'll understand. This is like when I took you two shopping for your first bras, or when you started liking boys. It's a part of growing up and coming of age. It's a celebration!"

Krystal crossed her arms over her stomach. "It sure doesn't feel like it. I burnt my dinner last night, because the oven overheated."

Catherine was still grinning. "Oh, you poor thing. What else has happened?"

She told her everything about feeling feverish when she was emotional, and about the fire growing in the fireplace. So far, that was all that had happened, and she was thankful it wasn't anything worse.

"That's not so bad. One of my good friends on the council has elemental dark magic, but with air and he can suck the oxygen out of a room as quick as that." For extra emphasis, Catherine snapped her fingers.

Krystal grimaced. "Well, I could probably burn the house down and I'm sure you don't want that."

Catherine took a hold of her shoulders. "Don't worry. Mama is here now, and we'll get this all taken care of. It doesn't take much to learn how to control fire."

"You know how?" Sierra asked in disbelief.

"Of course! I birthed two fire babies, after all. An Aries and a Leo. I thought one or both of you might have a knack for fire conjuring, so I did my research. Especially after you set fire to your bedroom curtains when you were five." She gave a pointed look to her eldest daughter, who only shrugged helplessly without a hint of remorse for the trouble she had gotten into that day.

"We've been trying to look through the catalogue," Krystal said, "but we didn't find anything. Why didn't you add that in when you were learning?"

Catherine shook her head. "Because this is not a charm or a spell, dear. This is just good ole' fashion witch training. We'll get started tonight. Call all your friends and tell them to meet at the house. They need to bring all the candles they're willing to use up."

"Mom, I have to work tonight."

She waved off the excuse. "That's fine, dear. We'll get started after the coffee shop closes. Besides, you shouldn't wait until the last minute to start your training. This isn't something you can just get a handle on as you go."

Now, she was glad that she hadn't made a date with Devin. It would take a bit of time to explain that her mother decided to make a surprise visit, because she could sense that her daughter just came into her dark magic and needed to start her training.

Then again, she would have much rather taken care of the mountain of work on her desk. The unthinkable had happened, and her coffee shop was beginning to slip through her fingers. Too much was going on too quickly and she couldn't juggle everything. Work and Devin might have been easy enough to get a grip on after a while, but throwing dark magic and her mother into the mix was like trying to herd cats. She would definitely need a cup of charmed coffee to get through this week.

Chapter 12

"What is that supposed to mean, anyway?" Devin asked as Aaron turned from Twin Hills Lane to Reichman Street and toward Our Lady of Peace Catholic Church.

By this point, Aaron must have been thinking that Devin had taken something to make him so wired. He was beginning to wonder the same thing. After just three or four sips of the special coffee Krystal had made for him, he was ready to run a marathon while carrying three full grown men on his back. It must have been the bitter espresso he tasted. Potent stuff.

"In my limited experience," Aaron replied as they eased through the school zone, "it's a soft warning that the girl is about to dump you. But, that's me. Krystal is nothing like any of the girls I've ever dated. I'm sure it means something completely different."

"She said it had nothing to do with me." Devin watched as three elementary school children made their way across the crosswalk.

"Then I would believe her until she starts to show otherwise," Aaron said.

He looked to his partner. "What signs should I be looking for? The last time a girl said she needed time to think, I never heard from her again and she never answered her phone."

Aaron winced. "Well, there's that. If she keeps turning you down for dates, if you see her with another guy, you know, that kind of stuff."

Devin ran his fingers through his hair for what must have been the hundredth time since they started off on their mission to interview everyone on the list. Those who lived on Jackson Creek Road didn't hear any screams or notice any suspicious activity last night either. So far, almost no one had given them any real clues except for this lead they were following.

Elizabeth's boss at the Torn Sails Bar and Grill said she did come to work that day. The chubby man with the overgrown mustache said the girl was in pretty high spirits, smiling a lot and laughing more than she usually did. He did mention her particular side gig she had, which the bar owner didn't approve of necessarily, but he didn't reprimand her at all.

Their murder victim was a known whore, taking extra money from guys she met at the bar who were looking for a good time. In Goldcrest Cove, there might not have been a big outlet for that kind of business. Elizabeth was popular with the men who needed a little extra release that alcohol couldn't give them.

Her boss said that last night, she was approached by a potential client, but she turned him down. It was pointless to interview the guy, because Elizabeth's employer confirmed that he stayed at the bar. He was getting shitfaced until two in the morning, long after they found the body. It would have been the perfect motive, but once more, they were at a dead end.

The body was found around nine o'clock at night, far too early for a barmaid to be leaving work, and the medical examiner said she was killed approximately around eight o'clock. Her employer said that she had to meet someone, but she wouldn't say who. However, she seemed pretty happy about it. From what he could tell, there were no other men who made a proposition to her that night. Nor anyone to his recollection that were going steady with Elizabeth. She didn't have any regular "customers".   They continued down the list of interviewees until about halfway when they talked to Elizabeth's landlady. She hadn't talked to Elizabeth since the beginning of the month, but she did recall something specific on the previous Saturday. She saw Elizabeth talking with Father Frank for a long time at the festival. As she said, they looked to be in a rather emotional conversation and Elizabeth seemed upset at first.

When they probed further to ask if Father Frank might have been the one upsetting her, the landlady quickly denied it. If anything, Father Frank was encouraging her. She didn't see how the rest of the conversation went. If Father Frank had anything to do with Elizabeth's good mood, if he had been the one she went to see last night, they needed to confirm it.

They pulled into the relatively empty parking lot of the church. Father Frank's little Toyota was there, along with the vehicles of other church officials that would be there on a Monday afternoon. "I think the after-school youth group will be meeting soon, so we need to make this quick," Aaron said as he shut his car door.

Devin could tell that his partner didn't enjoy the idea of putting his priest under a microscope. He didn't like it either, but if he could at least give them more to go on, Devin was more than willing to grill him.

The sanctuary was empty and deathly quiet, but Devin could hear the low rumble of voices coming from the offices and additional rooms down the hall that branched off from the left side of the altar at the front. As the two cops walked down the aisle, their keys and other police standard equipment slapping against their hips with each step, Devin felt that strange spiritual energy that seemed to suffuse the sanctuary. It only intensified as they came closer to the altar. There was something sacred about this space. He knew that yesterday when he sat in the pews and listened to Father Frank speak.

Though it wasn't unthinkable, Devin would have hated to put the priest on the suspect list. He seemed like a pretty upstanding guy. But, he kept his mind open.

After all, the sign of the cross was carved into Elizabeth Thatchman's chest. Was it coincidence or a clue?

Father Frank walked through the hall doors, carrying a cardboard box. At least they wouldn't have to go far to find him. Aaron hurried forward.

"Need some help with that, Father?" he asked, but took the heavy load from the priest anyway. He seemed surprised to see the two cops, but not afraid. That was in his favor.

"Thank you, Aaron," he said. "I was taking this out to my car. The canned food drive just started, and I was going to take these donations down to the distribution center."

"How many more are there?" Aaron asked, taking a peek into the box of soups, canned veggies, and other non-perishable foods.

"Just a few. They're in my office."

Aaron looked to Devin and jerked his head toward the hall. "Why don't we help him out a bit?"

Father Frank didn't see the frown Devin gave his partner, but he agreed anyway. They didn't exactly have the time to help out, but perhaps doing a good deed for the priest would help loosen his tongue for a little later.

When the priest said there were a few boxes, Devin imagined two or three left. There were ten. Though he could easily take two at a time, the task of lugging them across the sanctuary and to the parking lot had worked up a good sweat.

By the time all three of them sat down in one of the front pews in the sanctuary, Devin thought he had used up all that extra energy the espresso had given him earlier that day. Father Frank passed each of them water bottles he had grabbed from the church's kitchen. "Thank you, boys. I appreciate your help."

"Anytime," Aaron said as he took a long gulp.

"Is there anything I can help you with?" the priest asked as he slipped a finger under his stiff collar and tugged to let some cooler air in.

Devin leaned forward, resting his elbows on his knees and looked to Father Frank who sat on the other side of Aaron. "Yes, we actually came to ask you a few questions."

He frowned. "Is this about the murder from last night?"

Damn, word did travel fast. Even all the way to the church. "Yes. Do you have some time to talk?"

He nodded. "Absolutely. I'm always happy to help out the police whenever I can."

Aaron pinched his water bottle between his knees and pulled out the notebook from his back pocket. "We heard that you were seen with Elizabeth Thatchman at the Fall Festival this past Saturday. Is that true?"

The blood seemed to drain from Father Frank's face. "Is Elizabeth your suspect?" At least one thing hadn't gotten around already.

"No, Father," Devin replied. "She was the victim. We're trying to form a list of suspects."

Father Frank's mouth hung open and Devin went to studying his reaction. It appeared to be genuine. The way his pupils dilated, his loss of speech, the way he sat so perfectly still. It was the same look Elizabeth's boss had given when they questioned him earlier that day. The priest didn't see this coming.

"Please answer the question," Devin gently requested. "Were you with Elizabeth on Saturday?"

His mouth closed, and he slowly nodded. "I was."

"May we ask what you two were talking about, or was it confidential?"

Father Frank's throat worked as he took a moment to collect himself. "We were talking about the Lord. We had run into each other on Friday and she mentioned that she had been meaning to talk with me. We met at the festival, because we agreed it was a nice, public place... I'm sure you know about her reputation."

Both of the cops nodded.

"Anyway, Elizabeth said she had been struggling with some personal dilemmas, and she asked me for help. Of course, I gave her the best help that I could. She came to church on Sunday and I believe she and the Lord made a real connection."

That lined up with what her boss had said about her being in a more chipper mood.

"When you say she was struggling," Devin began, "did she mention anyone who might have been trying to hurt her? Was she struggling with anyone in particular?"

Father Frank gave him a weak smile. "Only with herself. She had a troubled life. She seemed very encouraged after our talk."

"So, you don't think anyone would have a reason to harm her?" Aaron clarified.

Father Frank shook his head and looked to the carpet in front of their pew. "No, I don't. God rest her soul," he said as he made the sign of the cross over his chest.

Devin let a few beats pass before he asked the one question he dreaded. "I have to ask where you were last night around eight o'clock."

The priest's eyes went wide when he looked to the cop. "You don't suspect me of killing Elizabeth, do you?"

He held up his hands in a placating manner. "We're trying to eliminate all the possibilities. We know that Elizabeth was going to meet someone and the medical examiner said she was killed around eight o'clock. Since she had made meetings with you before, we are just trying to ascertain if she tried to meet with you last night."

After the shock wore off, Father Frank shook his head. "No, I was here at the church. We host Bingo night for the senior citizens. I was here until nine."

Aaron spoke up. "And you have witnesses that can confirm this?"

Father Frank nodded. "At least fifteen came to play last night, not to mention some of the other church deacons."

Devin was satisfied. Father Frank didn't kill Elizabeth. He had an alibi, and no motive whatsoever. He stood from the pew. "Thank you for your time."

Aaron wasn't so ready to leave. "Father, I hate to ask this, but do you think any of your congregation are capable of doing this? There was a... a cross cut into her chest and down her torso. Do you think that has any religious significance?"

Disclosing so many details to a civilian wasn't smart, but Devin listened for Father Frank's answer. The priest blanched again, but shook his head. "It could, but I don't think anyone in my church would do such a thing. As for the cross, I don't know. I would hate to think that anyone who belongs to the body of Christ would think this sort of behavior was righteous."

The cops looked to one another. Devin was satisfied with that answer, but Aaron probably held firm to his suspicions. He hadn't seen the kind of psychotic, senseless murder like what happened in Boston. Devin did. He thought this had as much to do with religion as it did with anything else. It might have just been a coincidence, rather than a symbol.

"Thanks for talking with us, Father," Aaron said as he stood to join his partner. "I trust our conversation won't be spread around."

Father Frank made a gesture toward the towering crucifix behind the altar. "Only the Lord will know we had this talk. I hope you find the murderer, boys. I really do. This isn't something that belongs in a town like Goldcrest Cove."

Devin couldn't agree more, but once again they were without a lead. Now, at least, they knew they could rule out the community's religious leader.

Krystal was glad for one thing. The house was big enough to accommodate a lot of witches. Krystal and Sierra were in the living room with their mother, moving furniture while Valerie and Amber were busy in the kitchen fixing drinks and snacks for later. The only two they were waiting on were Alexa and Taylor. The latter had called earlier to say she was having trouble finding her candles, but then she would be right over. Valerie said that Alexa was stuck at the coffee shop with a late customer. Poor Artemis, disgusted by the noise and bustling around, retreated upstairs to one of the bedrooms to sleep through the commotion.

"We have to make the circle big enough for everyone to sit around you," Catherine said as she directed her two daughters to push the sofa against the far wall. The coffee table with its heavy slab of marble was a little tougher to pick up and move across the room.

"Move the carpet too," their mother advised. "That was a souvenir from your great-grandmother when she came back from Persia."

"We know," Sierra and Krystal said in unison as they rolled up the heavy woven rug. It took both of them to lift it over their shoulders and set it down in the foyer.

From the kitchen, Valerie called out, "Don't you have anything stronger than wine?"

Krystal opened her mouth to deny it, but Sierra beat her to it. "Check in the cabinet above the refrigerator."

She shot her older sister a glare. "I thought we agreed not to keep any hard liquor in the house?"

Sierra propped her hand on her hip. "You try dealing with girls who don't know what they want for their hair all day and see if you can come home without taking a shot or two."

Catherine clapped her hands to get their attention. "Girls, where are the candles?"

Krystal motioned toward the two boxes sitting on the hall butler bench. "Those are from Valerie and Amber."

The purple-haired witch came from the kitchen, a half-eaten cracker between her fingers and a few more tucked into her palm. "I brought my own ritual candles and snitched a few from the guest rooms that I use for decoration."

Catherine rolled up her black sleeves and gave her the thumbs up. "Excellent. Where are ours?" she asked her daughters.

Sierra rolled her eyes and trudged up the steps to the second floor. "I just got home, mom. I haven't had time to get them."

"Hurry up," her mother insisted as she took one of the boxes. "We don't want to be here all night."

"Do we really need that many?" Valerie asked as she came back with a tumbler glass in one hand and the frosted bottle of vodka in the other. "We don't want to set the house on fire."

Krystal followed her mother into the living room with the other box of candles. They were of many colors and sizes, but according to Catherine, this training didn't depend on the type or shade of red in the candles like some required.

"We won't set the house on fire, dear," Catherine, the senior witch replied. "We just need lots of tiny flames to manipulate."

"Why does this still sound like a really bad idea?" Amber mumbled to Valerie.

"Because I think it is," she agreed.

Sierra came bounding down the stairs with a meager box of candles to contribute. Compared to the donations of the others, it was unimpressive. As soon as Catherine took a look, she made a face.

"Girls, I taught you better than to let your supply go this low."

"We don't do that many rituals, mom," Krystal said as she and Sierra began to evenly space the candles in a circle in the middle of the living room.

"Still, a witch should never find herself without a good candle when she needs one."

"That's what my mama always said," Amber remarked with her mouth full of cracker.

Krystal stuck her tongue out at her, as if to say that the innkeeper wasn't helping. She stuck her tongue out in return.

Everything about this had her on edge. All day at the coffee shop, she couldn't help but go over how all of this could go terribly wrong. She tried to convince her mother to just tell her how to do the training and she would take care of the rest. She didn't want to burn anyone by accident or do just as Valerie suggested and burn the house down. If she did any damage, she would have rather done it by herself.

Then again, there hadn't been a big meeting of the witches like this in a while. They hung out with Amber and Taylor on occasion, but to have all the girls together really instilled a new energy in the house. It was like having all this magic in one place was going to bring about some wonderful things. At least, she hoped so.

Krystal knew she needed to get this fire under control or her relationship with Devin would be nonexistent. She still hadn't told her mother about Devin and as long as Catherine didn't ask what provoked the fire in the first place, Krystal would not tell her. There was no need to give information when it wasn't asked for, after all.

The front door opened, and Krystal heard Alexa and Taylor come shuffling down the foyer.

"We've got the goods!" Alexa shouted as she came to stand beside the two other girls. "Oh, I see you already have the goods."

Taylor came in with her own heavy box and her messy braid looking especially tousled. "Oh, you'll need more than that, though."

"We're all going to catch on fire," Valerie muttered. She had already poured herself a tiny bit of vodka and was downing it. She handed the glass to Amber, who proceeded to take a swig herself.

"You girls put that down and come help," Catherine reproached.

Krystal had already taken her place in the center of the ring of candles as Alexa and Taylor came in to assist. "Did you kick the customer out or did they leave on their own?"

Alexa seemed mildly entertained by what she was about to tell her friend. "They left on their own, but guess who it was." She didn't wait for anyone to ask. "Father Frank and Harry Middleton." "Excuse me?" Sierra questions, sitting back on her heels with a look of utter bewilderment.

"You heard me right," Alexa said as she began to set the candles in a third row around Krystal. "Father Frank and Harry Middleton had a coffee date... Well, not a date, but they had coffee."

Amber came back from the kitchen after she put away the rest of her crackers. "Did you see Harry pull out his flask to spike the coffee?"

Alexa shook her head. "Nope. He was sober for a change. He even looked like his clothes were clean for once."

"What did they talk about?" Taylor softly asked from where she squatted next to Catherine, passing candles and placing her own. They were starting on a fourth row already.

"I couldn't tell, but whatever they were talking about, it made Harry cry after just a few minutes."

Krystal's forehead wrinkled with confusion. "Cry? I didn't think he could cry. Just stumble through the streets asking for money."

Catherine was the first to scold her. "Watch your mouth, young lady. Harry's a good man... Or, at least he was. He and your father got along very well. They had long talks outside the hardware store."

"So, they were just talking?" Valerie asked as she came in to help, but there were already too many hands snatching up candles from the boxes and positioning them. She sat cross-legged at a distance and seemed to be content to stay out of everyone's way.

Alexa nodded. "Yep, just talking, and crying, and maybe a bit of praying. They had their heads down for a while anyway and Father Frank was muttering something."

Krystal went silent as they continued to speculate what could have been taking place. Was this another one of Father Frank's mercy missions, like with Elizabeth Thatchman? She never found out how their talk went at the festival the other day, and unless she asked Father Frank, she'd probably never know.

Her heart truly ached for Elizabeth. She hadn't told anyone that she was the murder victim from the night before. It wasn't her place to tell them. It would be in the newspapers the following day and with it, she hoped there would be the good news that Devin had already caught the culprit.

She hadn't heard a word from Devin all day. That could mean two things. He was either hot on the trail of the killer and far too busy to bother with her. Or he was giving her the time and space she had requested of him. That was a good thing, because if he stopped by the house, thinking he could catch her alone, he would be vastly mistaken. The last thing she needed was him trying to walk in on a witch gathering like this one.

When they had five complete rings of candles, they finally stopped. Krystal rearranged her long skirt, so it wouldn't get close to the candles, and tucked her legs beneath her.

"All right, ladies," her mother began. "I want you to all sit around the circle."

The five other witches did so, along with Catherine. Krystal took deep breaths to calm her nerves, though she had a feeling that this ritual would require her to get a little excited. The heat didn't engulf her when she was calm, after all.

Catherine flicked her hand toward the switch on the wall and the lights went out in the living room. By the light in the foyer, she saw her mother grab for a box of matches and she struck one.

"Are you ready?" she asked.

Krystal nodded, even though it was a lie. She feared this power more than she would let anyone else believe. She might not have truly claimed herself as a daughter of Gaia, tethered to the gods and goddesses of the wiccan religion, but she did value all life and nature. Fire, though it was associated with the sun, which shined light upon the world to give it life, was destructive. She never wanted to be linked with something that could kill. She wanted control, stability. Fire was anything but that.

Perhaps she was already setting herself up for failure, thinking that fire was evil or something that would need to be extinguished instead of harnessed. Without fire, after all, the human race wouldn't have all of the technological marvels that they did today. But, in the end, what use would a witch have for fire?

She watched the dancing flame at the end of the match as her mother lowered it to the first wick of the candle immediately in front of Krystal. The white, unblemished wick adopted the fire from the match and darkened as the flame consumed it, burning bright.

Her mother lit the two other candles on either side of the first. Krystal's heart pounded in her throat as she looked around to the other, unlit candles of various sizes and wax colors. Somehow, she couldn't help but think that they should have kept a bucket of water nearby in case this got out of hand.

"Krystal," her mother began in a soft voice, "I want you to focus on these three flames. They are the Goddess Trinity. Feel their energy. Feel their spirit. Feel the life within the fire and let it become your own."

Just like her mother said, she focused on those three, slowly undulating flames in front of her. She stared at them until her eyes burned from the intensity of their light and heat. She glanced up to her mother, who held the smoking match between her fingers.

"Nothing's happening. Am I supposed to do something?" Krystal asked.

Her mother sighed. "Whenever you felt that heat, you said that it was during moments of high emotion, right? Bring back one of those instances. Replay it in your mind."

"If I do that, the flames might get bigger."

Catherine smiled. "That's exactly what we want. You can't be challenged unless you increase the risk."

Krystal could feel her fingers shake in her lap. She didn't want to do this. If it were possible, she felt more scared than she had been when Devin took her out on the boat. At least then, she could lean on him for strength. Here, he was the reason her powers raged out of control. He couldn't help her. Or could he?

She closed her eyes and brought back the memory of every kiss, every touch and smile he ever blessed her with. The thought of last night resurfaced and the warmth plumed within her chest, spreading through her limbs and core.

All at once, she could feel that energy her mother spoke of. She could feel the swaying and jerky movement of the candle flames in front of her as if it were a physical entity moving in that space. It drew upon her life source just as she fed upon it in turn. She and the fire became one, sharing the energy between them. The heat exponentially grew, just like it did when Devin's kisses graced the sensitive skin along her neck and chest.

Her body responded to her thoughts and she could feel her nipples press against her bra, peaking just as they had when Devin was there with her, touching her, caressing her body with such need. Her lips parted as her imagination exploded with all the things that Devin could do to her until it felt as if her skin were set ablaze.

She opened her eyes and saw the three flames were level with her, so skinny and erect. Hot wax dropped down the sides of the candles.

"Oh, shit," she whispered, her breath teasing the flames. Her heart pounded out of her chest, searing her bones with the heat that had spread through every organ in her body. Soon, her blood would be set on fire and she didn't know how to come down from that high.

"No, no," her mother insisted as she watched the three straight flames with a smile. "This is good. Extend your hand and make the flames jump."

"What?"

"Spread the fire. Bend it to your will and light the other candles."

Krystal lifted her trembling hand and held it in front of the flames as if to shield herself from its power.

"No, not like that. Hand open. Like this." Her mother showed her palms facing upward and Krystal obeyed, mimicking the way her two hands were lifted in a receiving way.

She inhaled and let it out slowly, letting some of her magic leak through to aid her. The three flames shivered, just as her hands did. With a flick of her finger, part of the right flame sputtered. She tried again, and it did the same, but it wasn't moving as she intended.

Krystal felt the toxic swirl of impatience meld in her chest, adding to the heat. She flicked her fingers one more time. It was as if the flame were cut in half and the second half fell straight into the unlit candle beside it. It caught fire and now, there were four spindly towers of fire in front of her.

She actually did it. Upon the encouragement of the other witches, she did it again and again. Soon, almost half of the candles were lit, and the living room was bathed in the flickering amber light from the fire she was able to control.

All the while, she kept Devin alive in her mind, shirtless and glistening with sweat as they were surrounded by the fire that was hers to tame. She imagined him on top of her, his arms encasing her and holding her naked body beneath his. In her fantasy, he kissed her, suckled her breasts, teased the folds between her legs and finally thrust into her.

Krystal felt the heat pierce through her core and she gasped as the energy around her surged. When she opened her eyes, she could see the flames had merged together, creating something like a wall that separated her from her friends and family.

Sweat beaded and trickled down her temples and along the slender curve of her neck, but it only added to the thrill of having such power. Every candle was lit across all five rows, every drop of blood coursing through her veins like liquid fire. Her imagination took her places she had never dreamed of going, soaring higher until the tips of the flames reached over her head.

It felt so good she never wanted it to end.

But it had to. Reality came crashing through as she realized what was happening. They disabled the smoke alarms as soon as they got home, but the danger was still near. If she allowed herself that release, that one last burst of pleasure inspired by her imagination alone, someone was going to get hurt. She couldn't even see the faces of her mother or sister through the wall of fire.

She took a shaky breath and let Devin fade from her mind. Her heartrate slowed as she pushed back the images of the fantasy that she hoped one day would become real. Krystal turned her hands until her palms were facing down and the flames lowered once more.

She didn't stop fighting the passion until she could see the eyes of her mother, watching her with such calm, as if she had every confidence that her daughter would conquer this lesson. Her friends, not so much. A few of them had scooted backward and through the pandemonium, Amber had brought a popcorn bowl brimming with water. As if that would do anything.

The wall of fire became individual candle flames once more and though the energy in her spirit didn't ebb away as easily, the fire was still under her command. Her bangs stuck to her damp forehead and she thought steam was rolling off her exposed arms as her own sweat evaporated. Her clothes clung to her. The place between her legs was especially wet, but not with sweat.

She smiled as she and her mother looked to one another.

"You did it," she said, her words a little choked with pride.

Krystal felt relief wash over her. Quite literally, she had been put through the fire and came out unscathed. It would be a long time before she could really control her dark magic, but this was the first step to dominating all she was expected to as a witch. Once her dark magic was under control, nothing was out of reach.

Chapter 13

It was a long shot, but Krystal crossed her fingers that Devin would not come into the coffee shop that day. It had nothing to do with her dark magic or the idea that she didn't want to see him. Nothing could be farther from the truth. After last night, when she learned the key to controlling her powers was to simply control her own passion, she knew she could handle being in Devin's company. She would have to keep a tighter rein on her emotions. If things got out of hand, all she needed to do was stop and take a breath. It was simple enough and she wanted to get the practice in with the stimulus for her dark magic. So she was eager to see Devin again. But, she wasn't going to rush things.

They had worked through most of the night and evening, working on raising and lowering the flames of the candles until everyone else was ready to step outside in the cold night air for a breather. Even her mother was a bit worn out after they had been at it for hours. Krystal, on the other hand, continued to feed off the fire and she wasn't the least bit tired. If anything, she was more keyed up than ever. The kind of rousing energy the fire gave was better than any caffeinated drink she would ever drink.

No, that's not the reason why she didn't want him to make that little brass bell over the door jingle to life. It had everything to do with the fact that she was wearing a skin-tight green jumper wrapped in fake vines and a red wig.

Every year, the three girls played along with the added traditions of Samhain, also known as Halloween. They put out a big bowl of candy for the customers and dressed up in the costume of their choice.

Alexa paraded as a fairy in her glittery top with long bell-sleeves and tulle skirt with leotards, Valerie simply racketed up her usual attire by wearing every piece of studded jewelry in her possession and smearing on black lipstick, while Krystal decided to dress as Poison Ivy from the comic books.

The comic book villain had actually inspired her love for plant life more than her family's obsession with nature because of their magic. So, every year Krystal pulled out the green wig. Of course, she kept the outfit relatively modest for the sake of her professional appearance at Perfect Books and Brews. She didn't want Devin to see her in case he got a little too excited over the way the thin material hugged her frame. It would have been the first time he had ever seen her in anything but a skirt or dress.

Thankfully, the two cops hadn't come in yet for their coffee. In fact, hardly anyone came in. Their usual customers, who admitted they could never go a day without coffee, stopped by rather quickly to grab their usual and go. They didn't even stay for a while and chat like they usually did.

When Krystal finally got up the nerve to ask if something was going on, Mr. Thompson told her that the newspapers finally released the story about Elizabeth Thatchman's murder.

"Officer Daniels and Officer Wright have been looking for the murderer, but the article said they don't have any conclusive leads yet," Mrs. Thompson added.

She had been afraid of that. Perhaps that was why Devin and Aaron hadn't come in yet.

Behind her, Alexa and Valerie abandoned their machines and asked for more details. This was the first time they had heard about who the murder victim was, but this was her first time hearing about the nature of the murder. Devin said nothing about Elizabeth being carved open or where exactly her body had been dumped.

There was no way she would ever see Jackson Creek Road the same way again, and surely the rest of the town wouldn't either. Once the kids learned about the murder, their parents would probably forbid them to go to Jackson Creek. They would go anyway, of course, and within a few years there would be ghost stories told about the spot where they found Elizabeth Thatchman's body. Friends would dare one another to spend the night in the woods along Jackson Creek Road as a rite of passage and Krystal ruefully shook her head at the concept.

As long as the police department was without a lead to go on, it was unlikely that many people would be out on the town as much as they once were. There was a murderer loose, after all. And even though the murder happened in the evening, some people wouldn't see it that way and they'd shell up in their homes until the perp was caught. Mr. and Mrs. Thompson even admitted that they wouldn't be leaving their home after the sun went down.

That meant two things for Krystal. Business was not going to be as steady for a while and Devin would be busy. A lot.

Alexa and Valerie talked about the incident, while Krystal simply listened. They weren't getting as hysterical as some would, but they were just as stunned as she was.

When Aaron finally came in after the Thompsons left, she expected to see Devin waltzing in with him, looking deadbeat tired like he had the morning before. Devin wasn't with him, and it was Aaron who looked exhausted this time.

"Where's Devin?" Krystal asked hastily as he came up to the front counter.

"Good morning to you too," he mumbled, then looked up. He flinched at the sight of her bright red hair and nearly exploded in a laugh.

Krystal propped a hand on her hip. "You see this every year, Aaron. Doesn't it get old?"

His blue eyes danced. "Nope. Not a bit. It's still freaking hilarious to see you in a wig." Then he looked to Valerie. "The demon looks like she's flying her usual colors too."

As expected, the gothic barista flipped him the bird and he laughed.

"So, really," Krystal said again, "where's Devin?"

All humor left the cop's expression and he let out a long sigh. Before he replied, he looked around the coffee shop to make sure no one was paying attention. "There was another murder last night. Same way as Elizabeth, same drop off location, but only about half a mile east." Instantly the other girls were at the counter, hanging on every word.

"Who was it?" Alexa whispered, her glittery artificial eyelashes sparkling in the lights. Her overdone makeup gave Aaron pause at first, but he recovered quickly.

"He was actually here last night," he said in a low whisper. "Harry Middleton. Who was on duty while he was here? We have other eye witnesses who were on Johnson Avenue last night that said he was coming out of here with Father Frank."

Krystal's chest ached for Alexa. She might have been one of the last people to talk to Harry. Save for Father Frank. And to think that the poor drunk was killed in the same way with his chest cut open and throat slashed. She shivered, knowing exactly what this meant. Whoever the murderer was, he wasn't done after Elizabeth. What was the likelihood that he still wasn't done after Harry? If a murderer in Goldcrest Cove wasn't bad enough, they had a serial killer now.

"Yeah," Alexa replied, her voice breathy and quivering. "He was here last night."

"Can you tell me anything about how he and Father Frank were getting along?" There was a certain streak of emotion in Aaron's question that made her wonder if he had dreaded to ask it at all. Then, it occurred to Krystal that Father Frank had ties with both victims. She only hoped that the kind priest wasn't at the top of their suspect list. There was no way he could have committed these murders.

Alexa didn't speak. Her gaze turned distant, unfocused as if she were in a mental fog. At the risk of getting glitter all over her Poison Ivy outfit, Krystal wrapped her arm around Alexa's waist, hoping to serve as that grounding presence like her friend had been so many times for her.

"Can you come back a little later, Aaron? I think she needs some time."

Alexa blinked and lifted up her hands. "No, I'm fine. Really." She took a breath before continuing. "They were just talking." Then, she went into the little details of Harry crying and Father Frank trying to comfort him.

When her friend was done, Valerie quickly asked, "Do you think Father Frank did it?"

Aaron made that same, wry face Devin had made just before he told her that there had been a murder in Goldcrest Cove. That same face that said he didn't want to talk about it, but he was about to anyway. Krystal didn't want to hear it, though.

"Right now, Father Frank is the only one that links to both victims. He was seen with Elizabeth at the festival, the day before she was murdered, and he was the last one to talk to Harry last night before we found him. He had an alibi for the first murder, but we haven't seen him about Harry yet. I know Devin's going to want to talk to him again, just to find out what they talked about, if any of it's important to the investigation."

Krystal nodded hopefully. "But, he had an alibi for the first murder and if they were done in the same way, it can't be Father Frank, right?"

Aaron shrugged. "We have to look at every possibility. I have a theory, though." He leaned forward across the counter and the girls leaned in too. "I think the cross that was cut into their chests is a major clue. If this was just a random killing, they would have just slit the throats and bolted. The cut was done post-mortem, meaning it was done after they were killed. Why would someone go through the trouble of making those cuts unless it was just for show? With how the murderer just left them by the road instead of hiding them in the woods, maybe he wanted them to be found. He might be trying to make a point. And then," he said, stabbing the counter top with his fingertip, "you have to look at who the victims were. Elizabeth was... let's be honest, she was a whore. And Harry was the town drunk. Whoever this guy is, they're targeting textbook sinner profiles." It made total sense.

"If that's the case," Krystal said, "then the murderer might be some self-right-eous psycho, right?

Maybe he's trying to send a message to the town."

Valerie grimaced. "Like the whole 'turn or burn' thing."

Aaron nodded. "Again, that's my theory, but the problem is that we have to find out who that is. Father Frank doesn't fit the bill in my opinion. I saw the look on his face when we told him about Elizabeth. He was totally devastated. I can't believe he would willingly hurt another person that way.

But, it might be someone from his congregation. That's a lot of people to interrogate."

Krystal finally turned away to start making his usually espresso with coconut. With the chalkboard empty, she wished there was a charm she could put in his drink to help them find the killer. It had only been a couple of days, but they needed to find out who was doing this and quickly before any more innocent people were hurt. Maybe a little bit of luck?

She charmed the coffee with a subtle wave of her hand and delivered it, along with Devin's normal black coffee, to Aaron while he was still working out his theory with the girls.

"So, is Devin out in the squad car or something?" she asked the cop when he was taking his first sip.

Aaron shook his head. "No, he's back at the station. He told me to tell you that he'd be in touch soon. He's just really swamped with the paperwork for all of this."

"You'd think Chief Nickels could take care of that shit," Valerie remarked.

The look on Aaron's face told them that he perfectly agreed, but he wasn't about to vocally admit it. "You girls watch out, okay? I recommend you close the shop when it gets dark and go straight home. I don't think any of you would fit who this guy may be targeting, but it never hurts to be on the safe side."

He paid for his espresso and left, leaving the girls to talk about everything they had just learned that morning. They stood off in the far back corner of the brewing station, far enough away from any listening ears or prying eyes.

"We have to do something," Alexa said first.

Valerie made a sound of disbelief. "Are you kidding? What if Aaron's theory is actually right? We're witches. We could all be fucked if this guy finds us. I agree with the cop. We should close down early."

Krystal crossed her arms, rustling some of the fake ivy leaves on her costume. "I agree too. We'll close at four and post a sign on the door. However, I don't agree that we need to get involved."

"Why not?" Alexa pleaded to her friends. "If the cops can't find this guy, maybe we can? Is your mom still in town?"

She shook her head. "She went back to Albany this morning. She didn't tell my dad about what was going on and she didn't want to be away from the council for too long."

"Okay, so we go to Amber and get her to scry and find out who this guy is. We can send an anonymous tip to the police and they can go hunt him down."

Krystal gave an incredulous look. "Amber would never agree to that. She's just as hard core about not using magic on non-magic folk as my parents are."

The dejection coming off of Alexa was almost palatable. "What about the rule saying that if another magic folk is in danger, we can use our powers to help them?"

"None of us have been directly threatened or affected by these murders," Valerie pointed out.

"Elizabeth and Harry weren't relatives or magic folk. We still can't get involved."

"And I highly doubt that a huge anonymous tip like that would just slide under the radar," Krystal added. "I don't know if the station has voice recognition wired into their phones or have some way of locating where the call is coming from. If they do pin it back to any of us, we could risk exposure. They'll ask how we knew about the murderer and I can't think of one good, logical, non-magic excuse how we would know. They might think we were associated with him."

Alexa threw back her head and let out a sigh, the overhead lights making her outfit shimmer. "I can't believe neither of you is willing to do something." She looked back to Krystal, indignation flavoring every word. "We started this coffee shop, because we wanted to help the community. We have the means to help and you refuse?"

Krystal hated it when they were right. Finding the murderer would have been the best thing they could ever do for Goldcrest Cove, but it still didn't feel right. Maybe it was some new cautionary trait that came with her dark magic. "This is way out of our league, Alexa. This isn't just adding a bit of magic to a drink and sending them on their way. This is full blown psycho killer danger. We aren't experienced enough to handle this. Not even me, Sierra, Amber, or Taylor."

"I believe we are," Alexa argued with a proud tilt of her chin.

"I believe we are too," Valerie joined. "But, I still think it's way too dangerous and too risky to screw around with whoever this guy is. For all we know, he's done with his crimes and moved on. I can't think of anyone else in this town that commits some crazy cardinal sin. Besides himself, that is. Maybe he'll be the next body they find on Jackson Creek Road."

Though Alexa seemed far from content to let the argument slide, she had little else to say on the matter. Two overruled the one and Alexa had to know that none of the other witches in town would be willing to lend her a hand like this.

All they could do was wait and hope that Devin would find the killer soon and life in Goldcrest Cove would return to normal.

As Devin walked up to the front porch, he wondered if he should have called or texted first. In reality, he hadn't expected to end up at Krystal's home. He just took off from the police station when he was done with the last of the paperwork for

Harry Middleton's murder, with the intent to go home. Somehow, he had pulled alongside the curb on Pinkerton Street instead, right in front of the historical landmark sign by Krystal's home. He must have been too tired to realize that he was taking that many wrong turns, but it was too late now.

He was here and maybe it was something in his soul or subconscious that had led him to her. The lights were on, but Sierra's car wasn't in the driveway. Krystal must have been home, but he hated the idea that Sierra was out at this hour. She had to know about the murders by now. Everyone in town did.

He rang the doorbell and heard some fumbling from inside. With his chest aching and heart pounding, Devin wondered if this was wrong. She said she needed time to think, but here he was disturbing that peace. He had to see her though.

The last couple of days had been pure hell. While the other cops at the station were content to go down to Torn Sails Bar and get a beer or two to wind down, Devin knew that wasn't good enough for him. Krystal was better than any alcohol or other distraction he could think of. If he could just see her, hold her for a little while, then maybe he could relax enough to get some rest.

Just before she opened the door, he came up with the only excuse he could think of. But when he laid his eyes on her, all mental function simply stopped. Krystal was in her pajamas already and it wasn't even nine o'clock. However, he couldn't hate the view. He had never seen her in anything but skirts and to see her shapely legs clad in soft flannel did predictable things to his crotch. Her white camisole, too, made his heartbeat shoot through the roof.

For a moment, she seemed just as speechless as he was.

"I was in the neighborhood and I saw the lights on," he said, jerking his thumb toward the empty street. "I wanted to make sure you were all right."

It just occurred to him that the citizens were taking the news of the murder quite seriously. The traffic on the main road was practically non-existent and despite the fact that it was Halloween, there were absolutely no trick-or-treaters to be found. Their parents must have thought it unwise to let their children out at night while a killer was on the loose.

They were right.

Krystal blinked, her lips parted in that sexy, confused way. "Oh... Well, as you can see, I'm fine."

Devin swallowed hard just before asking, "Can I come in?"

It was a dumbass move. If she wanted him inside, she would have offered when she opened the door. Somehow, she seemed just as hesitant as he was.

The past two days found him perplexed, stressed, and in desperate need of some relief. And Devin knew that fishing wasn't going to help him make sense of the mess in his head. Not now. He needed Krystal, the only thing that felt right and good to him anymore. This whole murder business and her strange declaration that she needed space had created a warzone in his mind. He needed some stable ground to stand on, so he could sort it all out. And as inconvenient as it was, she was that stable ground for him.

Krystal stepped aside to let him through and the delicious scents of garlic, butter, and browning beef met him.

"You're cooking this late?" he questioned as she shut the door. Devin wondered if he should take his jacket off, but thought better of it. It might have spooked her into thinking he was going to stay long. He wanted to, but not unless she offered.

"Yeah," she replied, moving toward the kitchen, her bare feet slapping against the hardwood floor. "I tried to go to bed early, but I couldn't sleep. I thought I'd try something new to replicate Mrs. Pazzini's meat sauce recipe."

Devin followed her into the kitchen and saw the chaotic mess of dishes, dirty chopping boards, glass containers full of the food she had prepared, boiling pots on the stove and both the ovens were glowing.

"So, you decided to bake food for the whole town while you were at it?" he teased.

"Not for the whole town," she said as she took up a wooden spoon and began stirring the noodles. "I've also been cleaning."

He could tell that too. The floors seemed shinier and the wood banisters on the stairs gleamed, even in the dim light of the foyer.

"I hope you weren't having trouble sleeping because of all the... you know."

Krystal let out a sigh and set the spoon down on the countertop before she took up a spice container of something that looked like parsley, but he was a dunce at cooking, so he could have been wrong. All the green stuff looked the same to him. "Not just that, but other things too."

"Like about us?"

Before he could stop himself, the words came spilling out. Krystal didn't even flinch or pause in her cooking, but nodded. A bit of her raven hair fell over her shoulder and she pushed it back behind her ear.

He stepped into the kitchen, hoping that his work boots wouldn't dirty her clean tiles. "Did you figure anything out?"

Krystal's shoulders rose and fell as she took a deep breath. "Some things, yeah."

Hope may have risen up in him a little too soon, but Devin had to try. He stood by the kitchen island, watching her push the ground beef around in her skillet as the meat sizzled.

"So, does that mean you're done thinking?"

Finally, she looked up, blindly shoving the meat in front of her as steam rose up into the air between them to partially shroud her face in a mist. "I don't know."

Devin gripped the edge of the island. "What I don't understand is, what is there to think about? If it's nothing that I've done, does it have something to do with your family?"

Krystal set her spatula down on the dirty napkin next to the range. "No, it's not my family. Not exactly anyway."

The torn, slightly scared look in her eye propelled his mind into cop mode. If he wasn't still in his uniform, it might have been easier to ignore the troubled way she stared at him. This was the thing she had been hiding since the beginning, the thing she couldn't speak of or didn't want to talk about. Maybe tonight, everything would come out in the open. Even for him. He would bare his soul and tell her everything that happened in Boston, if she would just let him in.

"Then what is it? You can tell me, Krystal. I know we haven't known each other for long, but you can tell me anything. If it's about what your family business is — "

"No, it's not exactly that," she said quickly, a bit more panic rising in her voice.

The water on in the pot that was cooking the noodles began to boil at a faster rate. Luckily, Krystal noticed and quickly turned off that eye. While she was at it, she turned them all off.

"Not exactly? So, it's partially that?" he questioned, picking apart her words, so he could get to the bottom of this. He felt like the cop he had been back in Boston, before the accident, before he was afraid to even touch the nasty, gritty cases.

Krystal winced. "Sort of... It's all kind of connected, really." Her eyes darted toward the oven and she dashed over to quickly flip them both off. It still took a while for the heating elements to cool down.

Devin didn't want to be the reason she stopped cooking, but maybe then she wouldn't seem so distracted. "So, the reason you don't want to go out with me again is connected with your family business? If they're tied in with some illegal – "

"No!" she snapped. "It's nothing illegal, I can promise you that. It's just... complicated. They expect certain things of me." Devin waited while she searched for the right words. "They have this idea of what I should do with my life, who I should date and marry, who I should associate with, that kind of stuff. It's all part of tradition and to deviate from that is a pretty big deal. I haven't told them about you because of that."

Devin wanted to understand, but this seemed like something straight out of medieval times. Who she should or should not marry seemed like such an archaic mindset. "This is the twenty-first century. How can they put you in a box like that?"

Krystal crossed her arms and he realized she was sweating a bit. He thought the kitchen was getting a little warm, but all of the appliances had been turned off. "It's not a box as much as it's a... a safe zone. They want me to date the right guy, so I'll be safe and secure."

That was a laugh. How much more safe and secure could she be with a cop than anyone else?

None of this made sense.

"Honestly, I don't even know what it is we're doing," Krystal continued. "Are we dating? Are we boyfriend and girlfriend? I know it sounds totally juvenile, but it would really help me to label this, so I can understand where we're at. I don't know if I can keep going with you unless I know."

That had been another thing he wrestled with since their first date. He wanted to believe they were dating, that they were a couple now, but apparently it wasn't that clear for her. Relationships weren't so black and white anymore.

"I'd like to think you are my girlfriend and I'm your boyfriend. Does that help? Or is all of that going to change now?"

Krystal chewed on her bottom lip and shook her head. "No. I don't want any of that to change. I want to be your girlfriend, I just..."

"You don't want to upset your family."

He never thought it would happen, but the bitter pangs of resentment rose up in him. He wanted to dislike her family and all the pressures they imposed on her. He hated that joyful family photo sitting on the mantle now. He wanted to take her away from Goldcrest Cove, so she could just disappear and never have to worry about their judgement again. All of these things, he wanted to do. But he knew that he couldn't.

Krystal's family meant the world to her. She wasn't like him. Devin felt absolutely no qualms with leaving his father and sister behind in Boston. He had no problem with deleting their phone numbers from his contact list and erasing them from his life altogether. He refused any call coming in from the Boston area code without so much as feeling that ache of regret in his chest.

She could never do any of that. She'd miss her family, her sister and this house. As much as he wanted to be against everything her family was doing to her, she agreed with them. If they stood on opposite sides of this battlefield, he lost the war already.

When Krystal didn't agree or disagree, Devin had to assume the answer. He gave her a nod and backed away from the island. "I may not understand where you're coming from. You can keep your secrets about whatever it is your family does, and be so fucking unclear about what it is you want from me... from us. But I won't stand in the way of your happiness."

He stopped in the foyer, just beyond the entrance into the kitchen. Devin could taste his final words on his tongue like a bitter poison dissolving the last of his composure. "Say the word and I'll leave. We can still see each other at the coffee shop and you can still drive me absolutely crazy with those eyes of yours. But, just one word from you, and I'll never bother you again. I wouldn't want to be the reason you and your family don't get along. God knows I've been through that and I wouldn't wish that kind of drama on anyone."

Devin zipped up his jacket. "Just say the word and I'll either stay... or I'll go."

Krystal shook her head. "Don't force me to make this decision right now." Her voice swelled with the heartache she must have been feeling. Whether it was heartache over the idea of him leaving, or the thought of her opposing everything her family stood for, he didn't know. But he wasn't going to hold his breath.

She had loved her family all her life. He was just the new cop in town that wanted something that might have been out of his league. He was already set up for failure and he didn't even know it.

The doorbell rang, and Krystal jumped. Devin stayed fixed where he was as she moved to answer it. He didn't have to look when he heard a few kids scream, "Trick-or-treat."

Despite the turmoil she must have felt, Krystal managed to put on a smile and coo over their pretty costumes as she dropped candy into their bags from the bowl that sat by the door. The parents thanked her and they hurried off the porch. Devin wanted to call after them and tell them to get off the streets. After all he pieced together about the two murders, he figured that innocent children would be safe. It was the sinners and social outcasts who were in danger. Aaron's theory was beginning to hold water.

Krystal stayed by the door and he turned to hold her gaze and the debating expression fixed on her face. Her breaths came heavy, her chest rising and falling, so enticing, but still forbidden until she gave him an answer.

He came toward her, his footfalls tapping against the floor as he came closer. Devin stood before her and the air around them seemed balmy, thick with the shared emotions they suffered for the decision she had to make. He hoped, he prayed that she wouldn't let him leave. The longer they stood like that, eyes locked in an unnamable struggle of unspoken morals, Devin lost it all.

He reached for the doorknob. "I'll show myself out."

Before he could turn it, Krystal leapt at him, her mouth claiming his with undeniable longing. Her arms wrapped around his neck, pulling him in tight, so he had no choice but to return the kiss. This wasn't his answer, not by a long shot, but Devin would take it.

He locked the doorknob and deadbolt without having to even look at it, and then enveloped her in his arms so he could feel her supple body against his. As if reading his mind, Krystal's hands got to work on his jacket, stripping it off and he helped her with his belt.

His cop gear fell to the floor. Neither of them thought of the scuff the hard plastic and metal would make in the wood. Without any communication, he picked Krystal up, his hands cupping her ass against him. Her legs hooked around his torso so he could easily carry her into the living room.

Even if this was the last night they could be together, he wouldn't question it. Devin was going to enjoy this and he had a feeling that Krystal would too. Whatever disaster waited for them in the morning, could wait until the dawn.

Chapter 14

Passion swirled in Krystal's core as she felt her nipples harden against Devin's chest. She moaned as he took her down onto the couch. Now that his jacket and cop belt were out of the way, she could explore that body she had been fantasizing about during her elemental training.

Her hands snatched at his shirt, tugging it free from his pants as his hands roamed just as they had the other night. Without a bra to encumber them, Krystal could feel every scintillating brush against her chest that made her sigh with pleasure. The familiar heat and electricity shot through her, setting her blood on fire.

She didn't want to think about everything he had said just a moment or two ago, about leaving or staying. The universe knew Krystal wanted him to stay, to be with her for as long as he'd have her. The excuse about her parents was true.

They wanted her to date a warlock, not a non-magic cop. They wanted so much from her, but she had to disappoint them. Her heart demanded it.

The bigger question, the one that had stolen away her sleep, was if she should listen to the demands of her heart or her magic. Being with Devin would be nothing short of a thrilling adventure. A kind of small town fairytale that she couldn't resist. Her dark magic, this fire that steadily grew within her the moment she saw him standing on her front porch, was what threw a wrench in her plans.

How long would it take before she could trust herself around him? How long before the fire could be contained and controlled – if that was even possible. Could she risk him, or should she give herself more time? Devin wasn't giving her more time, so this was the next best route. Test the waters, see if she could master this passion without it consuming the thing she loved most. If she could, then they could get right back to where they started.

She worked at the buttons of his shirt, breaking off a few in the process and she heard them patter upon the carpet by the sofa. Devin's mouth moved along her jaw and down her neck as he did before. She could feel his fingers tug down the waistband of her pajama pants. The cool air of the house crawled across her flush skin.

Krystal wanted this more than anything else. She needed him near, to have him hold her. There was another reason why she couldn't sleep. Thoughts of Devin had danced through her brain to the point she couldn't stand to be still any longer. She got up to cook and clean, hoping to expel some of that energy that had been building up inside of her since the night before. She needed that release and no amount of touching herself and fantasizing about him would bring it. She needed him. All of him.

She tugged his button-down uniform shirt over his shoulders, his arms nearly trapped at his sides. When he took the time to sit up and strip off his shirt, she curled her legs up to free herself of her pajama pants. It was moments like this that she should have been wearing any of her flowing skirts. That would have been easier than tugging off her pants to have them join his shirt on the floor.

Devin was more built, more magnificent that she had ever dreamed. She longed to touch every hard, sculpted muscle across his chest and abs. She wanted to feel the ridges and lick them all, one by one.

Her eyes caught something that she hadn't been privileged to see before. The skin across his left shoulder and a bit down his chest, looked puckered and scarred, as if he had been burned. Krystal quickly sat up to touch that wide, snaking patch marred flesh, but Devin wouldn't let her.

He leaned back down and pressed his lips into the hallow at the base of her neck. She moaned as his tongue and lips glided across every sensitive spot of her chest. Her thoughts drifted back to the scar. What happened to him? Was this what he didn't want to tell her about Boston?

All rational train of thought was shattered when he pulled down the front of her camisole to release one of her breasts. His tongue teased at her nipple and she bucked at the flood of ecstasy that rushed through her. More powerful than anything her magic could give her. More consuming than any of her fantasies.

Krystal cried out as he continued to excite her. One hand gripped at his hair, begging him to linger there while her other caressed the rigid muscles of his unblemished shoulder and arm. The heat and wetness between her legs came in tandem with the tantalizing movements of his mouth on her chest. She rocked against his pelvis and she could feel his hardness pressing through the front of his pants.

She rocked faster, moving her hips in time with his so that she could drive him mad with the promise of what it would be like when they didn't have any clothing there to hinder them. Devin took a break from flicking at her nipple to yank her camisole over her head. Now, she was completely bare to him and she no longer felt cold, but white hot, warmed by the passion that they shared.

He sat up to gaze at her, taking in her mostly naked body with smoldering, hungry eyes that she had missed so badly over the last few days. She reached down to seize the front of his pants, so she could unbutton them, but his hands beat her to it.

In one breathless moment of anticipation, he stripped off his pants and underwear, sliding his shoes off somewhere in the mad dash to get naked. His cock, glistening with his own wetness and throbbing for her touch, called to her. Krystal wrapped her hand around him and slowly moved her hand along his silky shaft. The way he closed his eyes and sighed made her even wetter, knowing that she could pleasure him just like he had her.

His hands refused to be idle and he moved down once more to tantalize her nipples. Both of them. The heat within her grew hotter and Krystal didn't care. She enjoyed this too much to think of what might happen, though she remembered exactly at what moment she knew to stop. Right when she was ready to climax. Krystal bit back the moan that came when she wished that moment would never come, that she could just enjoy this forever with his hands all over her and her hand around his cock.

He wouldn't allow it though. Devin kissed along her chest and down her core, toward the center of her desire. His cock slid from her fingers and she groaned at the unfairness. Yet, when his fingers hooked the fabric of her panties, she couldn't openly complain.

"Damn, you're wet," he whispered as he pulled them down. The evidence of her arousal was plain when the crotch of her pants clung to her folds before exposing that which he searched for.

Krystal grabbed for the edge of the sofa as his tongue lapped up her juices. She cried out once more. She was sure that the neighbors would hear their lovemaking. His mouth covered that most sensitive bit just above her folds and his tongue played with her.

Subconsciously, her hips began to move against him, his palms pressing into her butt cheeks as he lifted her off the couch cushion. Heat exploded within her and she knew that moment was drawing close. The more he teased her, bringing her closer to the end of her pleasure, she wanted to rebel, to pull back and make it last an eternity.

At the same time, she whispered, "Yes, just like that."

Her skin tingled, her core tightened. She could feel the climax travel up to her very soul, caressing it and pulling her dangerously close to insanity. She was insane for wanting this so badly, for carelessly playing with that fire that would devour them both.

But in that moment, she realized something so transcending. He was her fire. Just as she had fed upon the energy of the candle flames the night before, so now she drew on him for that overwhelming heat that sent her through this spiraling of ecstasy. And he drew upon her. She could feel it now, the warmth and fire channeling between them as he touched her and pleasured her.

Krystal grew dizzy, breathless, and she didn't know which way was up or down anymore. All that existed was them and this amazing moment as she came. She cried out, loud, and she bucked against his mouth, begging for more as the shocks rattled her body.

But Devin wasn't done. His tongue brushed in and out between her folds, prolonging the climax in the most amazing way. His mouth slowly detached from her and he moved up to trail kissing across her quivering core.

"I love it when you scream," he said before kissing her parted lips. She could taste her own cum upon his lips, and she didn't care.

When Devin's tip brushed against her pulsating folds, hot and slick from his own arousal, Krystal managed to hook her legs around his thighs. "Take me," she begged.

He complied, and slid into her with one, agonizingly slow push. Krystal sighed and threw back her head as the grips of passion took her once more. She never imagined she could be ready for another organism, but Devin continued to prove her wrong. She thought she could never love a man and still be successful at business. She thought she could never need something so completely that she would do anything, short of murder, to obtain it. She thought she'd never be so willing to cast aside the traditions of her magical family for something as primal, as eternal as the love of a man.

Yet, here she was, realizing all of the sudden that she did love him. Krystal loved Devin with every cell in her body, with every ounce of the magic that coursed within her. How could she have ever thought that she could let him walk out her front door, forever?

Devin moved within her, pushing and pulling his cock in and out between her folds, filling her and leaving her yearning for more. She arched her back, making her taut nipples brush against his chest as he slowly, but forcefully pumped into her.

"Harder," she begged, whispering in his ear as he nipped at her neck.

At first, he didn't. He did the exact opposite. Slowing his movements until she pleaded for it in the way she rocked her hips toward him. Her legs tightened around his waist, pulling herself clear off the cushion until she felt him fill her again.

Only then, when she grew frustrated with the mounting tension within her, did he do as she asked. Devin's hard cock pounded into her, jostling her body and sending the most unimaginable sensations through her.

His skin was hot to the touch, just as hers was, but the second organism came just as powerfully as the first. She shuddered and cried out as she came again, and she could feel his own member pulsate within her as he came at the same time.

Krystal fell slack against the sofa, weak and shivering from the wild high Devin had just sent her on. Devin, too, eased down, his arms still supporting his own weight, so he wouldn't crush her. They panted together as one, trying to catch their breaths as the last tingling thrills of their lovemaking faded away.

The heat, however, did not fade as she had expected.

Krystal opened her eyes and rolled her head toward the fireplace that was blazing. The tips of the flames escaped through the metal screen to lick at the wooden mantle. She had never started a fire that evening.

Her eyes went wide. Her mind was suddenly clear as she looked around and saw every candle in the living room boasted a tall, rigid flame just like the ones from the night before during her training. Her senses came back to her and she smelled both the scorched meat in the skillet and the heard the boiling water in the pot on the range.

Krystal began to hyperventilate as she reached out to calm the flames before Devin noticed.

"What's wrong?" he asked, lifting himself up a little more. His cock eased out and she shuddered at the feeling of total disconnect. She wished he could have stayed in all night, but there were more pressing matters.

The flames weren't going down. None of them were. She tried to focus and wouldn't answer his question.

Shit. Shit. Shit.

Devin finally looked up and turned toward the fireplace. "Was that lit before?"

Krystal tried to act as if she were simply stretching her arm muscles, so he wouldn't suspect what she was really trying to do. "Uh, yeah. I started it just before you got here."

Yet, there was something in the way he watched the fire that reminded her of the first evening they shared together in the house. That troubled, almost panicky look in his eyes made her even more desperate to control the flames in the room.

She was really fucked when his gaze jerked toward the candles on the table on the far wall of the room. "Holy shit!" he exclaimed and scrambled off of her. Krystal's face wrinkled with worry as she didn't try to hide it anymore. There was no way he was going to just ignore two-foot-tall candle flames.

Krystal rolled over on the sofa cushion and outstretched both of her hands toward the candles, seeped the life from the fire until they were completely snuffed out. Tiny wisps of smoke curled upward from the wicks. Thankfully, they had never turned the smoke detectors back on.

Devin was on his feet, staring at the fire that wasn't completely out of control, but almost. The paint on the mantle began to chip and flake away, dropping onto the rug and smoldering there with residual heat.

Once more, Krystal reached out to quell the fire. It took a bit more effort, but she got it down to a reasonable level to the point that it wasn't going to eat away at the mantle any more. She didn't even want to look at Devin. She didn't want to see the fear and questions in his eyes. And she definitely didn't want to think about how much it would cost to touch up the wood on the mantle.

Instead, she readied herself for the inevitable shit storm that was about to come barreling through her living room. Krystal reached down to retrieve her clothes and tugged them on, her hands trembling as she waited for the explosion.

Nothing.

When she finally slipped her panties on, she looked to Devin. His crystalline blue eyes watched in wide fascination. His mouth hung open as he stood completely naked and vulnerable by the sofa. The scar across his shoulder and chest drew her attention again, but now wasn't the time to ask about it. She could make her own assumptions. By the way he had been terrified of the out of control fireplace, Devin must have been involved in some accident that burned him while in Boston. The details weren't important right now, but it made her feel even worse about losing control like that. He was afraid of the one thing that would follow her for the rest of her life.

"What the hell was that?" he asked, his voice carefully soft, so unlike what she had expected.

Krystal blinked back the tears that pricked at her eyes, wishing it hadn't come to this. She thought she was being careful. Thought she had it under control, but hindsight showed her that even during earth-shattering sex, she still didn't have any restraint.

If given the chance, she wouldn't have done anything differently. The utter bliss that came with his touch, his caress, his sex, none of it could be regrettable. She'd do him all over again if he'd let her. After this night, he probably wouldn't.

"It's hard to explain," she replied.

"Try," he demanded, the boldness in him resurfacing. That same boldness that presented her the ultimatum earlier.

There was no easy way to say what needed to be said now. There was no way to break the news gently to someone who must have never even entertained the idea that there was anything supernatural in the world. Devin was a realist. He appreciated honesty and openness, but he didn't show it to others. He didn't want anything to water-down his reality. Would he try to shun the truth when she spoke it?

Taking a deep breath, Krystal said, "I'm a witch."

She had never said those words to non-magic folk before. Whenever she met another witch, there was an instant connection. They already knew what she was, and she didn't have to tell them.

Even fae and other magical creatures could sense the magic within her and didn't need an explanation. But to a human, she would have appeared just as normal as any other. Devin would have never thought she was anything magical. Not until now.

At first, she thought he would deny it, reject her response with a laugh or sneer. Instead, he narrowed his eyes and studied her, as if looking for something to prove what she said was true, apart from what he just witnessed.

"A witch?" he repeated. "Like, wiccan and pagan shit?"

She shook her head. "No, I mean like real, magical, witch. I have been all my life. It's not a religion. It's who I am."

Devin ran his fingers through his hair and she noticed the way his body glistened with sweat as the light in the fireplace made him shine. If the situation allowed, she would have wanted to run her hands all over his chest. Right now, he probably didn't want her anywhere near him.

"You're a witch... That explains so much."

Krystal was sure her heart stopped beating for a split second. "What?"

"Did you cast some spell on me to make me fall in love with you?"

She didn't know how to feel about that question. Joy made her breath hitch at the idea that he might have fallen in love with her just as she had fallen for him. Then rage mingled in that he might have thought her so conniving that she would actually charm him into wanting her. It wasn't unheard of. She always thought those witches and warlocks were rather desperate to think they could make someone love them with their magic. Love had to be organic to be lasting.

"No, Devin, I never used magic on you."

It was a fib and somehow, he picked up on it. How could he tell when she wasn't being honest like that?

"Don't lie to me!" he snapped. "Did you cast a spell on me?"

Krystal held up her hands. "Okay, I did use a little magic, but it was in your coffee yesterday, that's all. You were so exhausted, and I just wanted to help."

Devin's face contorted with suppressed fury as he snatched his pants and underwear off the ground. He dressed, and Krystal was scared he would storm out of the house. She crawled across the couch cushions and wanted to reach out to hold him there, but he flinched away.

Her heart was ripped into two jagged pieces when he turned on her.

"Why didn't you tell me from the beginning?"

She huffed in disbelief. "What would you expect me to say? That kind of conversation isn't exactly something you bring up over dinner."

"It's better than hiding it."

Krystal gripped the arm of the sofa. "We have to hide this, Devin! What if the world knew about witches and magic? What do you think would happen? They would just be fine with this? Or did your history teachers not talk about the Salem Witch Trials?"

Devin jerked back and shook his head. "We? There are more?"

Each breath came out shaky and she could feel the fiery anger build up in her. Krystal had to calm down or the fireplace would get out of control again. "Yes, there are more," she replied delicately. "That's what my family does. We're all witches. My parents are on the council that keeps track of every magic folk in this part of the country." Might as well spill all the ugly truth now while he was still receptive.

Devin stared, unblinking, but she could see the way he was grappling with all this new information.

"I didn't want you to find out this way," she said softly, glancing to the burning logs in the fireplace.

"How was I going to find out? Was I going to see you flying around Goldcrest Cove on a broomstick instead?"

So much distain sullied his words and Krystal wanted to wail out in frustration. "We don't fly on broomsticks. I didn't know how I was going to tell you. Please," she pleaded. "Please understand that this isn't easy for me to tell you. I only hid this from you, because I didn't know how you would react."

Devin shook his head in disbelief. "I never thought that this is what you were keeping from me. I thought maybe your family was part of some crime syndicate, or something. This would have never occurred to me."

"For any normal person, it wouldn't." Krystal sat up a little straighter, hoping that they were at the end of the shock phase, so they could talk this over rationally. "My entire family line is made up of witches and warlocks, people who were born with the ability to use magic. We can do almost anything. Remember that broken brake light on Alexa's car? I fixed that with magic without ever having to get out of the car. That time you spilled coffee, I used magic, so it wouldn't mess up your clothes."

"And what you just did?" he questioned, gesturing toward the fireplace.

Krystal gulped, bracing herself for the ultimate confession. "All magic folk have this thing we call special magic, or dark magic. We kind of come into it when we're adults. I'm just finding out that I can manipulate and create fire."

Devin nodded. "That explains what happened the other night when you made the smoke alarms go off."

Excitement took the place of fear. He was beginning to understand, and she could sense he was finally beginning to settle down. That harried, frantic look in his eye was nearly gone. "Yes. It was completely by accident, though. I didn't realize what was going on until after you left."

"And that's why you needed time to think?"

Krystal thanked every god and goddess she could think of. Devin was a smart, rational man. Relief mushroomed within her, though it might have been too soon, and she closed her eyes. "Yes. I had to make sure this is what I wanted. Whenever we're together, a little more of my special magic was coming out and it was becoming dangerous. Not only that, but my family would much rather me marry a warlock. Mostly because this is a hard conversation to have with non-magic folk. It's just a lot easier for witches to marry within their own circles."

She opened her eyes and watched the way his face softened with understanding. There was still a hesitance there, but with time, maybe that would go away altogether. Would he give her that time, though?

"But you want to be with me anyway?" he questioned. "Even though you know this could never work?"

She hastily shook her head. "No, this can work. It's worked before many times with other couples."

Then she thought of the scar on his shoulder. Did that have something to do with what he said? It could work for her, but would this relationship work for him? Every time he kissed her, he'd be playing with fire, the kind of fire that burned him. The kind of fire he was afraid of.

Devin moved toward the coffee table, his steps laden with hesitation as if he were ready to pounce and run if she moved too quickly. He was within reach now, so close she could reach out and touch his cheek, but she refrained.

"So, what is it that you do, exactly?" he asked as he sat on the coffee table.

Krystal shrugged up one slender shoulder. "We just live like anyone else. You know I have a job, a family, friends, a cat. I'm normal, just like anyone else. I just have magical powers, that's all."

It sounded so corny, but it was the truth. Question was, would he even believe that? Could he accept it?

He leaned forward on his elbows, studying her face, probably to see if she was lying. They had no more secrets now. At least, not on her part. She could tell him everything about her life and her family. She could finally explain about that family photo on the mantle. She could tell him how the very thought of him was what made her elemental magic come to life. She could be completely open and free with him. Despite her initial fears, Krystal had never been more in love with him.

Devin didn't run, he didn't scream. He stayed. Thank Gaia, he stayed.

"Are witches responsible for these murders?"

It was so left field that Krystal jerked back in disgust. "What? No! Absolutely not. We value all life, no matter how simple. Remember how I told you that I didn't like to cut flowers? A lot of my upbringing has to do with that."

"Do you have the ability to find out who the murderer is?"

Krystal's slight smile failed her. Was she talking to the Devin that she loved, or the detached cop who was just doing his job? Her shoulders slumped a little, but she replied, "We can find out, and we do want to help, but I don't think we can."

Devin squinted in confusion. "What do you mean?"

Krystal settled back against the sofa and curled her legs beneath her. "The number one rule amongst magic folk is that we don't use our powers on non-magic folk. That can include helping them. I break that rule every day, but I don't have the ability to find out things like that."

"What do you mean you break that rule?" His fingers tightened over his knuckles.

She took a calming breath and explained to him about the coffee shop, their mission, and the good they were trying to do for the community on whatever small scale they could manage. It wasn't much, but they were proud of what they did accomplish. There was no reason to tell him about Amber's special scrying magic, even though that could be the key to cracking open their case.

"In a lot of ways, we hold the same values. You become a cop, so you can help the innocent. I started my coffee shop, so I could help the people of this town. We're not that different, Devin."

He nodded, a certain calmness seeping through the muscles that had once been taut. "I can see that... But I need you to do something for me."

"Anything," she breathed, leaning toward him a bit.

"Don't get involved in the murder investigations," he said with all the coolness in the world. "If Aaron's theory is right, and this guy is going after people that don't line up with religious standards of 'righteous'," he said with air quotes for emphasis, "then you're just as much at risk as any other witch or magical person in town."

He might have been right, but Krystal knew they were safe for now. "I under-stand that, but unless the murderer knows that we're witches, we should be safe."

Devin shook his head. "I don't want to risk you."

It was a simple phrase, made up of simple words, but to Krystal, it was the most beautiful thing she had ever heard. He not only seemed to accept her, but he cared for her. Maybe he wouldn't recant what he said earlier about loving her, but she wasn't going to push it. Not tonight when he still had so much to process.

Anyone would be dazed by the amount of information she just tried to cram between his ears. It wasn't going to be easy for him to grasp the idea that magic and witches existed. That's why she didn't mention werewolves, vampires, fae, or anything else that she knew existed. Not yet. Not now.

"I can promise you that as long as we don't become targets, we will stay out of your investigation."

Devin's gaze dropped to the space between them. "I hate to say this, but I need some time to think."

Whatever was left of her heart splintered and cracked as those words flowed out so smoothly, so casually like it wasn't supposed to mean the end of her world. But they did. All sanity left her and turned to ash in the fire.

"Take all the time you need," she said. And before her brain could tell her mouth to not form the words, she said, "Just know that I'm still willing to be with you, to be your girlfriend. I don't care if it goes against the grain. I... I love you."

Devin didn't move. He didn't reply or return her sentiment and she could feel her heart fracture more with each passing second of silence. She wondered if any magic in the world could put the pieces back together. Then, she knew that one type of magic could, but it was nothing she personally possessed. Only the love of the man in front of her could heal her wounded spirit.

Devin picked up his shirt from the floor and inspected the empty spots along the front of his shirt where only tiny threads poked out from the fabric. In a daring move, Krystal reached out her hand and used her magic to retrieve the buttons that had popped off earlier. He watched the plastic buttons float through the air and then refasten themselves to the shirt with brand new thread that seemed to materialize out of thin air.

It was all Krystal's doing and though he watched with odd fascination, he said nothing. Not even a thank you. When she was finished, he slid his arms through the sleeves and stood to tuck his shirt back in.

She said nothing as he moved around the sofa and toward the foyer with his boots in his hands. Krystal bit her lips together as silent tears burned along the edges of her eyelids. She wouldn't cry. Not while he was still in the house. She shouldn't have been crying at all. It wasn't like he totally denied her. He just said he needed to think. She had pulled that line on him once before, but did he mean the same thing?

She listened to him sit on the hall butler bench and slide his boots on. A soft meow drifted down the stairs along with the light patter of cat paws coming down the hall. Krystal looked over the back of the couch and saw Artemis trot toward Devin with absolutely no hesitation.

This, she had to see.

Krystal jumped off the couch and went to the cased opening into the foyer. Artemis was brushing himself against Devin's pant leg, purring like a loud motorboat as he looked up to Devin with expectant eyes. She had fed the cat earlier, but this wasn't the usual supplication for food. He wanted attention, and from a complete stranger. That never happened.

Devin finished lacing up his boots and then carefully scratched Artemis behind the ears.

If there was ever a sign that Devin was the one who was destined to stay, it was this. Forget the dark magic and the way he made love to her. If Artemis actually liked Devin, it was a universally accepted truth that he should stay.

She wanted to run to him and throw her arms around his neck to beg him to stay just a little longer, but that wouldn't have been fair. He gave her space when she asked for it, and Krystal would do the same for him.

Devin stood from the bench and walked to the door. He took one last look over his shoulder as his hand wrapped around the knob. She met his blue eyes and tried to smile, but the unbidden tears kept her from fully expressing how grateful she was for the benevolence he had shown her tonight.

"Your secret is safe with me," he said. "I promise, I'll let you know when I'm ready to talk about this again."

Krystal nodded in understanding and watched him walk out the front door. With his absence came that cold loneliness that she couldn't shake. Artemis looked up to her as if questioning why the perfect man was just leaving her like that.

She shook her head to the mute question. She didn't know either. There was no use understanding why she loved him. Why she was willing to give him the world if he asked for it. Why she was willing to give up everything she ever knew – including her powers – just so she could be with him.

Chapter 15

Krystal sipped on her chai tea latte, wishing that painful ache in her chest would just go away.

"And then he left?" Valerie asked. The two girls had been clinging to every word of Krystal's story of how she finally came out of the broom closet with Devin. Of course, she didn't tell them about the sex that preceded the talk. That was none of their business and she couldn't handle any questions about whether there were rights read or handcuffs involved.

She nodded and swallowed what was in her mouth. As always, every sip reminded her of her family, the traditions that had been such an integral part of her life. It reminded her of evenings spent in craft stores with her mother, browsing for fall decorations or candles to use in some ritual she wanted to try. Right about now, she was beginning to think that she wanted to change her drink choice to something less nostalgic.

"He left and I haven't heard from him."

They had just opened for the morning. Not one customer had come in. They were probably reading the headlines of that morning's newspaper. Big bold letters screamed that the murderer was still on the loose and Harry Middleton was the second victim. She doubted that anyone would come walking through those doors all day, not even Aaron or Devin.

And for once, she didn't care.

The business meant little to her in the wake of this new personal tragedy. She had done a lot of thinking, going over his reactions and how she had the fleeting hope that he would understand. He probably understood, but that didn't mean he was comfortable with any of it. That look in his eyes, the way he said he needed time to think. It wasn't good. Even his promise as he was walking out the door meant little now.

"Maybe he'll call later today?" Alexa offered. "He's got to come in for his coffee anyway."

Valerie passed her a look. "Or he could just send Aaron to get it."

"I don't think either of them are coming in," Krystal said as she set her cup down on the counter, tired of the drink after just three or four sips. "I don't think Devin would have told him about us, but he'll probably make up some excuse for them not to come in. Either that, or he's going to be swamped with work. They still haven't caught this murderer yet."

Alexa shivered. "I know. I don't know what news is worse. That you may have lost Devin or that this killer is still on the loose."

Krystal shook her head. "I don't think Devin was ever mine. Last night, we kind of came to the conclusion that we wanted to be a couple, but that was before... you know." She crossed her arms over her frumpy light blue sweater, the one she always wore at home when she needed something soft and comfortable to wear. She didn't care if it wasn't professional looking.

"I've seen the way he looks at you," Valerie said. "He's totally in love with you and he even admitted it. Just give him some time to adjust. This is a small town. It's not like he can avoid you."

"He can transfer out." The words came out cold and bitter from Krystal's lips. "That's what he did when things got tough in Boston. Who's to say he won't do it again?"

Alexa put a reassuring hand on her friend's arm. "Because he's crazy about you and you're crazy about him. He just needs to realize that."

The long breath she took wouldn't ease the pain in her heart, but it was worth a shot.

Valerie took Krystal's coffee mug from the counter. "Let me charm this so you can at least think straight."

She shot out her hand to stop her friend. "No," she said. "I don't want to be charmed."

"Why not?" Valerie asked. "You'd do the same for any other customer that would come in with a broken heart."

"Because... I don't want my reality to be watered down. I don't like this pain, but masking it won't help me now."

Her two friends looked at her as if she were a masochist. Maybe she was. All Krystal knew was that if Devin was in her shoes, he wouldn't want his coffee charmed. He'd want to feel this pain to its fullest extent. He'd want to experience every agonizing lurch of his guts when he thought of what caused his heart to shatter into a thousand tiny pieces.

Krystal had charmed herself too many times and she knew plenty about sorrow. Seeing how much Devin had been through and survived without the aid of magic, she knew she could survive this.

The familiar bird song ringtone cut through the silence of the coffee shop. She reached down hastily to her purse and saw it was Sierra calling. Her heartbeat rose into her throat. Sierra didn't come home the night before from the costume party she went to with the other girls from the salon. At first, Krystal just wanted to assume that she got drunk and spent the night over there. It was unlike Sierra to not send a single text to let her know.

"It's my sister," she told the others and hit the green button before it could go to voicemail.

"Where are you?" she nearly screeched into the receiver.

"I'm at the police station."

The light quiver in her elder sister's voice stifled every bit of anger she might have had. "What's going on? Did you get arrested?"

"No," she said a little calmer this time. "No, I didn't get arrested. I was attacked last night. I'm fine and I've been to the hospital, but I need you to come get me. I left my car at Monica's house."

Krystal's hand flew to grip at the collar of her sweater. "Who attacked you? What happened?"

"Krystal," Sierra barked in that voice she used whenever her little sister was getting frenetic. "I will explain everything when you get here. Please, just come and get me." She agreed and ended the call.

Questions came flying at her from the other two witches, but Krystal silenced them. "I don't know anything yet. I will tell you when we get back." She grabbed her purse. Then it occurred to her, she had walked to work. She turned back around. "Can I borrow your – " Alexa was already throwing her keys and Krystal caught them.

She had a pretty good idea of what must have happened, but Krystal didn't want to assume anything. It was Halloween, after all, and there were always creeps, even in Goldcrest Cove. Krystal just hoped to Gaia that whoever attacked her sister was ready to pay for it. This might have been the excuse they needed to get involved.

The police station was fairly empty that morning. The officers were already on their patrol circuits. Only Aaron, Devin, and the chief remained to look after Sierra and fill out the last of the reports detailing her attack. In the open office space that Devin and several of the other officers shared, desks were situated in two long rows. File cabinets lined the back wall where they kept every traffic stop, ticket duplicate, and other reports.

Devin watched Sierra from across the hall as he poured himself another cup of coffee from the station's only coffeemaker. It was so old that it rarely worked, and even when it did, there were always grounds left in the bottom of his cup. It was either drink the subpar coffee or go to Perfect Books and Brews, which he wasn't ready to do just yet. Even the thought of seeing Krystal within mere moments didn't thrill him in the same way anymore.

He loved her. He knew that now. Witch or no witch, he loved her, and it confused the shit out of him. He had loved her all along. He didn't realize it until last night when she confessed she was willing to throw away her family's approval and everything they expected of her. That was before they had sex.

Last night, they had made a connection. He couldn't explain it or put it into proper words that anyone would understand. If it were possible, Devin was more drawn to her now than ever. When they made love on the sofa in her living room, he had felt something come alive deep within him. Call it a soul, spirit, essence, whatever. When it came alive, burning like a smoldering coal within him, it was like he could breathe for the first time. He felt the world more vividly now. Every color brighter, every sense heightened. Every nerve lay bare and raw, ready to be torn to pieces by this love that gripped him so tightly. And it did tear him apart. Learning Krystal's truth injured him far more deeply than he would ever let anyone know. She couldn't help being what she was, and he couldn't help but love her anyway.

He loved her long before that, though. Devin loved her when she admitted the rose wasn't the ideal present for her. He loved her when she was willing to face her fears just to be with him. He loved her when they were cooking dinner together in her kitchen. He loved everything about her from the way her nose wrinkled when she laughed to the way she spoke her mind to how she looked at him with those captivating, bewitching brown eyes.

Maybe she never cast a spell on him, but she certainly charmed him even before they officially met. Devin had been waiting all his life for a woman like Krystal. It seemed to be just his luck that he should fall for a girl he couldn't have.

He poured the second cup and made his way back to his desk where he told Sierra to wait for her sister. Her stare was unfocused and far away, as if her mind were somewhere else. No doubt, she was thinking of the attack. If only she would tell him more. He wasn't buying that she didn't see the guy at all.

Aaron, who happened to be on patrol last night, came upon Sierra and the man, and they had already been in the middle of a tussle. It was a lucky break that he happened to be there, or Sierra might have been hurt more. As it was, the nasty bruises on her neck told the story of a violent struggle that could have killed her. It was just one of the other injuries she had in common with the two corpses they had found already.

Devin wondered if he should tell Sierra that he knew about her and her family. Maybe it would get her to open up a little more. He was content to try a gesture of kindness first.

"Here," he said, offering out the hot cup to her. "You look like you need this."

Sierra came out of the fog for a moment to simply look at the cup. "I don't drink coffee."

Devin cracked a smile. "Your sister owns a coffee shop and you don't drink coffee?" he asked as he sat down in his swivel office chair across from her. He set the cup down in front of her while he took a sip of his own. Bitter, nasty stuff. It was hard not to make a face when it touched his tongue.

The older witch pointed at him. "That's why."

He swallowed and chuckled. "Well, it gets me through the day."

"Black coffee, right?" she said. "No sugar, no cream, nothing."

He nodded. "Yep. Krystal tell you that?"

"Yeah. The last I heard, you two weren't talking. Care to explain that?"

It was unlikely that she knew anything about what happened last night. Aaron picked her up around ten o'clock, which was shortly after he left Krystal's house. She must have been talking about how Krystal had told him to give her time to think. She didn't know, though, that Devin knew all about that. About her special magic and the big decision she had to make as witch trying to have a relationship with an unimpressive mortal like him.

"You tell me," he said, taking another sip. After a few gulps, it all started to taste the same and it wasn't so bad.

Sierra smiled sweetly. "Whatever you think is going on, it has nothing to do with you."

"That's what she said, but it's like that old saying girls give when they're ready to break up. They say, 'It's not you, it's me.' And I'm wondering if that's pretty much where this is headed."

"No," she said with a shake of her head, rather lucid now that she was sitting in front of the cop.

"Krystal's too crazy about you to ever do that."

He wondered how far he could push this conversation without fully showing his hand. "What if I told you that I got this feeling she was hesitant about being with me? I am a cop. It wouldn't the first time someone's dumped me because of my line of work."

Sierra made a dubious face. "Really? You think that she would dump you just because of your job? Sorry, but my sister isn't that shallow."

"So, you don't think she would dump me because I was different than her? Even if your parents disapprove of me?"

A glint of something unreadable shone in Sierra's eye, but it was gone just as quickly as it came. "I know she wouldn't. You don't know her as well as I do. She's always been a bit of a rebel, ever since she was little. She was better behaved than I was, that's for sure, but she hated to follow anyone else's rules but her own. When she started the coffee shop, our mom had a fit."

His brows shot up. "Really?" Krystal had told him that none of her family knew about her mission when initially starting up the coffee shop. That meant her mother hadn't been as truly supportive as she had led him to believe. Why would her family not want her to follow her dream or own her own business like that? Did it have to do with this witch council thing she mentioned?

"Really. Our parents thought having her own business wasn't a safe or smart idea. No one in our family ever started their own business. They always worked under someone else or worked their way up the ladder for another company. They never started from scratch. Krystal did it first, and then I followed her. We are the first women in our family to ever have something of our own." Sierra leaned forward. "Krystal wanted that coffee shop bad enough to defy our parents. She certainly wants you bad enough that she'd do it again."

It confirmed what Krystal had said the night before. Somehow, he had wondered if she was just saying those things to make him more at ease about this whole witch thing. Now he knew. It wasn't just something she said. She meant it with all her heart. If her sister could testify to that, then perhaps he needed to give this more thought.

Devin had to ask himself whether he would be okay with having a witch for a girlfriend, for a wife, for a lover. Was he okay with being part of this new and fantastic world that he knew absolutely nothing about? That tiny, impulsive voice in his head, the voice of the man who let his emotions run wild without logic or reason, screamed that he should take the chance. Take Krystal for himself before she changed her mind.

That was the struggle that led him to this place where his heart and his mind competed for the final say. Would he take her hand and accept this, or would he turn away? He knew which path was easier, but since when had he done anything the easy way?

He heard the police station doors swing open and he stood from his chair as he saw the flash of blue dash down the hall.

"Krystal!" he shouted as she was running in the wrong direction, toward the chief's office.

She skidded to a stop and then trotted back to the open glass door. Sierra ran to embrace her, and Devin thought he saw Krystal's eyes wetted with impending tears. Those same tears he saw film over her eyes last night.

He wasn't sure whether to stick around and try to eavesdrop for any extra clue Sierra might drop to her sister, or leave the office to give them some private time. While still in the middle of deciding, Krystal looked up and met his stare.

She gave him a weak smile and mouthed a thank you, even though he didn't do anything but question Sierra.

Above all, he needed to know if the killer was Father Frank. One thing that didn't match up with the other murders, was that Father Frank didn't talk with Sierra like he had with the other two victims. The priest had his alibi for the first murder, but not for the second. He claimed he was home when Harry Middleton was murdered, but no one else could confirm that. If Sierra could have IDed the man, who didn't even wear a mask to cover his face, then maybe they could at least get a sketch of the perp.

No such luck. For whatever reason, Sierra wasn't telling him shit about the killer and he couldn't figure out why. According to Aaron, she had looked straight at him. Unfortunately, his partner didn't get a good glimpse either.

"Does she need to stay for anything else?" Krystal asked after she and Sierra had exchanged a few words that he couldn't quite make out from where he stood.

"Not unless she has anything else she needs to tell me." He gave a pointed look to Sierra, but the witch just shook her head.

"I told you everything I know."

Devin wasn't buying it, but torture was illegal in the states, so he couldn't force the truth out of her. For Sierra's sake, he hoped that she wasn't covering for anyone. That would mean she was abetting a murderer. If anyone found out, Krystal would lose her sister to the system and Sierra would go to jail for a long time.

As soon as the Volkswagen car doors were closed, the sisters turned to one another.

"What happened?" they asked in unison.

Krystal gave her sister a perplexed look. "You just got attacked and you're asking me what happened?"

Sierra waved her hands. "Devin was acting all weird, but we can get to that. The guy who attacked me is the same guy who's been going around killing people."

That's what she had been afraid of. Krystal sighed and pressed her palm to her forehead, willing the world to stop spinning. She was losing Devin and now her sister was a target of some psycho serial killer.

"I was leaving the party last night and my phone was dead, so I couldn't call you," she began as Krystal cranked up the car. She didn't want to have this conversation right in front of the police station. "I'll admit I was a little drunk, so I just decided to walk home. This dude jumped out at me from some bushes on Sandy Lane near the grocery store. He was shouting about vanity or something. He tried to strangle me, but remember I took those kickboxing classes in college? Well, they paid off some, but I was so sloshed, I couldn't get a good shot on the guy. Aaron was out patrolling, and he scared the guy away."

Krystal continued down Twin Hills Lane toward the park. "Did you get a good look at the guy?"

Sierra sighed. "Enough to know I don't recognize the dude. He was kind of short, dark curly hair and dark eyes. Well, everything was dark, so maybe his eyes were different. I don't know." Her sister held her head in her hands. "I just can't believe I came that close to dying."

"You said he was shouting about vanity? Do you think that has to do with your salon shop?" It lined up with Aaron's theory about some self-righteous prick trying to pick off sinners in Goldcrest Cove. Though, she hardly considered her sister to be conceited or lavish. Yeah, she knew plenty about what it took to look pretty. But if she really cared about her image, she would have done something about the smeared mascara under her eyes by now.

"I don't know, maybe." She gestured toward the road. "When you get to Johnson Avenue, just keep going onto Seaside Drive."

Krystal slid her sister a look. "I thought you said you wanted to go home?"

Sierra nodded. "I do, right after I go talk to Amber about this asshole."

"Amber? Why?"

Was the unthinkable happening? Was her sister going to break the cardinal rule of the witches and try to use their powers on non-magic folk?

"She knows how to scry, just like mom does. Before mom gets involved again, I want to find out who this guy is." She pointed angrily at her little sister. "And don't you dare tell mom about any of this."

Yep, her sister had crossed into the deep end. This was a good thing for all of them. Krystal and her friends would finally get their chance to intercede, and she wouldn't break her promise to Devin. She said that as long as the killer wasn't directly affecting her or her family, she would stay out of it. He had to know that this was her loophole. They could all pitch in with their magic to help the police. Then, maybe Devin would see that witches were a good thing for this community and he wouldn't be so hesitant about being with her.

Krystal went silent and when she turned onto Reichman Street to head toward Main Street and Johnson Avenue, she took a deep breath. "I want to go with you, but not right now."

Sierra wagged her head. "Excuse me? No, you're taking me to Ambers today."

"It's too early," she said. "Rose House is going to still be packed with guests. Wait until the afternoon or evening after some have already checked out. Then, you can go, and I'll go with you. Alexa and Valerie too."

"Hell no!" she shouted. "I'm not getting any of you involved. This is my fight."

"This is our fight!" Krystal screamed back, feeling the fiery heat of irritation pour from her. "This guy threatened my sister. Do you really think I'm just going to let that slide? If mom were here, she'd agree that this is our business. This is our town and this guy can't just come in here and start killing innocent people."

That seemed to quiet Sierra, and Krystal couldn't help but feel a bit victorious. She finally shut her sister up. Then again, she might have just stunned her sister into silence. It was rare, if not unheard of for Krystal to have an outburst like that.

"What was Devin asking about?" she asked.

Sierra shrugged and gave a flippant gesture. "He was asking about you and if you would dump him just because he was a cop or because our family wouldn't approve of him. I mean, I can see how dad might not think he's good enough for you but – "

"I told Devin," Krystal blurted out.

Sierra's eyes would have popped out of her head if she opened them any wider. "You did what?" she screamed.

She would not be daunted though. "I told him I was a witch and so was my entire family."

Before Sierra had a chance to call her an idiot, Krystal went on to explain how this bit of truth had to be exposed, how her dark magic made a lovely appearance in the fireplace and burned the beef she had been planning to make with her meat sauce.

When she explained it like that, Sierra seemed to calm down. "So, you didn't have much of a choice."

Krystal shook her head. "Nope, and it looks like I scared him off. He told me that he needed time to think."

"He's probably just digesting everything," she said, seemingly pacified by her explanation. "It's a lot to take in."

She was right and that's what Krystal had believed at first. But the way he looked at her in the police station, with such placid indifference, she couldn't believe that he was anywhere close to making a decision.

"Don't give up on him just yet," Sierra continued. "I think he really likes you and I put a good word in for you when he was asking all those questions. I said you'd go against our mom any day just to get what you really want."

Krystal glanced her way. She wasn't entirely wrong. "How did he react?"

"Oh, you know," Sierra shrugged. "He started babbling on and on about how he was so madly in love with you and hopes to make lots of half-magic babies with you."

She laughed and shoved her sister's shoulder. "Quit it. I'm being serious."

"Well, he didn't say it with his lips, but he said it in his eyes." Sierra batted her own lashes in an exuberant, flirty way.

Krystal rolled her eyes and turned onto Johnson Avenue to head toward the coffee shop. "Well, until he says it with his mouth, I'm not holding out hope. You didn't see the way he looked last night."

"Maybe not, but I saw the way he looked this morning. He looked exhausted and lovesick, just like you do." Sierra reached out and tucked some of Krystal's ebony hair behind her ear. "At least know that he's suffering as much as you are, even if he's not saying anything. I could sense it."

That was some consolation, but Krystal couldn't get swoony over this tragedy for long. They had a mission. Now that they were given some license to go after this murderer, it was all hands on deck. All emotions set aside for one evening while they worked their magic and did what only they could do.

Chapter 16

"Yes, Mr. Cleveland," Krystal heard Amber say cheerfully from the front door of Rose House. "I can't wait to see you next year too. Did you tell your grandson happy birthday for me?"

Krystal, her sister, Alexa, and Valerie all sat at the antique dining table, waiting for the remaining witch to see the last of her customers out the door. It was late evening and her other guests were out to dinner or visiting with family. Most had checked out of the bed and breakfast as soon as they read the morning paper headlines about the second murder.

Valerie tapped her black nails on the tabletop, the sound slightly muffled by the white cloth that was spread across it. She hadn't seen the table so clear before. There was always at least a flowery centerpiece in the middle that dripped with plastic crystals or peacock feathers. Amber had it set aside on the sideboard table against the wall. The sun had already set outside, but their hostess only lit a few candles around the dining room to set the ambiance for what she needed to do.

From what Krystal understood, she needed minimal distractions in order to do her scrying. Krystal's mother could scry at the drop of a hat, but Amber didn't have her special magic so developed yet.

None of them spoke, but an anxious energy filled the air. They had told the others about what happened to Sierra the night before. They all knew, just like Krystal knew, that this meant war. They hated to see the non-magic folk suffer at the hands of this murderer, but it was another thing to have one of their own kind threatened in this way. They had to act and that meant sometime tonight, they would confront the killer. They were all young, inexperienced in combat, unlike the Warlock Enforcers. But they couldn't pull them in without getting the council involved, which would put more pressure on Goldcrest Cove. Attention they didn't want.

They listened to Amber bid the final farewell to Mr. Cleveland and his wife before shutting the door and locking it. She hurried into the dining room and straightened out her long, knitted shawl that draped over her shoulders. "That man doesn't know when to shut it."

Krystal smiled at the way her friend's voice, both in tone and manner, changed so much compared to when she was talking to one of her guests. She called it her "customer service voice" and Krystal could see why. It was as if she had dropped a mask. Though, no one would ever second guess if she was sincere to her patrons.

She took a seat at the end of the table, Krystal on her right and Sierra to her left.

"All right, let's get started," she said with a little grin and wiggling in her seat. Alexa and Valerie stretched across the middle of the table to clasp their hands together, and also held the hands of the other two witches at the table.

Amber reached out to them both and closed her eyes. "Where exactly were you when this jerk face attacked you?"

The girls all smiled at her colorful, informal language. That was one thing they loved about Amber. She could break the tension with such ease that she didn't even realize she was doing it. "Right in front of Mrs. Miller's house on Sandy Lane."

It took a moment, then Amber nodded as she pinpointed that part of the street. "Time?"

"I think it was around nine o'clock."

Amber cracked an eye open to peer at Sierra. "You think, or you know?"

"Girl, I was a little drunk. I wasn't paying attention to the time."

"Drunk at only nine?" Amber clucked her tongue. "Naughty girl. Get drunk after midnight next time."

"Why after midnight?" Valerie asked beside Krystal.

Amber shushed her. "I need silence."

Valerie rolled her eyes and the others went deathly silent as Amber tried to drop into the meditative state. The house, though it was empty, creaked and the floor boards groaned above their heads. Amber claimed it was just the old Victorian house settling, but Krystal's house never settled like that. She trusted that if the scrying witch didn't think the house was haunted, then it probably wasn't, but she had her doubts.

Amber hummed a long, flat tune and Krystal bit her lips together to keep from laughing. It was like something straight out of a cheesy séance scene from a movie, but if Amber needed it to focus, she wasn't about to argue.

It was only when the tune began to waiver into something comical that the others had to hold in their laughter as well.

"Is that the Dr. Pepper jingle?" Alexa whispered.

Sierra, one of the eldest witches there, shushed her and Amber continued to summon whatever forces she needed to see into the past.

The humming stopped, and Amber's shoulders went slack. Krystal half expected her to start acting possessed, but she only let out an aggravated sigh.

"Not this ass wipe," she mumbled.

"You see him?" Sierra asked.

Amber made a face, but kept her eyes closed. "Yeah, I see him. He's new to town. Just moved here from out of state after a divorce. His wife cheated on him.

He came to stay here for a few days and he left without paying for his room. At least now I know what he was doing."

Alexa leaned forward. "What's his name?"

"One second..." Amber said, holding up one of her fingers. "I'm trying to see where he is right now."

All four witches waited, their eyes fixed on Amber's calm face. They had a name, a face, and a positive identity. They even had a possible motive. If this guy was obsessing over his wife's affair, then it might have been safe to say that he was targeting other people who had sinned in a similar way. Or just sinned at all.

"Oh, shit!" Amber exclaimed before opening her eyes wide.

"Where is he?" Valerie demanded, banging her hand against the table. Alexa winced when the back of her own fingers were slammed into the hardwood.

Amber turned to Krystal. "You need to call Devin. This is way out of our league."

"We're witches," Sierra said. "How can this be out of our league?"

Amber turned a saucy look to her. "Do think you could stop a man from shooting up a bar with an automatic he stole from Mr. Voisin's gun shed? I didn't think so."

"Gun?" cried Alexa. "He's got a gun now?"

Knives were one thing, but Amber was right. Guns were harder to handle.

Amber nodded. "Yep, and he's going all out with it. No holds barred, and he knows he's not walking away from this one." She looked back to Krystal. "Listen, I don't care what angsty drama you two are going through, but you need to call Devin and Aaron right now. Get them to come to Torn Sails Bar. We don't have a lot of time." Then, she looked to the others with genuine concern in her eyes. "This guy isn't going to come down easy," she continued. "This isn't just your normal psycho killer dude. He's second-hand charmed."

All four responded with a, "What?"

"Second-hand charmed," she repeated. "It's where – "

"We know what it means," Sierra interrupted.

Alexa spoke up excitedly. "Wait, I don't."

Krystal turned to her friend. "It means whoever this guy is, he caught something like an aftershock from someone who was given too high of a charm dose. Some of it spilled over from the first receiver into this guy."

What it really meant was that one of them screwed up. Someone came through the coffee shop with a problem, they solved it too well, and this killer was a prime candidate to catch the charm as if it were an airborne virus.

"That means someone's been charming," Sierra stated with a note of obvious displeasure. And her eyes went straight to the three younger witches. She might not have known about the coffee shop, but she could clearly guess who would be stupid enough to charm a non-magic, just like they weren't supposed to.

"It also means that the only way to get this guy off his killing streak," Amber added, "is if the caster of the initial charm retracts it onto themselves to negate it."

As Krystal predicted, Alexa blinked in confusion. They had never been over this with her. She was still too inexperienced, too naïve in the craft to know anything about things so complex. Even Krystal wasn't quite sure how to absorb and negate charms. Most of the time, they just wore off, but second-hand charms were different. Once they were caught, they were nearly impossible to shake, because the magic didn't come directly from the witch, but from the non-magic it was first cast upon. Its energy signature was different.

"Do you know who cast the initial charm?" Valerie asked, her eyes brimming with anxiety that was so unlike her. She must have been wondering if this was her fault, but Krystal had her own suspicions.

Amber closed her eyes again. "It's going to take me a minute, but I think I can find out."

The witches joined hands once more and tension returned to suffocate each of them once more. Krystal could feel the tremor in Valerie's hand and sense the unease from all the others. Even within herself, she wondered how this all would end. If only they could have called on her mother, or even her father for help. If they had time, they could have gotten the Warlock Enforcers to take care of this guy. But, none of them could negate the charm.

At the head of the table, Amber nodded. "I see it. The moment when he was charmed... At the church... Father Frank's sermon..."

Krystal looked straight to Alexa and watched as the color drained from her face. The petite witch withdrew her hands from the others to cover her own mouth. It was her charm that overflowed. Krystal had thought Father Frank's zeal was a little too strong that Saturday at the festival. Normal enthusiasm charms only lasted twenty-four hours and his lasted all the way to Sunday, maybe even Monday.

Sierra and Amber looked right to the young, half-magic witch with scathing glares.

"You were charming?" Sierra exclaimed.

Krystal jumped to her friend's rescue. "Only because I asked her to."

Her elder sister turned to her in disbelief, her eyes full of hurt as if Krystal had betrayed the entire magical world. "I could expect this from a witch who doesn't know better, but from you?"

"We don't have time to get into this right now," Krystal growled as she pulled out her phone. Against every irrational, emotional thought she had about what she and Devin could have been, she kept his number in her contacts.

There was no denying that this might be the end of everything they had set out to do with the coffee shop. When this was all over, Sierra would know the truth and no doubt, she would tell their mother. Their mother would tell their father, and then the Warlock Enforcers would be after them. The coffee shop would be nothing but a distant memory and an empty shell of a building by the end of the week if the council had their way after they found out the girls had broken the cardinal rule. And where would that leave them?

Krystal's hands couldn't stop shaking as she scrolled through her long contact list and she wondered how long it would take for this crushing ache in her chest to go away. Weeks? Months? Never? She was losing Devin, and now she was going to lose the coffee shop. Everything she ever truly loved, everything she worked so hard for, would be gone. And there wasn't a damn thing she could do to stop it. At least they could do one thing and right the wrong they had done to this town by letting a second-hand charm leak through.

Valerie added, "She's right. We need to find this guy and take him out before he hurts anyone else."

Even in the dim light of the dining room, tears glistened in Alexa's pretty blue eyes. "I don't know how to negate a charm," she whimpered.

Sierra, despite the roiling storm of anger in her, turned to Alexa and nodded. "I'll be with you three when you take him on. I'll show you how."

Amber stood from the table with a sigh. "And when you do, he owes me four hundred and seventy-five dollars and some change... I need a drink." She walked away from the table and through the swinging door to the kitchen beyond.

Krystal also stood from her place at the table as the phone began to ring.

"I'm insane, aren't I?" Devin asked his partner, smiling to himself while they sat in the patrol car.

Aaron was busy checking his phone and not watching the house of their only suspect in this case. They didn't want to be sitting outside of Father Frank's home, but after Chief Nickels looked at everything in the case file, evaluating the evidence and Sierra's testimony, there was no arguing with their boss's decision to stake out the priest.

"What?" Aaron asked.

Devin couldn't force his lips to rest from the wide grin that split his face. "I'm insane. Every bit of logic tells me that I should leave Krystal, but I just can't."

Aaron threw his cellphone into one of the empty cupholders that divided their seats. "Whoa! When did you start debating on dumping Krystal?"

There was so much that he could say, but Devin had made a promise to the witch that he wouldn't tell her secret. And he was determined to keep it. "We just got into a long talk last night and she told me some things."

That's all he said, but Aaron wasn't going to leave it alone.

"Okay? What kind of things?"

Devin shook his head. "Stuff that would make any sane man turn tail and run, but I just can't shake her."

"What?" he asked. "Does she have a kid hiding somewhere?"

He chuckled. If only that were it. That might have been easier to deal with than the fact that she could use magic. She could turn him into a frog, make his tongue turn blue, or probably flip this entire town upside down. If Krystal had all this power and magic, there was nothing she couldn't do.

That thought had him thinking. If she was telling the truth, if he was still this torn about being with her, she could have cast a spell to make him forget what she had told him. She could have used her magic to force him to love her. But she didn't.

How could she anyway? Devin was attracted to her long before she ever spoke a word to him.

How could she have cast a spell just by standing there and looking beautiful?

"No, she doesn't have a kid," Devin replied, leaning his elbow on the passenger side window as he stroked at his chin and lips.

"Is it something we need to arrest her for?"

Devin laughed again and shook his head, his eyes fixed on Father Frank's front door illuminated by porch light. "No, nothing illegal."

A few beats of silence passed before he said, "You're not going to tell me, are you?"

"Not a chance."

This revelation, this sudden epiphany that he wasn't going to be able to live without Krystal had shaken his entire world. The tiny, fractured pieces of his childhood and former life in Boston came loose, leaving behind a whole and complete man again. Nothing, in all of his post-traumatic stress therapy, could have readied him for the healing that he hadn't been expecting.

His life in Boston, though far from perfect, had been ruined by the very thing that Krystal could control. Fire had burned away a part of him that he never thought he would get back. Sure, the skin was healed, but he knew a piece of him had burned to cinders that day. Krystal reclaimed that lost piece and gave it back to him, unblemished.

Devin caught himself laughing at the absurdity of it all.

Beside him, Aaron squinted. "Are you feeling all right, buddy?"

"I've never felt better, to be honest."

That final insight set him free somehow. He was about to open up and tell Aaron all about his former partner and everything that he had neglected to tell a single soul. How Krystal played into this grand scheme of recovery, when his cellphone buzzed in his pocket.

After thinking about her all day and letting her walk out the station without a word, finally, she was calling him. He answered quickly.

"Krystal?"

"Devin," she said, her words slow and annealed by urgency. "I need you to go to Torn Sails Bar and Grill right now."

"Why?" he asked, sitting up a little straighter in his seat. He looked to Father Frank's living room window and saw the man was still seated there reading his Bible with a pair of glasses perched at the end of his nose. "What's wrong?"

"The killer. We know where he's going to strike next."

Devin looked sideways at Aaron and hoped his partner couldn't hear her. "I told you not to get involved."

"We had to get involved when he decided to attack my sister. We know who he is, too. Jacob Nathanson. He just moved to town."

The memory of Sunday Mass came back to him and Devin slammed his fist on the console in aggravation. He should have known something was suspicious about the guy, but just thought him nervous and cynical. "I know the guy. We met on Sunday." He turned to his partner. "Aaron, go to Torn Sails Bar. Now!"

Instead of questioning the snot out of him, Aaron must have seen the ire in Devin's eyes and knew better than to ask anything. He revved the engine to life and peeled down the road toward the harbor, leaving behind Father Frank and all the wrongful suspicions they had toward the priest. They had been focusing on the wrong man the whole time.

"Krystal," Devin said, his voice dropping. "Do not do anything without us there. Do you understand me?"

He didn't hear a response.

"Krystal!" he barked.

"We have a plan, Devin. Jacob's been charmed. We have to undo it before you arrest him. It won't take long, and everything will be fine. I promise."

Devin shouted her name again, but it was no use. The phone beeped to let him know the call had been disconnected. If he were driving, Devin would have flicked on the sirens and broken every traffic law to get to the bar before Krystal had a chance to do whatever it was she was planning.

He didn't care if the guy was charmed, a warlock, or anything else supernatural. He couldn't risk her safety. Images and flashbacks of his final day on the force on Boston resurfaced. He couldn't let that happen to Krystal. If it did, his whole world might have fallen apart all over again, and no magic would be able to put him back together again.

"Are you done drawing it yet?" Valerie whispered to Sierra, who was crouched down in the alley beside the bar. They had moved the dumpster to partially hide what they had planned to do. Krystal could still see part of the binding circle her older sister was drawing into the asphalt with the chalk.

"It's a little tough when the ground is so wet," Sierra replied back, her whisper a little harsher than Valerie's.

Krystal stood at the corner of the bar, watching the door. The salty breeze from the harbor chilled her skin and she regretted not bringing a heavier coat to wear. She could hear the music booming through the walls, the sharp crack of billiard balls hitting one another, and boisterous laughter coming from inside. For a Wednesday night, they seemed fairly crowded. Apparently, even when there was a murderer in town, people still needed to get together for a few drinks.

Beside her, she could feel every bit of nervousness bounding in waves off Alexa, who continued to repeat to herself the instructions for how to negate the charm.

"If you don't calm down, it's going to be that much harder for you," she said, taking her friend by the shoulders and wishing she could have done something to sooth her nerves. If Krystal tried to charm Alexa into a more serene state, it would screw with the negation.

Alexa's blue eyes fixed on Krystal and she nodded. "I know. I just can't stop thinking about how all of this is my fault."

Sierra could blame the half-blood witch all day long, but that wouldn't convince Krystal that any of this was her fault. Accidents happened, lessons were learned. Second-hand charms happened often, even with full-blood witches casting the charm in the first place. If anything, it was Krystal's fault for putting too much faith in her friend. But she couldn't think about that now. They had to focus or all of this could go sour.

"This isn't your fault. You couldn't have known this was going to happen."

Alexa's cheeks were already wetted by the tears she had shed earlier that evening behind their backs. "I was only trying to help Father Frank with his sermon."

Krystal hugged her. "I know you were. You had good intentions, and that's what matters."

"We're ready," Sierra announced. "Is he here yet?"

Valerie checked her watch. "It's almost eight twenty-two. Right when Amber said Jacob would be here."

Krystal fled to the corner of the building at the end of the alley, her eyes fixed on the door and surrounding parking lot. "I don't see him yet."

"Does everyone know the drill?" Sierra questioned as she joined the three other witches in front of the dumpster.

"I'll distract him away from the bar with an illusion," Valerie said.

Krystal turned to face her sister. "Then the four of us bind him in the circle, so he can't escape."

Every pair of eyes drifted to Alexa and she stiffened under their stares. "And I'll negate the charm," she said, a complete lack of confidence in her statement.

Krystal's guts twisted at the sight of her friend so distraught. She opened her mouth to try and give a few more words of encouragement before she heard a car door slam. She turned and saw a man charging toward the bar. There was a suspicious bulge beneath his long coat.

"Valerie," she whispered harshly, signaling her friend to begin the illusion as they scrambled to hide behind the dumpster.

Devin spotted Jacob as soon as they pulled into the parking lot. If the way his dark hair curled out from the edge of his ball cap wasn't enough to give him away, then it was the bulge underneath his trench coat. He unholstered his gun, ready to go at a full run to catch up with him from across the parking lot, but another sight made the very blood in his veins freeze.

It was a wonder he saw Krystal at all. Her jet-black hair blended in with the shadows of the alleyway next to the bar. Only the flash of the blue sweater she was wearing earlier that day drew his attention. He muttered a curse under his breath.

"Is that him?" Aaron asked as he shut off the engine. His partner must not have seen Krystal. Devin didn't answer, but watched as something peculiar happened.

Jacob stopped, just a couple of yards from the bar. He turned and looked to the alleyway and took one stumbling step backward as if he were surprised. Only, there was nothing there. Krystal had disappeared behind the green dumpster that poked just out of the mouth of the alley, blocking his view.

"Stay here," he told Aaron, suspecting that there was something witchy going on.

Jacob slowly walked toward the alley and Devin gripped his gun a little tighter as he quietly angled out of the car. Whatever Krystal was doing, he didn't want to upset it just yet. If he could take Jacob alive, he would. If the perp ran, he might have to shoot.

"No way am I letting you go in there alone," Aaron resisted. "I see what he's packing."

Devin kept his eyes fixed on Jacob as he neared the alleyway. "No, just stay here. I'll explain later."

That was a lie if he ever told one. There was no way he was going to explain any of this to Aaron in the end. He didn't have any substantial proof that Jacob was the murderer. He was only going off of whatever source Krystal was pulling from. Maybe she saw it in the mist of some crystal ball, or she threw some bones and they spelled out Jacob's name. He didn't know how she knew, and he didn't care. If he could get the murderer, he was willing to follow her lead. She wouldn't have called him there if she wasn't absolutely sure.

He kept a firm hold on his gun with both hands as he avoided the streetlamps and followed Jacob. The man in the trench coat disappeared behind the dumpster. Devin crept forward, and pressed his side to the cool metal. Before he even stepped foot into the alleyway, he could feel that familiar spiritual, otherworldly pull of energy like he felt while in the church and at Krystal's home.

He now understood that it must have been magic, or some other kind of unseen force that they both shared. How ironic that the power of the witches could have something in common with the power of the church. Only, what he felt flowing from the mouth of the alleyway was stronger, bolder, and more aggressive than anything he had ever felt in Krystal's presence.

There was a shout, and then a grunt, followed by something that sounded like a whirlwind coming from the alley. Devin raised his gun and jumped out from his hiding place, his heart pounding in his throat. Even after years on the force, he still felt that adrenaline pump hard when he was faced with danger.

What was going on behind the dumpster defied science, logic, and everything he thought he knew about the natural world.

He saw four witches standing around a chalk circle, their hands outstretched as magic billowed from them. Jacob stood in the center of the circle beneath confusing and twisting lines that must have only made sense to one who knew magic. The gun he had been carrying was tossed to the side, far out of reach and unable to harm anyone.

Devin pointed the barrel at Jacob, who struggled against the invisible force that whipped around in the circle. The only evidence of it was in the way the girls' hair fluttered and flew out around their shoulders. It was something straight out of a movie, yet this was totally real. There were no props, no tricks or fans to make their hair and clothes move like that. The bay wind wasn't strong enough to blow Jacob's cap clean off his head the way it did.

Their lips were moving, muttering something that he couldn't discern over the rising howls of the power that surged between them. Whatever they were doing, it was keeping Jacob trapped there, unable to escape.

"Alexa!" Sierra said. Devin kept his gun aimed at Jacob, just in case whatever they were planning didn't work, but he shifted his eyes toward the little blonde witch.

What he saw wasn't good. He knew that look on her face. It was the same look new cadets at the academy had when they were faced with their first real offensive fight. She was panicking. Usually, it took a good hard slap to the face to get someone to unfreeze like that.

By the way they all looked to her, Devin knew the next part of this scheme was up to her. He didn't have to know what it was. All he had to do was see that Jacob had taken another step toward the edge of the circle, and he knew he had to help. This guy wasn't going to slip through their fingers again.

"Alexa!" he barked, utilizing the same demanding voice he was forced to use on the rookies who couldn't get their shit together in a fire fight.

Her blue eyes darted to him and she seemed to get a hold of herself. She closed her eyes and brought her fingers together, creating a diamond shape directed toward Jacob. Her quivering lips formed the words for the spell she must have been casting.

A misty, formless green aura drifted through the space between Alexa and Jacob, transferring from the murderer to the witch. Devin shifted, unsure of exactly what she was doing. By the way he continued to thrash against his captors, he knew the witch wasn't stealing his life force or anything so sinister. That would have been a hard murder to explain.

The green flowed through the center of the diamond she had formed and channeled straight to her chest. Her arms buckled and the lips that had been muttering her incantation slowed. Her eyes squeezed together as if she were in pain.

But it wasn't pain. Devin watched as Alexa began to cry. She fell to her knees as the sobs rattled her body with such force it looked as if she were having a seizure.

The mystic hold on Jacob weakened as the witch became crippled by the energy she absorbed.

Krystal broke from her post in the circle to aid her friend. Sierra looked up to Devin and gave a nod. This was where he came in.

The cop charged forward, stepping into the circle as the two remaining witches dropped their hands and released the magical hold over the murderer. He tackled Jacob to the ground and holstered his gun to make his hands free, so he could whip out his handcuffs. Only when he heard the final clinking of the locking mechanism, did Devin finally relax.

"Jacob Nathanson, you're under arrest for the murder of Elizabeth Thatchman and Harry Middleton. Also for the attempted murder of Sierra Hayden."

Jacob turned his head and looked up to the cop with wild eyes. "I dispensed justice!" he shouted in his defense. "Those sinners deserved to die."

Before Devin could stop her – like he was going to anyway – Sierra came up and kicked Jacob hard in the ribs. She called him some pretty nasty names and began scuffing out the chalk lines with the bottom of her shoe, so anyone walking by wouldn't see the circle they had drawn.

Devin pulled Jacob to his feet and finally looked toward Krystal and Alexa embracing one another.

"It's not your fault," Krystal kept saying to her over and over again.

He gave a questioning look to Valerie who approached him and Jacob. She reached out and tapped the murderer's forehead with the tips of her fingers.

Immediately, his body went limp and Devin had to adjust his hold on the man to keep him standing.

"What's wrong with her?" he asked, his curiosity for their strange, magical way of life finally slipping through. He wanted to know everything about what they just did, how they did it, what that green smoke was, and how four girls single-handedly caught a violent criminal.

Valerie looked to her two friends and let out a tight breath. "Alexa absorbed the enthusiasm charm that Jacob caught second-hand from Father Frank. It intensifies whatever she's obsessing over. It looks like she was really preoccupied with the fact that she was the one who cast the charm in the first place."

Before Devin could ask more questions, Valerie set to helping Sierra get rid of the trapping circle. If he hadn't had a criminal between his hands, he would have stayed.

"You can't blame yourself for what happened," he heard Krystal console to Alexa, who continued to weep so bitterly over her own intensified grief. "It was an accident. There was nothing you could have done to save them."

Those words, though they weren't spoken to him, swirled around his mind and his heart. He had heard those words before, many times. The therapist told him that, his former co-workers in Boston, even his sister told him the same before he left for Goldcrest Cove. None of them had the power to speak those words and have them hold any meaning whatsoever.

Not until Krystal said them. He paused, bearing most of Jacob's weight against his chest as he listened to her continue to comfort Alexa with her adages. He watched her, loving her even more as she continued to heal the wounds of those around her, not just his.

She looked up and their eyes met. He wanted to tell her so much, to explain his behavior and tell her that he wanted her in every way possible, even if she was a witch. She was a good person, a kind soul. Devin needed her as more than a lover, but as a friend and companion. He needed her just as much as he needed air. That's what he had come to realize earlier in the day, when he knew that he couldn't live without her. As crazy as it was, that was the truth he had to tell her.

But this wasn't the time or the place to go into that. There would be another chance for him to make things right between them, but not tonight. One gentle look from Krystal told him that he needed to move on. He had a job to do.

This was going to be a hard one to explain in his report.

Chapter 17

As Krystal sipped on her black coffee, she wished she had at least added a little sugar. Maybe Devin could handle such a strong, bold roast, but she wasn't as strong. Last night proved that. It took hours to calm Alexa down to the point that she could finally negate the charm.

It was no surprise that it took her so long, or that Alexa struggled so hard to get a grip on her emotions long enough to have a single, clear and positive thought. But for Krystal, it wasn't so easy. Through the trail of blame, Krystal knew that it wasn't Alexa's fault. It was her own. If she had just charmed the coffee herself, then perhaps Father Frank wouldn't have ingested the overly charmed coffee, and Jacob would have never been exposed to the overflow of magic, and both Elizabeth and Henry would be alive today.

She tried to use some of her own logic that she had dished out to bring Alexa back from the brink. But Krystal still couldn't help but wonder that if she hadn't made that fatal error, things would have been a lot different right now.

It was enough guilt to make her lock herself in her office at Perfect Books and Brews for the majority of the day. Outside, she could hear the flow of customers coming in and out of the store, talking and laughing as Alexa and Valerie made their drinks. She made the excuse that she needed to catch up on paperwork, which she did, but the negativity continued to pummel her in torrents.

It might have been a worthless endeavor to organize any of the receipts and reports on her desk. It wasn't like the coffee shop would see the end of the year. After they had negated the charm, and everyone had gone home for the night, Krystal and Sierra had their talk. She told her sister everything about the coffee shop, and about what her friends had been doing to the community for the last five years.

The way Krystal saw it, they had done no harm up until now. This was just a fluke, a mistake, a bad judgement call that should have never happened. Alexa needed the practice, but Krystal should have seen that it was damn stupid to practice on someone like Father Frank. Second-hand charming was never even a thought in her mind.

Once Krystal explained her motives, Sierra seemed to calm down. She didn't say one way or another if she would spill the beans. Krystal listened all night for her sister's hushed words, suspecting that she would call their mother late that night, but she heard nothing.

Even if Catherine never found out about the shop, even if the Warlock Enforcers never came blasting through their front door, demanding they be shut down, Krystal's faith in her dream had been shaken. What if this mission to help their town had been a disaster waiting to happen from the beginning, and it just took five years for it to finally catch up with them?

Krystal was in the middle of looking up the proper procedure for shutting down the coffee shop when someone knocked on her office door.

"I'm busy," she called out, never taking her eyes off her laptop screen.

"Not for me, you're not."

Krystal's hands went motionless over her keyboard when her mother's voice rang through the wood, clear as a summer day. "Come in," she said with a sigh. If getting an earful from her sister wasn't enough, she was about to get it from her mother too.

The older witch stepped in and closed the door behind her, the knitted scarf dangling from her neck told Krystal that she must have just arrived. She pushed aside her laptop and waited for the verbal lashing that was to come.

"They told me you've been in here all day," Catherine said as she sat down in the chair across from her desk.

Krystal motioned toward the somewhat straightened piles of papers. "I've been working on getting all this together, so when we shut down, it'll be easier to haul out. I still have taxes to file in the spring."

Her mother's dark eyes went wide, the wrinkles around them deepening. "Shut down? Honey, you can't shut this place down. It's your dream."

She leveled a look at her mother. Just like Devin, she appreciated honesty and if her mom was going to try and cajole her into thinking all was well, Krystal was going to have none of it. "Have you talked to Sierra lately?"

Catherine blinked at the turn of conversation. "No, why? Should I?"

"I highly doubt that she hasn't told you everything already," Krystal said, crossing her arms over the tabletop. "Why else would you be here?"

"I'm here, because I sensed a great sadness in you and I knew I had to come see what was going on." Catherine's gaze roamed over what she could see of Krystal. "Does this have to do with Devin?"

Now it was her turn to be shocked. "Sierra told you about Devin?" Perhaps it was like confessing that she was guilty before she was even accused of the crime, but there was really no use in playing stupid with her mother. She saw through everything.

"I knew about Devin since Monday, dear," her mother said with a little shake of her head. "Mrs. Macy told me all about the cop from Boston and how you two have been sweet on each other."

Krystal took a deep breath and let it out slowly. "You don't have to worry about him, mom. It's not going to work out like I hoped."

Her eyes narrowed upon her daughter with that wordless look that demanded more information. So, Krystal told her about how Devin summoned the dark magic within her, how she felt about him in the beginning, and how it all came crashing down around her ears that night when they had sex on the couch. Of course, she didn't mention the sex part, because her mother would have throttled her. That couch belonged to their grandmother and she sewed the cushions together herself. It was as much of a family heirloom as the entire house was.

"I thought he took the news really well, but he said he needed time to think. We haven't really talked since then."

A slow smile crept across Catherine's face. Such an incongruous expression when Krystal's world was still crumbling to pieces like a dry autumn leaf under a heavy boot.

"Do you love him?" she asked.

Krystal shrugged and rubbed her cheek against the soft knitted fabric of her sleeve. "I don't know what I feel anymore. All I know is I hate that it's come to this." She looked back up to her mom. "Remember how Missy Thompson lost her virginity in my freshman year and the guy dumped her a week later? Now I know how she feels."

Catherine nodded. "You gave Devin a precious jewel when you told him your secret for the first time, and now it feels like he's tossed it into the dirt."

"Exactly," Krystal replied, slightly surprised that her mother could be so intuitive about something she really didn't have a clue about. "I know you've always been with dad, so you can't really relate, but it hurts so bad not to hear from him, not to talk to him."

The knowing smile on her mother's face prompted her to wonder what was going to come out of her mouth next.

"Darling, I know it's hard to believe, but I know how you feel. I loved a non-magic man once."

Krystal gasped. "No way."

Catherine, her eyes twinkling with reminiscence, nodded. "I did. It was James Nickels, actually. Now, he's the chief of police, but we used to get into a lot of trouble back in the day." She laughed. "I could tell you stories and stories of how we sprayed graffiti on the water tower and stole things from the neighbors all the time."

A contagious smile made its way to Krystal. "I never knew that. Does dad know?"

"Of course, he knows," she replied. "He was the one there to pick up the pieces when your grandmother told me that I could never be with James."

Krystal nodded. "Just like you're going to tell me that I can't be with Devin."

Catherine scooted to the edge of her chair and grabbed at the front of the desk. "No, dear, I'm going to tell you to go after that handsome cop. If he wants you, if he loves you like I suspect that he does – because you know that I know things – then you need to grab him up before some other girl in town tries. That's what happened with James. He moved on, found another non-magic girl, and I fell in love with your father. That is our love story, but yours is with Devin, I know it."

To have a scrying witch tell Krystal that her fate was to be with Devin shined a bit of light into her dark and gloomy heart. Perhaps they did have a future together, but she wasn't about to force anything. She'd doubt every nagging hope until she knew for certain that Devin did want her, magic and all.

To know her mother had dated and run around town with a non-magic was a far more interesting story. There wasn't a single witch alive that frowned upon mixed couples more than her mother. Krystal could remember her and other members of her family gabbing about the scandalous relationships in other parts of the country and how her mother suspected they would lead to ruin. Catherine even predicted how Alexa's parents would eventually split up just before their half-magic baby was born.

Mixed couples could work, but her mother always seemed the pessimist toward them. Whether it was because Krystal was on the brink of having her own outrageous matchup with Devin, or if she had seen things come up in the council that put the idea in a new perspective, she didn't care. As long as her mother wasn't going to yell at her for it, or disown her as a daughter, Krystal was content to hope again.

"If he wants me, he knows where to find me." Krystal shrugged. "At least, for now."

Catherine grunted as she grabbed the arms of the chair and pulled the chair closer to the desk. "What's this nonsense about you closing down the shop, then? If it doesn't have to do with Devin, does it have to do with the murders?"

Krystal shouldn't have been surprised that she knew about that too. "Did Mrs. Macy tell you about that too?"

"No, the newspapers did." Catherine gave her a cunning look. "I don't have to gossip or scry for everything, you know."

Bracing herself for the long story, Krystal took a breath and told her mother about the murders, Alexa charming the coffee under her orders, and everything they've tried to do over the last five years. Maybe since her mother was on the council, she could put a good word in and the punishment wouldn't be so severe. She left Alexa and Valerie out of it, of course. The coffee shop had been her idea in the first place, so it was only right that she take the fall for it. She claimed her two friends as completely blameless.

Catherine didn't show one hint of violent or distressed emotion in all the time she confessed her sins. There was no greater rule than the one stating that witches should not use their powers on a non-magic, and Krystal had done just that. She was a disappointment to her family, and to the magical community. She could already hear the lessons years from now, where her story was told to teach young witches and warlocks the consequences of using their magic improperly.

When Krystal was done, she waited for Vesuvius to blow, but nothing came.

"So, you're going to close your shop, because you made a bad judgement call?"

Krystal flattened her hands over the stack of papers she had been leaning on. "Mom, I broke the rules. I broke the one rule a witch should never break. This isn't just a bad judgement call. This is a whole five years of risking exposure and you're acting like I just gave you the weather report."

Catherine held up a thin hand to hold back Krystal's growing mania. "I've known what you and the others have been doing here. I've known for a while now."

It didn't happen often, but Krystal fell speechless. Something must have happened after Catherine took her position on the council. She had always been the picture of straight-laced, no nonsense, follow the rules or die sort of woman. Now, she seemed to be the complete opposite. First, she approves of Devin. Now Krystal learns that her mother had known about the coffee shop and Warlock Enforcers weren't dispatched to take care of the threat to the magical world.

"Honey, don't look so shocked," Catherine laughed. "I admire what you're doing here. You may be breaking the most important rule, but you're also following the witch's creed to never do harm and help others. How could I possibly be mad at that?" She sat back and shrugged. "Your father, on the other hand might not be so lenient, but I keep plenty of things from him. This would be no different."

The witch's creed wasn't so much as a dogma tenet as it was a simple way of living. To do unto others as they would do unto you sort of mentality when it came to interacting with others, whether in the magical world, or the non-magical.

Krystal buried her face in her arms and let out a long groan of relief.

"Did you think I would come here to tell you not to follow your dreams?" her mother questioned. "I know this coffee shop means the world to you. And now that I know there's a man for you in that world, I'm overjoyed that you've found everything I've ever wished for you. Yes, it would be easier if you came to work on the council and had a nice warlock husband. But you have to know that I've only wanted the best for you, and wanted you to be the happiest you can be. You've made your own path in life and I'm proud."

Krystal heard the whisper of fabric as Catherine stood up and came to wrap her arms around her daughter's shoulders in a motherly hug. Grateful tears burned in her tired eyes as she swiveled in her chair and hugged her mother in return.

She was right. The coffee shop was her dream, her world, and her life. Yes, they had been careless, but they learned their lesson the hard way. Charms would be kept to a minimum, maybe only five a week instead of five a day. Krystal would find a way to check each of them to make sure that this second-hand charm mess wouldn't happen again. They could charm those they knew, but risking a charm on a stranger, who was unpredictable and maybe as volatile as Jacob wasn't worth the trouble.

"Thanks, mom," she whispered against the older witch's silver-streaked hair as a single tear spilled down her cheek.

"Any time, my fire baby."

They pulled away from one another and Krystal scrubbed at the tear with the edge of her sleeve.

"Speaking of fire," her mother continued, "you have a visitor."

Not two seconds later, another knock came at the door and Valerie invited herself in. She looked from Catherine to Krystal and then cleared her throat, probably wondering if this was a bad time.

"Krystal, Devin's here and he wants to see you."

Krystal's heart began to palpitate, and a faintness swept through her at Valerie's declaration. Devin was there? And he wanted to see her? This was far sooner than she had expected. Before she realized it, her mother escorted her out of the office and into the hall.

The air was filled with that rich, coffee aroma that had a strange way of clearing her head and welcoming her back to the land of the living. The coffee shop was buzzing with activity, the way it had been before the big serial killer scare earlier that week. The newspapers were quick to let out the announcement that the murderer had been caught and was safely behind bars. That wasn't only good for business, but good for the town. The community could breathe easier, knowing they were safe once more.

Behind the counter, Alexa and Valerie were sipping on their afternoon dose of caffeine, both as happy as they could be after a long night of battling charms and psycho killers. Alexa, in better spirits than she had been, seemed to recover and accept what happened. Though, Krystal knew they weren't out of the woods quite yet. There would be days when the terrible guilt monster would come to pay them a visit.

Devin stood near the front door, clad in his officer uniform, and not attended by Aaron as he usually was. Her mother gave her arm a reassuring pat and went to join her two friends at the counter. Krystal knew exactly what her mother would order too. She adored their house blend latte with lots of whip cream and cinnamon on top. That foamy pile of white paired well with her personal burgundy mug with the words "World's Best Mom" written on the side in a childish hand.

Catherine looked over her shoulder, casting a knowing glance toward her daughter. Just a gentle reminder that Krystal was still a woman and allowed to make her own decisions about life and love, now that she had left the nest. It was all the permission she needed.

Krystal approached him, keeping her eyes on anything but Devin, because she didn't want him to know she had just been crying.

"Can we talk in private?" he asked, his voice like a soothing balm to her churning stomach.

She made the mistake of meeting his gorgeous eyes and caved. He seemed neither mad, nor fearful in her presence. His expression was carefully neutral, unreadable like the first day they met when she predicted his personality based on his coffee choice. That seemed like a lifetime ago, and she knew him so much better than that now. Yes, he was still a realist, but also flexible, kind, funny, an amazing kisser, and so much more. Coffee could never tell her all of that.

"Sure," she agreed.

Without a single look back to her mother or her friends, she walked out the door with Devin, feeling her spirit a little lighter as she stepped out onto the sidewalk along Johnson Avenue.

When Devin asked Krystal if she wouldn't mind going to the park for their private talk, he was surprised to hear her suggest the marina instead. He hated the silence that filled the cabin of his Dodge once they were moving down the residential streets to get to the bay. He didn't know what to say, what to ask. He had requested a few hours off from Chief Nickels so he could have this time with Krystal, but he hadn't really prepared what he would say to her. They needed to sort things out and now that the state officials could take over with Jacob, his boss was more than willing to give him as much time off as he wanted. In the chief's eyes, Devin deserved it.

But to Devin, he played a significantly small role. He was just the guy to arrest the perp. Krystal and her friends were the true heroes. Of course, no one would know that. He didn't mention any of them in his report, not even when Krystal called him in front of Father Frank's house.

As they turned onto Orchid Crest Road, Krystal finally broke the silence. "What did you put in your report?" she asked, her voice soft and gentle, like a feathery touch on his skin that made him shiver. It didn't matter what she was saying, as long as he could hear her voice.

"I said that we were passing by and saw Jacob pull out the gun before going into the bar. We arrested him and upon questioning, he confessed to the murders. He's being transported to the state prison for holding until his trial. I think his lawyer may go with the insanity plea, because he wouldn't stop raving about his wife's affair that led up to their divorce."

Beside him, he saw Krystal nod in understanding. "Valerie said that she cleared his memories, so he won't say anything about us binding him in the circle. All he'll remember is going into the alley and then when you arrested him."

Devin had a feeling that was what the tap on Jacob's forehead was about, but he didn't have the chance to ask. "What exactly did you do to him? What was that green stuff that came out of Jacob?"

Krystal, as coolly as if she were explaining a recipe to him, detailed about the binding circle, the charms, the second-hand charm, how to negate the charm, and everything in between. He stayed quiet, letting her talk, not just because he loved to hear her speak, but because he wanted to understand. If he was going to be cast headlong into his weird world of magic, he needed to at least make an effort.

They came to the harbor and walked down to an empty pier where no boats were moored. Along the other docks, he could hear the fishermen and other sailors talking and shouting back and forth to one another, but out here, they could be alone.

There was a wonderful lack of tension in Krystal as they sat themselves down at the very end of the dock, their legs hanging just a few inches above the water. To know she wasn't afraid anymore, or at least not as afraid as she was, gave Devin hope that one day he could truly conquer his own fears. That day could be much sooner than he thought. Even going through the therapy sessions in Boston, he didn't think this would ever be something he could just get over.

"I didn't know if you'd ever want to talk to me again," she said, her feet kicking beneath her, in a slow, steady rhythm.

Devin watched how the breeze tickled the fine dark hairs around her temples, and how the sun gave her a glow that made him stare, breathless and longing for her even more. "It didn't take me long to figure everything out."

Krystal risked a glance his way and the corners of his lips tugged up into a smile that was completely involuntary. She had that effect on him. She always would.

"What did you figure out?"

Devin edged his hand closer to hers until the tips of their fingers touched on the rough wooden plank they sat on. "That I'm all right with this. With us."

He felt her fingers twitch, as if she wanted to take his hand in hers and hold it. He beat her to it and found her hand to be clammy, as if she were nervous. He hated that he had made her that way. He hated how much time it took him to realize what he had known all along. It had only been a couple of days, but that was far too long to leave her waiting.

"I may not understand how you can be what you are, but I hope that one day, I will. I hope I'll have a lot of days with you, learning about this stuff... about you."

She grinned and started to laugh. "You don't know how relieved I am to hear that." Her free hand reached up and wiped just under her eye, as if to catch a tear before it had a chance to fall. "I was so scared that you didn't want to have anything to do with me. I totally get where you were coming from about thinking I charmed you or something, but you have to believe – "

Devin leaned forward and kissed her. It was the only way to make her shut up and accept his apology for being a jackass about the whole thing. He hadn't realized how much he missed her warm, sweet lips until just then. He wanted to kiss her every day, every hour if he could.

"I believe everything you said, everything you're going to say," he said when he pulled away.

"You trusted me and the least I can do is trust you... I love you."

Krystal's grin widened, and she held onto his hand that much tighter. "I love you too. Not just because you're okay with me being a witch. I think I loved you the night you took me out on that boat. You helped me face my fears and I knew that I would always be safe with you. I never knew I need that feeling until I met you."

Devin touched his forehead with hers, relishing the smell of her perfume as it drifted around his head. "Whether you know it or not, you helped me face my fears too." Her eyes beckoned for an explanation and he leaned back, so he could gaze at her, the picture of strength and beauty. "I haven't told you everything about my time in Boston."

Krystal's stare drifted down to his left shoulder, the one marred by the scars of his past. "Does this have to do with..."

He nodded. "Yes," he said, then steeled himself one more time to tell the story he didn't want to hear himself say. "We got a call one day. Some nutcase had a homemade flamethrower and he thought he could use it to rob a bank. He hurt a lot of people before we got there. He had several hostages and we were sent in to take him down. I was wearing a standard bulletproof vest, and so was my partner, Paul. We were safe from bullets, but not from fire. I managed to get a few shots in on the guy, but he turned the flamethrower my way. Paul jumped in front of me, taking the bulk of the attack."

Devin swallowed hard, pushing out the sounds that haunted him. The roar of the flames, Paul's screaming, the popping of guns going off all around him. "I blacked out and when I woke up, I was in the hospital getting treated for the burns on my shoulder. Paul died on the scene. They couldn't put him out fast enough. We got the guy, but..."

"You thought it was your fault your partner died?" she asked, her voice barely above a whisper.

He nodded, his throat thick with the warring emotions. Self-hatred, guilt, all of it wanted to consume him. But as long as Krystal was holding his hand, looking at him with those brown eyes, none of the demons could have him.

"I know it's not my fault now. When you were talking to Alexa last night, something of that day in Boston came back to rear its ugly face," he brought her hand to his lips and kissed the back of her fingers. "But what you said chased it all away. I couldn't control what happened. It wasn't my fault. I couldn't have known that Paul would try to sacrifice himself for me. It's what we're trained to do, and Paul died doing his job. He'd been a cop for much longer than me, and you'd never meet a guy more dedicated to his job." He paused, remembering his old partner with the same nostalgic fondness. "I really looked up to him."

Krystal moved in closer until their thighs were touching. She wasn't cold anymore, and he wondered if it had something to do with her special fire magic coming out.

"I didn't know you heard any of that," she said, leaning her head against his shoulder.

Devin let go of her hand, but only so he could wrap his arm around her waist to pull her tight against him. Damn, this felt so right. He would have been content to sit on that dock all day and watch the world pass by without a care.

He kissed the crown of her head. "I had almost thought to ask you for something, but I think I know what the answer would be." She edged away to meet his gaze. "When Valerie erased Jacob's memory, I started to think about that day in Boston. I started to wonder if you could take away those memories for me."

Krystal shook her head, just as he knew she would. To sleep through an entire night without waking up in a cold sweat, or flinching away from the tiniest of harmless flames, would have been such a relief. It was the easy way out, a coward's way out. It was a good thing Krystal wasn't so willing to give into everything he asked.

"What happened in Boston made you who you are today," she said. "I could never take that away from you, no matter how difficult it is to deal with the memories. If I didn't do it to myself when I was terrified of the water, then I won't do it for you."

Devin couldn't help but smile at her and squeeze her a little tighter. "That's exactly what I

thought you would say."

There was a sudden sassy flash in her eyes. "Besides, what happened to experiencing life in all its bold and bitter moments?"

He chuckled. "Well, maybe I need to start putting a little sugar in my coffee, then."

"Maybe you should," she giggled. "I tried drinking black coffee this morning and it was so terrible! I mean, the blend was great, but oh dear goddess, I couldn't drink the whole cup. Way too strong for me."

Devin burst out into a laugh. Yeah, he missed her way more than he ever imagined. "I guess to be fair, I'll have to try your chai tea latte now."

She ribbed him. "It's still on the house whenever you're ready."

Devin placed another gentle kiss on her lips. "As long as I can get plenty of these on the house as well."

She quirked her face up in a funny, thoughtful way. "I may start charging for those."

"And what do witches use as currency? Seeds?"

Krystal swung her feet up, draping her legs across his lap and he reached around to lace his fingers at her opposite hip, holding her there so she wouldn't fall over. "We don't use currency, but I'll have to make something up. How about for every kiss I give, you have to give me something just as sweet?"

"Like chocolate?"

She made a pleasing sound and grinned. "That sounds good to me."

Devin moved in and winked. "I can think of a few other sweet things I could give you." He captured her lips one more time, caressing them with his own until he could feel her body grow hot and feverish.

He quickly pulled back, but he could see the hunger in her eyes. He remembered how she explained that he was the one to ignite this fiery ability within her. If they weren't careful, they could burn the whole town to the ground.

"You're not going to burn my clothes off with all that special magic, are you?" he asked with a laugh.

"I'll certainly try," she said before grabbing the front of his shirt and pulling him down to her once again.

Dating a witch was not going to be easy, but it promised to be a hell of a good time.

About the author

Sheritta Bitikofer is an author of paranormal and historical fiction. She lives for the deep, engaging stories that enthrall readers from cover to cover. As a wife and mother of eclectic tastes, she can be found roaming Civil War battlefields, haunting her local coffeeshop, or relaxing with a plate of chili cheese fries.

Follow her for upcoming novel releases

www.sherittabitikofer.com

Also by Sheritta Bitikofer

The Native

The Irishman

The Scholars

The Convicts

The Soldier

The Outlaw

The Deviants

The Unsinkable

Keeper of Light

Bulletproof

The Nexus

Bewitching Brews

Bewitching Fire

Bewitching Darkness

Bewitching Hearts

Wolves in the Open

Highland Howls

Silver Screen

Mourning Moon

The Decimus Trilogy

The Beast of Verona

Amber Ashes

Saving the Beast

Redemption Duet

The Rose

The Lion

Standalones

Escape

Clouds

Passions

By The Book

www.ingramcontent.com/pod-product-compliance
Lightning Source LLC
Chambersburg PA
CBHW051537260626
47170CB00003B/981